Merry Christmas and love from
Margaret and Dad

12/25/00

The Soulbane Stratagem

To Steve Abbot,
    Best wishes,
        Norman Jetmundsen

The Soulbane Stratagem

DIABOLICAL SUBTERFUGE THAT THREATENS TO DESTROY US

John
HUNT
Publishing Ltd

To my wife, Kelli, for her unflagging
love and encouragement

— *Proverbs* 31:10-11

Also, in loving memory of
The Rev. S. Graham Glover, a faithful parish priest,
and Tony Jones, a devoted Oxford scout,
who were men of deep faith and
abiding joy, and great friends.

— *Philippians* 1:3

CONTENTS

PART I

PART II

I

"There are more things in heaven and earth, Horatio,
Than are dreamt of in your philosophy."

William Shakespeare, *Hamlet, Act I, Scene v*

1

A Winter's Solstice

THE BITING WIND whipped up whirlwinds of delicate snowflakes as I walked alone on New College Lane this December night. The street, narrow and winding, was surrounded by tall, soot-streaked stone walls. The fresh snow crunched under my boots, and I pulled my scarf more tightly over my face. My frosty breath quickly dissipated into nothingness. The main sign of life in Oxford had been along High Street, where passengers in impatient cars or occasional bicycles sped by, faceless and nameless, into the darkness. I was the sole evidence of human existence on this deserted lane, a fact confirmed by the single line of footprints in the snow behind me. The silent, winking stars that peered briefly between the invisible clouds seemed to mock my lonely sojourn. These distant celestial sparks offered no portent of unusual significance to this bleak night. Later, the recollection of this night – *the night that forever altered the course of my life* – always invoked that sense of the strangeness of a dream. Only, it was no dream.

The few lights along the lane created a surreal halo effect as they reflected off the new-fallen snow. The silence was disturbed by the deliberate, measured tolling of the Tom Tower bell, ringing one hundred and one times, as it did every night at five past nine, in the century-old tradition of ringing the curfew for the one hundred and

3

one students of Christ Church College. The single bell reminded me of a funeral death knell, and I shivered involuntarily. I hurried my pace and turned into a narrow passageway between two buildings, almost like entering a small cave. I soon came upon the welcome sight of an open-air courtyard. The grey stones of the old Oxford city wall enclosing the courtyard were capped by snow, and the lamps gave the illusion that the courtyard was bathed in moonlight. I wondered about the events those six-hundred-year-old walls had witnessed. This evening seemed to transcend time, as if the eternal had somehow touched the temporal: the sensation was at once strange and familiar.

Next to the courtyard stood a small, low building with white walls and dark, hand-hewn wood. A yellow-orange light shone from the crooked windows. As I entered, the glowing flames dancing in the fireplace of the ancient Turf Pub offered immediate warmth and masked the night's stark, foreboding character. I glanced around and noticed people at several tables looking over at me. I straightened my shoulders and smiled at no one in particular. A tall, blond American in down jacket and hiking boots, I felt conspicuous in British pubs, and my Southern accent rarely failed to raise a smile.

"Cade, over here," I heard a voice calling me. I turned to see my three friends gesturing from a table in the corner.

"What took you so long?" asked Colin, as I pulled up a chair.

"I was reading a novel and lost track of time," I replied. "Sorry."

"We were afraid we'd miss you, mate," said Adrian, our Australian friend. "We were just about to leave."

"Won't y'all stay a while longer?" I asked, trying not to sound desperate.

"Only if you'll buy the next round," chimed in Nigel, in his mild English accent.

"Here, here," said Adrian. "Cade Bryson, scholar and gentleman, is unanimously elected to buy the beer!"

"All right, all right" I said, as I strode to the wooden bar. The Turf, tucked away in the heart of Oxford, was one of our regular meeting places, and this was the last chance for all of us to get together until next term. Adrian and I, as overseas students, were staying in our colleges. Nigel and Colin had come up this weekend to a party for a friend of theirs who was getting married, and they were staying over with Adrian at Oriel. As the barman returned my change, I noticed he had mistakenly given me a ten pound note along with my pound coin change. I started to pocket the windfall, then turned back to him.

"I'm afraid you made a mistake," I said, holding the ten pound note out. "I gave you a tenner, not a twenty."

"Right you are," said the barman, who had greased-back hair, an earring, and pale skin. "Thanks for your honesty."

I returned to our table holding four tall beer mugs in my large hands. A low buzz of voices muffled other conversations in the pub, while my three companions and I engaged in our usual pub banter. My mind wandered, however, as I recalled that strange sensation of timelessness I felt just before arriving at the Turf. Why was it so odd and yet so comforting?

"Time, please." The barman's now-familiar pub call jarred my reverie.

"To the winter's solstice," toasted Nigel.

"Cheers!" we all replied in unison, as we raised our mugs.

"Time, please, and empty your glasses," said the barman after a few more minutes. We quickly downed our beers and began bundling up for the walk back to our colleges.

"Nice to see snow for a change," remarked Adrian, as we entered New College Lane and walked under the Bridge of Sighs.

"What are you doing for the Christmas holidays, Cade?" asked Colin.

"Not much, really," I said. We turned left near the Sheldonian Theatre, watched by the large sculptured heads peering from the tall fence surrounding the Theatre, and proceeded down Catte Street. "It's too far to go home, and my family couldn't come over here from Atlanta. I'll just stick around college for the most part. Christmas is nothing special to me. I don't go in for those myths about virgin births and wise men. I think it's all humbug."

"Sure, Scrooge," replied Colin with a snort. "It's a good time for partying, though. You're welcome to come home with me to London.

Adrian is coming. We're having a feast at my house Christmas Day, with plenty of libations."

"Thanks, Colin," I replied. "It does sound fun. Would it be all right if I came down on Christmas Eve and returned on Boxing Day? I need to get some work done over the vacation and catch up on my sleep."

"Jolly good," Colin replied. "We'll look for you in a couple of days."

"You wouldn't be planning to visit Rachael during the vac, would you now?" needled Nigel.

At the mention of Rachael Adams, I felt my face flush and was glad it was too dark for anyone to see me. ˙ let the comment pass.

When we reached High Street just past the Radcliffe Camera, we said our good nights and parted. Normally, my compatriots would have headed toward their respective colleges: Colin to Christ Church, Adrian to Oriel, and Nigel to Merton. Tonight, they all went off with Adrian.

Trudging down the High in the snow, I paused to look at Magdalen College. Spotlights illuminated its massive, golden, fifteenth-century stone buildings. I stared at the imposing tower, the landmark of Magdalen. In the half light and eerie shadows, Magdalen reminded me of some medieval castle. I had been in Oxford just over a year, after graduating from the University of Virginia, and I had become completely besotted by this ancient and beautiful place. I was taking a second degree, in PPE: the Oxford curriculum was equivalent to an American graduate program, and I found I had to buckle down pretty hard to keep up under the tutorial system. I had also managed, however, to learn my way to a number of pubs, and I had secured a position on my college rugby team.

I resumed my walk, and my thoughts wandered to Rachael Adams. I first saw Rachael just over a month ago on Guy Fawkes' night, when Colin, Nigel and I had gone to the Trout pub in Godstow. Out in the meadows near the river Thames, just past the Trout, someone had a huge bonfire going. We decided to investigate and crossed over the small stone bridge into the meadows, where we discovered a number of people toasting the guy. Just across the fire, her face lit by the flickering orange flames, stood a slender girl, with black hair, elegant facial features, and ivory skin. I was immediately taken with her, and as I wondered how we could meet, Nigel called out, "Hello, Rachael." My heart raced as Nigel introduced us and explained that Rachael was a second-year student at Merton. She had a lively smile.

Rachael and her friends joined us back at the Trout. When we got inside, her sparkling blue eyes were the first thing I noticed. Her well-defined cheekbones and nose gave her a noble quality, while her thin red lips and pink cheeks added an exquisite delicacy. Thick, silky hair hung down to her shoulders; at about five foot eight, she could easily be a fashion model. As Rachael and I talked, I learned that she was from Cornwall, was studying history and hoped one day to teach. We seemed to have a lot in common, since I had been a double major in history and English at Virginia, and we shared a love of books. Rachael's west country accent flowed smoothly, like a quiet brook. Yet beneath her calm was an undercurrent of enthusiasm and energy, and I was captivated by her smile and those incredible blue eyes.

There was something different about Rachael, something that I could not quite put my finger on. She was very engaging, yet also reserved, although not in a self-centred manner. After our encounter on Guy Fawke's night, I was ready to start the chase to get to know this attractive girl better. Unfortunately, I had only seen her once since then, when we had bumped into each other during the intermission of Shakespeare's *Henry IV, Part 1* at the Playhouse and compared notes on our favourite character, Falstaff. This brief encounter further piqued my desire to know Rachael better, and I decided that she would be my top priority during Hilary term.

"Good evening, Mr. Bryson," said the college porter as I hurried into the Magdalen lodge, brushing the white powder off my trousers. I had almost forgotten the cold while thinking about Rachael.

"Hello, Mr. Thompson," I replied tersely.

"I was about to lock the front gate. You just made it." He paused, then added, "Why so glum, sir? Ah yes, you Americans do get rather homesick this time of year."

"I guess that's it," I mumbled. "Any mail for me today?"

"I'm afraid not, sir. Do you have any plans for Christmas?" Robert Thompson was a large, round-faced gentleman, with reddish cheeks and thick glasses. His grey hair, balding forehead, and cheerful smile made him seem rather like Santa Claus. For some reason, however, his simple pleasantness irritated me tonight.

"Christmas doesn't mean much to me, Mr. Thompson. I plan to have dinner and lots of drinks with some friends. I was feeling a bit lonely tonight, though, and thought I'd see if I had any mail. I hope my packages arrived back home." I forced a smile.

"If it makes you feel any better, sir, I'm on duty until morning myself. I'll miss not seeing my family tonight, but I'm looking forward to the midnight service on Christmas Eve. Can I do anything for you?" he asked in a polite tone.

"Actually, I thought I might go up to the library and read for awhile." Then, seeing his puzzled look at my late-hour request, I added, "I'm not really tired and since all the pubs are closed, might as well do something productive. Do you mind?"

"Oh, I guess it will be all right this time," he replied with a friendly wink. "Just be sure to turn off the lights and close the door when you're done."

"Thanks, Mr. Thompson – and happy holidays," I called half-heartedly.

"Good night to you, Mr. Bryson, and a merry Christmas," said Mr. Thompson, with a twinkle in his eye.

I reluctantly left the warmth of the porter's lodge and turned toward the library. As I made my way down the dark passageway into St. Swithun's quad, I heard the bells in Magdalen Tower strike quarter to twelve. The college was virtually deserted for the vacation, and it was deathly quiet. I was among just a handful of foreign students staying over Christmas. There were few lights on in any of the rooms, and the various spotlights on the buildings cast huge, dark shadows over the sombre-looking grounds. No stars were visible now, and it began to snow again gently. Feeling quite sorry for myself, and wishing I was still at the pub, I wandered on to Longwall Quad and the library.

Facing the library's sombre oak door, I fumbled with gloved hands for my key card. I glanced up at the door expectantly – and somewhat apprehensively if truth be told – but no Dickensian Marley was there to greet me. The heavy door creaked as I slowly pushed it inward. A dim light inside illuminated rows of bookshelves dividing rows of tables, with a long aisle down the middle of the library, and the stale, musty smell of old books penetrated my nostrils. Shivering, I shut the door as quickly as I could, the resounding thud testifying to the weight of the library's massive portal, and turned on some more lights. Finding a cosy corner that suited me, I deposited my down jacket and gloves, and settled in with a book to attempt to escape my loneliness.

I soon lost track of time, the Tower bells being muffled inside the thick stone walls of the library. Something seemed unusual, however, to my restless eyes. I finally realised that the dark, leather-bound books within my view were all worn and dusty, except for one small nook at the bottom of an obscure bookshelf where the dust had been disturbed. Something white was just barely protruding from the shelves.

Curiosity and boredom got the best of me, and I got down on my knees to investigate. The strange sight that confronted me was a small roll of papers, like a scroll, tied with a bright red ribbon. I untied the ribbon and unrolled the papers. They appeared to be some type of correspondence written in jet-black ink. Because Oxford is known for its curiosities, however, at first I thought little of it. I glanced around, then sheepishly realised that I was, of course, very much all alone. Outside the window hundreds of snowflakes sparkled like playful fireflies in the golden glow of the street lamp. Giving in completely to my curiosity, I sat down on the floor and began reading the papers.

The correspondence was so strange that I was completely baffled by it. There were apparently two different authors, both of whom had very distinctive, queer writing styles. The letters were rather amusing, however, and looked like some kind of joke. I carefully retied the ribbon, replaced the letters on the shelf, and returned to my book. I must have dozed off then, and, upon waking, sluggishly pulled myself up. The Magdalen Tower bells struck three in the morning as I plodded up the dimly lit, wooden staircase to my third-floor room in St. Swithin's Buildings. I longed again for that fleeting sense of timelessness.

*   *   *

The next morning, I looked out my window overlooking High Street. It was a grey, overcast day, and this medieval city was adorned with a pristine shawl of snow. It was the Sunday before Christmas, and the air reverberated with a symphony of church bells. I had not ventured into an Oxford church on Sunday since I had arrived, and I certainly did not intend to alter that routine today. I leapt back into bed to warm up and remembered the strange letters. Then, I had an idea: I would make a copy of them and show them to Rachael. She would surely think they were humorous, too, and this would give me an excuse to go see her when term resumed.

I walked over to the College library after lunch. The papers were in the spot I had left them the previous evening. Not knowing if someone might come to retrieve them, I picked them off the shelf and dashed out to a shop around the corner to photocopy them. After hurriedly copying the pages, I again retied the ribbon and returned the letters to the library shelf. My hands and feet were numb from the cold by the time I arrived in my room, and I plugged in the kettle to make some tea. Sitting in the wooden chair at my desk, I picked up the photocopied pages. To my chagrin, they were blank. Had I been so careless as to copy the wrong side? I couldn't believe it.

The tea revived me, however, and I decided that it was now a challenge to copy the letters. I retraced my steps. This time, as the papers came out of the copier, I examined them. To my complete astonishment, they still came out blank. Deciding then that something was wrong with the copying machine, I tried the other machine, with the same result. I then picked up a book sitting on a nearby table and tried it on the first copier. The page came out perfectly. I was dumbfounded. My flesh prickled as I puzzled over my inability to copy the letters.

Was it Churchill who said, "Never give in?" Quite mystified, I decided to take the letters to my room and type them on my laptop computer. It was a tedious process, but I managed to do it and return the originals to the library. It was late afternoon, and the snow began falling again in earnest. Oxford was as quiet as I had ever heard it. I walked around Magdalen in the dusk, observing the deer quietly standing in the college deer park, seemingly oblivious to the snow. Their brown fur provided the only contrast to the white ground and leafless trees. I wandered past the Chapel, where I could hear the melodious sounds of the Magdalen Boys' Choir at Sunday Evensong, but hurried on to the dining hall without stopping.

2
LETTERS AND RIDDLES

THE BEGINNING of Hilary term was quite hectic. It was fun to see the college alive again, and to have my pub mates back. About a week after term started, I decided to visit Rachael one afternoon. She was in her room at Merton working on her history essay.

"How was your Christmas break?" I asked after our initial greetings.

"It was wonderful," she replied. "And yours?"

"Fairly uneventful, except for a quick trip to Paris. I actually worked a good bit on some philosophy essays."

We made pleasant small talk for awhile. Finally, I asked Rachael out for Saturday night to a party at Christ Church, and was relieved when she said yes.

"By the way," I said as I reached her door to leave, "you won't believe the correspondence I found in the Magdalen Library. It's so strange and funny . . . most amusing."

"Oh really, who is it from?"

"Well, there are several letters, in very queer writing styles. Their names are Foulheart and Soulbane."

Rachael laughed, saying, "Sounds like something from *The Screwtape Letters*."

"Screwtape . . . that's it!" I exclaimed.

"What?"

"That's another name mentioned in the letters I found."

"Oh, you mean you found a copy of *The Screwtape Letters*?"

"I don't know what letters you're talking about, but I found some letters with those names in them."

"Have you ever heard of C.S. Lewis?"

"Who's that?"

"He was an Oxford don, at Magdalen in fact. He taught literature, but he also wrote children's books and Christian books. Have you never heard of him?"

"I've heard the name, I think, but I don't know anything about him," I said, feeling stupid. "But, what does he have to do with these letters?"

"Well, Lewis published a book called *The Screwtape Letters*, which are letters from a devil named Screwtape to his nephew, Wormwood."

"Wormwood! He's mentioned, too." I then proceeded to tell Rachael about my discovery of the strange letters. She looked rather incredulous and had a faint smile.

Finally, Rachael tilted her head and said, "Can you show the letters to me?"

"Sure, let's go."

When we arrived at the Magdalen library, it was getting dark. There were a few students studying when we entered, and, without thinking, I put my finger to my mouth as if Rachael didn't know not to draw attention to what we were doing. My face reddened at my silly gesture. We walked at a deliberate pace toward the back of the library, until I motioned to her to go into one of the side aisles.

"They're right here," I said, pointing toward the shelf at the bottom.

"Where?"

"Well, they were right here," I said, my voice cracking. I began to search everywhere for them, but they were nowhere to be seen.

"I ... I ...", but nothing more came out.

"Well, I'm sure they *were* here," said Rachael with a sarcastic tone.

"No, they really were," I protested. "I even tried to copy them and couldn't, so I retyped them on my laptop."

Rachael giggled and said, "So you don't even have a copy? I guess next you'll tell me you can't find it on your computer either."

"Sure I can," I said with false confidence. We headed off to my room. I turned on my laptop and, to my great relief, retrieved the letters onto the screen.

Rachael read intently, but said nothing. I wondered if this had all been a big mistake on my part.

"Cade, did you make this up? Is this some kind of joke?" she asked, looking right at me.

"No, I swear it's not a joke," I said puzzled.

"And you've never read *The Screwtape Letters* before?"

"I promise I haven't."

"This is incredible," she said finally. "You could be on to something phenomenal."

"Are you referring to those Screwtape letters again?"

"Yes. It's one of Lewis's most famous books. I'll be happy to lend you my copy to read sometime. If you swear this is not a joke, then we need to see if there is really anything to this. I have a friend, a vicar, who has a church in the Cotswolds. I think we should go see him and tell him about this."

"I swear it's not a joke – at least not *my* joke. In fact, I'm the one who thought the letters were some kind of prank, and the only reason I retyped them was to let you share the laugh."

"They probably are some lark. That's why I want to talk to Mr. Brooke, the vicar. I'll call him and see if we can come see him."

"But why would you want to go talk to some priest?"

"Just to see if he thinks there is anything to these letters, since they mention Screwtape and Wormwood and the 'Enemy,' which in Lewis's book is the Christian God."

"Okay," I said with a shrug, not really understanding what she meant. But, I'd take any excuse to spend more time with Rachael. "It's getting late, would you like to go get some dinner?"

"Thanks, but my essay is due tomorrow, and I've got plenty left to do."

"Well, let me know if you talk to the vicar, and I guess I'll see you Saturday," I said somewhat doubtfully, waving goodbye to Rachael after I walked her back to Merton. I was puzzled by Rachael. She was so pretty and fun to talk to, yet quite reserved, almost coy. The subtle way that she resisted my flirtations intrigued me.

The next night, I was to meet Adrian, Colin, and Nigel at the Bear. The white plaster walls with the exposed crooked, wooden beams gave this thirteenth-century pub a unique look amidst the large stone college buildings. As I stepped inside the smoky, noisy room, the crowd of people forced me to be crammed in near the doorway. I found myself facing the display cases on the walls containing cut-off neckties from clubs and universities all over the world. I squirmed my way to the back room and found my companions already sitting at a table.

Colin Greene, a slim five-foot nine student with dark hair and eyes, was studying law. He had delicate features and a biting sarcasm. Colin had grown up in London. Adrian Neil, a balding, muscular, blue-eyed Australian, was studying biology. Adrian was well-known for his abilities on his college eights rowing team. People had even remarked that we looked like brothers, since we had similar builds. Finally, Nigel Stokes was a fair-haired, podgy lad, with glasses and freckles, who was studying literature. Nigel had a prodigious memory for poetry: I had once heard him recite Shakespeare's twenty-ninth sonnet to the object of his affection after a long night in the pub, then turn to a woman's portrait hanging on the wall and recite Browning's "My Last Duchess," and top off his performance with Yeats's "Second Coming." I was duly impressed. Despite our different backgrounds and interests, we enjoyed each other's company.

"What kept you, Cade?" inquired Adrian.

"I was just trying to finish my essay for tomorrow," I replied. "Old Randolph is a stickler for good essays, and I wanted to get it right this time–there's so much to read up first."

"That's what you get for studying PPE," said Nigel. "You should have stuck with one subject, instead of politics, philosophy *and* economics."

"I always seem to learn the hard way," I laughed ruefully.

"Are you coming to the party on Saturday?" asked Colin.

"Yes, of course. And, Rachael is coming with me," I added with a wink.

"Well, well ..." they said in unison. I knew I would get kidded by them, but I also knew they were envious.

Our conversation ambled on for a good while, ricocheting between talk of women, to sports, to literature. Oxford students pride themselves on being good conversationalists about a broad range of subjects, and I found soon after arriving that I had to work hard to keep up with their wit and knowledge.

Finally, I tried to sound nonchalant as I asked, "What do you know about a guy named C.S. Lewis?"

"He was a well-known literature professor here," said Nigel. "At your college, in fact. Very bright, keen mind and a prolific writer."

"Anything else?" I asked.

"He later kind of went off the deep end, if you know what I mean," chimed in Colin. "Got all religious and wrote a bunch of Christian books. Took it all rather too seriously."

"How do you mean?" I asked.

"Well, he did radio broadcasts, wrote books, and gave sermons, all about God and Jesus and stuff like that," said Colin. "Kind of sad, really, that such a good tutor should have ended his career hung up on religion."

"Have any of you read any of his books?" I quizzed them.

"I've had to read some of his literary criticism," said Nigel. "And, as school children, we were subjected to his Narnia tales, which are nice stories ... there's supposedly some religious symbolism there that I don't get. But, can't say that I've ever read any of his Christian books. I've spent a good deal of time studying creation myths, and it's obvious that Christianity is just another version of such myths."

"No sense getting too carried away with this God business, anyway," chimed in Adrian.

"That's what I figure, too," I said. "My dad's always told me that religion is a crutch for people who can't hack it in the "jungle", as he calls it."

"Isn't your dad a lawyer?" asked Colin.

"Yes, for a big firm in Atlanta," I replied. "He's told me often that it's a tough, dog-eat-dog world out there. That's one reason I'm here. He wanted me to come here for a couple of years to develop my skills before going to law school and broaden my horizons. He told me to take advantage of this opportunity to start networking. As he's always said, 'If you don't look out for yourself, no one else will.'"

"It's amazing that C.S. Lewis somehow fell for such myths. I don't understand how anyone could," chuckled Colin.

We all laughed together and then returned to our favourite subject: women. My feelings about the absurdity of religion in general, and Christianity in particular, had been confirmed. As the evening wore on, the crowd became rowdier. Nigel, caught up in the moment, suddenly stood in his chair and recited John of Gaunt's dying tribute to "This blessed plot, this earth, this realm, this England...!" Everyone cheered him when he finished. Thus encouraged, Nigel led a boisterous chorus of "Jerusalem." *What a marvellous night*, I thought, as I stumbled back to Magdalen. Did life get any better than this?

* * *

The following Saturday afternoon, I met Rachael at the bus stop, and we took the bus destined for the Cotswolds. We went to the top of the double-decker bus and sat in the front. I had no clue about why we had to go to see a priest, but I nevertheless welcomed a chance to be with Rachael and to see the Cotswolds again.

"Does this Reverend Brooke know why we're coming?" I asked.

"No, I phoned yesterday and just told him I wanted to come visit and might bring a friend."

"How do you know him?"

"Years ago, he was at our parish in Cornwall, when I was a young girl. Although I haven't seen him in years, I've talked to him several times on the phone since I've been at Oxford. I've kept meaning to go out and see him, so I'm glad for the excuse."

We rode in silence for a good while. The misty Cotswolds

countryside lulled me into a reverie as I gazed at the flocks of sheep grazing on rolling hills, narrow lanes bounded by hedges, and small towns of stone houses. This scenery seemed as if it were right out of an eighteenth century English novel.

When the bus jolted to a stop in one of the villages, Rachael abruptly pulled at my arm.

"Where do we go?" I asked. The February weather was chilly and dreary. There was a steady drizzle, and although it was just mid-afternoon, it was already growing dark, with grey clouds seeming to hang near the chimney tops.

"See the tall steeple of that church off the main street?" she asked, pointing off to the right.

I nodded as I saw a stone steeple, whose pinnacle was obscured by the clouds.

"That's his church," Rachel said with a sudden, optimistic lilt to her voice. Small stone houses fronted the narrow main street of the village. One or two people were walking down the pavement, but otherwise the village looked deserted. Smoke emerged from numerous chimneys, adding to the greyness. Surrounding the stone church was a rusted iron gate and fence leaning inward towards crumbling gravestones. A yew tree took up an entire side of the churchyard, with an overturned stone cross leaning against the trunk.

As we approached the large wooden front doors of the church, Rachael turned to the right. "The vicarage is back here. That's where he said we would find him," she explained, before I said anything.

Behind the church was a separate stone house with a slate roof. There was a yellow glow coming from the windows and smoke drifting from the chimney. Rachael knocked on the door of the vicarage, and a voice bade us to enter.

Rising to greet us was a tall, thin man, with thick silver hair, long dark eyebrows, and grey eyes. The vicar had deep creases in the skin near his eyes, and half-moon wire-rim glasses hung on his thin crimson nose. He removed the pipe from his mouth and smiled warmly. "Rachael, my dear Rachael, how you have grown," he said after we stepped inside. "Let me look at you – such a beautiful lady now."

Rachael grinned and gave him a hug. "Mr. Brooke, how are you? This is my friend, Cade Bryson."

"Jolly good to meet you, Cade," he said genially, extending his hand. He had long, bony fingers, with short, clean fingernails.

"And you, sir," I replied, noticing his grip was firm, but his hand was shaking.

"Can I offer you some tea … or sherry?" he asked.

"Tea for me," said Rachael.

"Tea is fine with me, too," I added.

He put the kettle on, and I glanced around the room. This was obviously his study, containing a desk cluttered with paper, and a wrinkled, faded burgundy leather chair in the corner. Hundreds of books filled the shelves and spilled onto the floor. A small fire burned in the fireplace. On a table next to the chair sat several sherry glasses and a full decanter. Behind the desk on the floor, I also noticed a half-empty bottle of Scotch.

As we sipped our tea, Rachael and the vicar talked about old times, and Rachael filled him in on her mother, her parish church in Tintagel, and on her studies at Oxford. Mr. Brooke was pleasant, but seemed somehow uneasy, and he looked very tired. His eyes saddened when he told Rachael about the death of his wife, Anne, from cancer. After some time had passed, he asked, "What brings the two of you to see an old country vicar on such a dreary Saturday afternoon, then?"

"I'm not sure where to begin," said Rachael. "In fact, we're a little afraid you may think us mad as hatters."

"Come, come, now, I promise I won't think that," he said laughing.

"Cade, tell Mr. Brooke what you told me."

I began to tell the story. The old clergyman listened and smiled, and I had to concentrate on what I was saying instead of on watching him pack and light his pipe. As my story progressed, however, the vicar quit fidgeting with his pipe and began to lean forward. He acknowledged me several times with nods of his head, and an occasional, "I see."

After I finished, he sat there for awhile, as if deep in thought.

Suddenly, he said, "Did you bring a copy of these letters with you?"

"Yes," I replied, handing him the sheets I had printed off my computer.

He adjusted his glasses, sat in his desk chair, and began to read. The only sound was the resonant tick-tock of the grandfather clock. I jumped when something suddenly nudged me and looked down to see an old, golden retriever trying to push his nose under my arm.

"Don't mind old Zeke," said Mr. Brooke. "He's quite friendly, and he's almost deaf now. His name is really Ezekiel, but Anne and I always called him Zeke."

I petted Zeke, who looked up at me with grateful eyes. I glanced at the vicar and saw that the papers were almost imperceptibly shaking in his hands. His eyes were moist, and he pulled out a large handkerchief, wiped his eyes, and blew his nose. He then turned around and poured himself a sherry. "Sure you won't have one?" he asked, but Rachael and I declined.

The vicar sat there silently for some time. It appeared that he was re-reading the letters. I looked at Rachael sitting in a wooden chair near the desk. She wore a white knit sweater and red plaid skirt, and her long, shapely legs were crossed. She seemed oblivious to my glances.

Finally, Mr. Brooke came around the desk and sat in his leather chair. "I knew C.S. Lewis," he almost whispered. "When I was young, I used to ride into Oxford to hear him lecture and preach. I even went to see him several times in his rooms at Magdalen. He was brilliant. He helped me decide to become a priest. In those days, I was young and idealistic, and thought I might change the world. That was a long time ago ..." His voice trailed off.

He laid down his pipe, then stood up, ambled over to his bookshelves, and began to thumb through his books. Finally, he retrieved one and brought it over. Without saying a word, he handed it to Rachael. She looked inside and smiled, and then handed it to me.

It was a faded hardback edition of *The Screwtape Letters*. Inside the front cover was some handwriting: "To James Brooke, a most promising young man. Yrs, C.S. Lewis."

Then Mr. Brooke said, "Cade, this is important, and I want you to be honest with me. Is this a joke? ... I need to know now if it is."

"No, sir. At least not from me. I don't know anything about C.S. Lewis and had never heard of *The Screwtape Letters* until a few days ago when I talked to Rachael. I've told you exactly what happened. I typed them because I thought they were clever and rather humorous. Rachael is the one who thought we should bring them to you."

The vicar smiled weakly and stroked his chin. He went over behind his desk and poured himself another sherry, then re-lit his pipe. I became aware again of the ticking of the clock, and I glanced over at Rachael. She smiled and shrugged, but said nothing.

Finally, Mr. Brooke broke the silence, saying, "What night did you find these?"

"Let's see," I said, "it must have been December twenty-first, because I remember one of us toasting the solstice."

"The winter's solstice," the vicar remarked pensively. "How interesting."

"What do you make of this?" interjected Rachael.

"I don't really know," said Mr. Brooke. "I'm not sure I'm the one you should be asking. Years ago, my Christian faith was strong, and this was in no small part due to C.S. Lewis. He was such an inspiration to me, and I wanted to make the priesthood my lifelong work. But, ever since my dear Anne died, what is it, six years ago now?"

He paused and appeared to be in deep thought. Then he continued, "I stopped praying after that, stopped believing really. For these last years, I've gone through the motions in my parish. Fortunately for me, out here in the country it's easier to get by. I'm just the nice old vicar around here, and most people in the church don't want anyone to rock the boat. That's suited me fine, and has allowed me to just drift on through life."

"But," interrupted Rachael, "you were so strong in your faith, so sure of it, when you were in Cornwall."

"Yes, I was back then. But times change and I've changed. God felt so far away, so distant and uncaring, and, finally, so irrelevant."

"He's not, though," said Rachael stubbornly. Her smile had disappeared.

"Perhaps. The question now, however, is what we do about young Mr. Bryson's discovery. It's all so puzzling, so unreal, in fact. It brings back many memories. When I used to visit Lewis, I came loaded with questions about Christian faith and doubt, and he always seemed to know just how to explain it or give just the right example. I learned a great deal from him. He was very kind and never made me feel that I was an imposition. Occasionally, I would try and get him to talk about the *Letters*, but he always seemed a bit reluctant to speak of them."

By this time, I was feeling very uncomfortable. I had long ago decided that I was, if not an atheist, at least an agnostic, and had looked down my nose at anyone foolish enough to take Christianity seriously. I assumed such people to be ignorant and naive, and it confused me to hear Rachael talk about God.

"... what do you think, Cade?" Rachael was asking. The fact that I hadn't been listening must have been obvious from my blank look.

"I'm sorry, Rachael, what were you asking?" I said sheepishly. By now, I just wanted to get back to Oxford, and I didn't want to miss the party at Christ Church tonight.

"I was saying, maybe we need to see if we can find the rest of this."

"But how? Besides, this is probably just a college prank."

"Maybe," interjected Mr. Brooke, "but maybe not. We owe it to ourselves, indeed to the church, to find out."

"Where would we even begin," I responded. "It's so vague and confusing." *Besides*, I thought, *I've had enough of all this*.

Rachael answered, "If these are authentic ... actual letters from a devil, we must find the rest of them. You're not afraid of finding them are you?"

"No ... I guess not. But this is so ... so ..." I stammered.

"So crazy?" filled in Mr. Brooke.

"Yes, I guess that's it."

"Why don't I read these letters out loud, and let's think about this," suggested Mr. Brooke. "Maybe something will come to one of us."

"That's a good idea," said Rachael.

He picked up the letters and sat on top of his desk, crossing his legs. He cleared his throat, gulped the glass of sherry, and began to read the letters out loud:

To Soulbane,

Although it is not our policy to believe in miracles, that is the ONLY explanation for Screwtape and Wormwood not being ousted from the Master's realm forever. The stupidity and carelessness they exhibited are truly unbelievable. It was bad enough that they let their human patient be won over by the Enemy, but to bottom it off, just as I was looking forward to a superb reward for exposing that egregious error, their inexcusable boneheadedness was discovered by someone else. How could they have been so moronic? I still shudder to think that Wormwood, a snivelling, stupid, whimpering, ignorant apprentice, could have allowed Screwtape's invaluable correspondence – containing the wisdom we fiends had gained over thousands of years about how to disrupt and destroy the Enemy's plans – to fall into the hands of such a despicable creature as that vile C.S. Lewis. That was a setback to our plans, to say the least, because that damned Lewis had the audacity to publish Screwtape's letters so that some of those drivels the Enemy calls his children could learn about our methods of operation. Of course, I hold that lout Screwtape responsible for this, because he was credulous enough to entrust his correspondence to his lunkhead nephew.

This was not without some rewards, however: I had the indescribable pleasure of watching those two cretins prostrate themselves before our Royal Hindness and plead with him to give them another chance. I experienced unspeakable ecstasy as they – Hell forbid – shamelessly begged the Master for ... I can hardly utter such a servile word ... forgiveness. Fortunately, the Master would have none of it: he was not taken in by their weakbellied, mealy-mouthed wailing. Our Royal Hindness has now banished them from our Hindom and sentenced them to be subjected to torture: they have been assigned to break the code of the Enemy's communication with these humans through prayer. We have not yet been able to intercept these transmissions, partly because the fiends who are assigned this task generally end up insane. What a fitting end to these two idiots!

Our Royal Hindness has now called in some real devils to do his work, and we have a chance to make up for their ineptitude. The Master wants a behind-the-scenes report on the Enemy's kingdom and the success of our multitude of strategies. But, let me warn you – there must be NO MISTAKES. Repeat, NO MISTAKES. As a result of Lewis's book, some of the upstart creatures actually learned to recognise our subtle attacks on them, and have crawled ever closer to the Enemy. As you well know, our mission is to destroy the Enemy by destroying his creation – particularly those weak, ignorant human creatures the Enemy claims to care about. (Why he does is totally inexplicable.)

This setback with Lewis – thanks to the incredible clumsiness of those two clods – has caused us to re-double our efforts. We are fortunate that the Enemy finally called that ignoramus Lewis back to the his spiritual realm. In order to make up for the inexcusable mistakes of our imbecilic colleagues, our Royal Hindness himself has authorised us to do a study of the effectiveness of the various strategies our Base Command has implemented to destroy the Enemy's work. Our brief is to evaluate the current status of our Hindom's efforts and make even more effective and diabolical plans for the future to wipe out the Enemy's influence once and for all. As part of the Base Command's global stratagem evaluation, we have been assigned to study the Church – how that word sticks in my mouth! – and the culture of the modern-day western world, from the vantage points of Europe and the United States.

You should immediately begin preparations for your study on the practices, habits, and most importantly, the thinking (an oxymoron if there ever was one) of these ignorant creatures, and report directly to me. Let me repeat, should you fail to provide a comprehensive report, the consequences for you are unthinkable.

Because of the nature of this research project, you'll need to assume appropriate human forms in order to infiltrate their society and observe it first-hand. In addition, given what happened with those numskulls, Screwtape and Wormwood, I want to take no risks. Therefore, I want you to provide reports directly to me. I will review them prior to sending them on to the Base Command, in order to exert any necessary editorial control. Do not send any information that might be intercepted by our fiend patrols, which could then be passed on to the Base Command before I have a chance to review it. Instead, prepare written reports, and I'll personally retrieve them. As an added precaution, produce everything in your own handwriting, so that I can be assured of authenticity, and I will do the same. Follow the procedures for exchanging reports outlined in MOCK, our Manual for the Overthrow of the Christian Kingdom. DO NOT FAIL!

Disrespectfully,
Foulheart

To the Most Dishonourable Foulheart,

I wanted to respond immediately to your letter. First, let me congratulate you on your well-deserved promotion to Archdevil. I know that it has taken thousands of years for you to achieve such lowly status. While we are not allowed to exhibit any of the Enemy's weak and silly characteristics, such as what he calls gladness, suffice it to say I commend you on your move downstairs. After the debacle you describe concerning the letters, I only wish I had been allowed to get my hands on that scoundrel Lewis … he would have been surprised all right, and not by joy!

I never did like that sycophant, Wormwood, anyway. He was always brown-nosing his uncle, and it serves them both right! They thought they were so smug keeping it all in the family, and look what their nepotism cost our Hindom. And his uncle, how low and mighty he thought he was! Well, they got what they deserved – and more.

I shall begin my new assignment at once. Do not fear, I will not let you down. Obviously, in order to carry out my Hellish mission, I will have to go undercover (excellent word!) to gather the necessary data for my report, which I shall personally prepare and deliver. As you suggest, when my report is prepared, I will follow the procedures set forth in MOCK.

I thank you for giving me this chance to prove my value as a fiend.[HN]

Your humble and ever obedient servant,

Soulbane

Soulbane,

This shall be my last communication to you until you have completed your report. No one – other than the Base Command and myself – is to know of your mission. You have been authorised to use the four urchins to assist you, but they are to be threatened in no uncertain terms that this secret mission has the Command's deepest priority and is of the lowermost importance.

Foulheart

Most Dishonourable Foulheart,

I am in the process of finalising Part I of my Report. As set forth in MOCK, and in order to avoid discovery, it will be available at the turncoat's shipwreck cave on the vainglorious day when drunkenness, gluttony and lust are celebrated before that horrid day of ashes and repentance.

Your humble and ever obedient servant,

Soulbane

*   *   *

When the vicar finished reading, there was complete silence, save the ticking of the clock. Finally, Zeke slowly roused himself from the corner and nudged him.

"What do you think this is ... someone's idea of a joke?" asked Rachael finally.

"I ... I don't know," said Mr. Brooke, stroking his chin. "I want to think it's just a student prank, and yet ..." he didn't finish.

[HN]*Might I add a "hindnote" and request that I be allowed to have the services of several of our fledgling underspirits to assist me in gathering the necessary information? If so, I would suggest, perhaps, Baldface, Scrunchmouth, Bleakblab, and Slobglob.*

"What is the day he is referring to?" I inquired.

"I think it must be Shrove Tuesday," Mr. Brooke informed me.

"Is that the same thing as Mardi Gras? I've been to New Orleans and Mobile, where they have Mardi Gras parades and parties."

"Precisely. It's the days leading up to the Christian observance of Lent. Mardi Gras means 'Fat Tuesday,' and it's a time of feasting and partying before starting the solemn fasting and prayer of Lent."

"When is it exactly?" I wondered aloud.

"Ash Wednesday begins Lent, which is always forty days before Easter," answered Mr. Brooke. "The date of Easter varies from year-to-year depending on – believe it or not – the moon. Easter is always the first Sunday after the first full moon after the vernal equinox."

He then went over to his desk and picked up a black book and thumbed through it. "Let's see, Easter this year is in late April, so Ash Wednesday is in mid-March. That means we don't have much time to figure this out."

"What's the big deal?" I finally asked. "What's so important about all this?"

"Well, it's a bit difficult to unpack," said Mr. Brooke. "This is probably someone's idea of a joke. But, if it isn't ..."

"Don't you see?" interrupted Rachael. "If this is actual correspondence from a junior devil, then this is a tremendous revelation. It allows us to have an insight into the unseen spiritual world."

"Rachael's right. This could be an incredible discovery. But I must caution you both to keep this completely quiet for now. If this is just a joke, we don't want to let on. If it's not, there are many people who would love to lay their hands on these papers. Some would want to destroy them and insure they never become public; others might use them for evil purposes. Because we don't know what we have here yet, we can't take that chance."

"But, how can we ever locate this report?" asked Rachael. "This is like a hunt for hidden treasure."

I could see that both the vicar and Rachael were getting more and more excited. I had a sinking feeling that maybe I should never have looked at those letters in the Magdalen library, and certainly should never have mentioned them to Rachael. Where would all this lead?

"I'll tell you what," said Mr. Brooke, "I'll come into Oxford on Wednesday and meet you at the Bodleian Library at half past two. We'll do some research and see if we can find anything that sheds some light on this mystery. Now, it's getting late, and I need to see if I can come up with something for a sermon tomorrow. You'd better run and make sure you don't miss the bus back to Oxford."

We said our good-byes and rushed out. We had only about five minutes to make it before the bus was due, and it was bound to be punctual on the day we were late arriving.

On the way back, I found myself confused about all this talk of letters from devils. I looked at Rachael with some bewilderment. She seemed quite troubled by our visit, but I decided not to address the issue. Instead, I asked about her studies, and she talked about her most recent essay on the Elizabethan era. Rachael was obviously well read, and I found myself becoming more attracted to her as she displayed her passion for the subject. After we arrived in Oxford, I walked her back to Merton. She seemed to perk up a bit as we walked.

"Are we still on for tonight?" I asked hopefully.

"Yes, of course," she said. "I'll see you about half past seven." She turned and waved good-bye from the porter's lodge as I headed back to Magdalen. And she smiled her wonderful smile.

3

COINCIDENCES

THE FOLLOWING WEDNESDAY, I was running late from a rugby match. Our Magdalen rugby team called themselves the Wilde Bunch, after Magdalen's famous alumnus, Oscar. Although rugby season was over, someone had got the bright idea of playing an inter-team match. It was below freezing today, with a damp, bone-chilling wind. None of us, however, had been willing to let down the others, so we all braved the weather. I had become so involved in the game, I lost track of time. When I realised how late it was, I rushed back to my room for a quick shower.

I went hurriedly up the High, rubbing my red hands for warmth, having forgotten my gloves. It was getting colder and the grey afternoon was quickly turning into night. My lips were very chapped, and I was grateful for my warm down jacket. My mind was planning how to explain why I was so late. As I turned the corner just past All Souls, a man was sitting on the ground, bundled up, leaning against the stone wall. I almost stumbled over him.

"Damn you," I yelled immediately. "Can't you watch out?"

The man just sat there, holding a dented tin cup. His tattered brown coat covered his upper body, and a dark green blanket was wrapped around his legs. He stared at me with huge brown eyes. Through his greying, unkempt beard, his yellow teeth were chattering.

"Can you spare any money?" he asked.

"No, I'm already very late," I said as I turned to go. Then, thinking twice, I found a fifty pence coin in my jacket pocket and dropped it into his cup.

As I walked quickly away toward the library, I heard him saying in a trembling voice, "Bless you, sir."

I finally caught up with Mr. Brooke and Rachael at the Bodleian Library about half past three. The vicar greeted me with a smile and handshake, but Rachael did not even look up from the book she was reading. Saturday night had been a disaster, to put it mildly. I had taken Rachael to the party at Christ Church, and the evening had started well. As it wore on, however, I drank more and more, and began to espouse my views on any number of subjects, whether I knew anything about them or not. I guess I thought I was still the All-American lacrosse player at Virginia, where such antics had played well at fraternity parties. I woke up Sunday morning with a train roaring in my head and no recollection as to how or when I got back to my rooms. My headache worsened when I realised I also had no recollection of taking Rachael back to her college. The message I had left for her at the Merton lodge had not been answered. I was inclined not to show up today, but my curiosity about this Soulbane business had been aroused, and I wanted to see what would happen next. I also wanted to see if Rachael would speak to me. She didn't.

Mr. Brooke appeared to notice the icy reception I received, for he suddenly launched into a summary of his investigation thus far. "I must confess I'm a bit befuddled by this. I really don't know where to begin. I've been doing some research on my own before coming up to Oxford, and I've actually been at the Bodleian since this morning."

"Have you come up with anything?" asked Rachael.

"Nothing. There are so many possibilities. There are thousands of caves around the world, and many associated with shipwrecks. For centuries, there have been reports of shipwrecks all over the Mediterranean, not to mention the Atlantic, Pacific, and other oceans. Why, I was even reading about the caves in the Caribbean, and that

Robert Louis Stevenson got his inspiration for *Treasure Island* from hearing about them."

"Do you have any suggestions?" I asked.

"No, I was hoping the three of us could come up with something. We only have a couple of weeks before Ash Wednesday, and I don't see any way we'll solve this puzzle by then. We'll have to narrow this down somehow. I say ... since the letters appeared in Oxford, maybe we should look only on this side of the world, say, the Mediterranean and the Atlantic. Even that will be a daunting task. It's worth a try at least, given the potential ramifications of the letters Cade found."

"Since I'm studying British history at the moment, why don't I take the British Isles and the Atlantic coast of Europe," said Rachael.

"All right, then I'll investigate the Mediterranean," added Mr. Brooke. "Cade, since you're American, you research the western Atlantic and the Caribbean. Don't forget to look at Bermuda, too."

"That's fine with me," I said.

"Why don't we meet back here at half past six to compare notes?" added Mr. Brooke.

I decided to try going to the Radcliffe Camera, that odd, round Christopher Wren building that reminded me of a Jules Verne spaceship, with its lead dome and porthole windows. I searched through numerous volumes of the archaic, hand-written book indexes and requested several books. When they were eventually brought up, I began poring through them, discovering many interesting things about shipwrecks over the centuries, but getting no nearer to solving the mystery of the turncoat's cave. I glanced at my watch finally, and realised I had five minutes to meet up with Rachael and the vicar.

When we rendezvoused, it was evident from the tired expressions on their faces that their luck had been the same as mine.

"It's getting quite late, and I need to be off," said Mr. Brooke. "Shall we meet here on Saturday for one more try?"

"Sure," Rachael said, as I nodded in agreement.

"Can I walk you back?" said Mr. Brooke to Rachael.

"No thanks, I'll be fine."

"I'll see you back," I volunteered apprehensively.

Rachael shot me a disapproving look, but said, "Well … okay, let's go."

We walked in silence most of the way. As we neared Merton, I summoned up what courage I had and said, "Rachael, I'm sorry about last Saturday. I made a fool of myself. I don't suppose you'd like to try again sometime?"

"Cade," she said in an angry tone, "you need to grow up. I was quite embarrassed by your behaviour Saturday night, and Nigel ended up seeing me back to Merton. You and I are in different places right now. I'll help you and Mr. Brooke on this Soulbane mystery, but that's it."

"I don't blame you." I could feel the lump in my throat. I had really blown it this time. Rachael was such a remarkable girl, and yet she was slipping through my fingers.

At the Merton gate, she said, "Come up for a minute. I have something I want to give you." When we arrived in her room, she walked over to her bookshelf, pulled out a small paperback, and handed it to me. "Perhaps you'll read this sometime. It might help you in your search."

"My search, what search?"

"You're probably not even aware of it, Cade, but I can tell you're looking for something. Maybe you don't know what it is you're looking for. Anyway, this book might help."

I looked at it and saw that the cover read, *Mere Christianity* by C.S. Lewis.

"Thanks," I said half-heartedly. The last thing I wanted was a book about Christianity. But I took it nonetheless and walked back to Magdalen in the dark. When I arrived at my room, I tossed the book on my desk and promptly forgot about it.

*   *   *

The following Saturday, we spent a great deal of time at the Bodleian, but again nothing jumped out at us. Finally, in mid-afternoon, we took a break and discussed the dead ends we kept hitting.

"Are you young people hungry?" said Mr. Brooke. When we both nodded, he suggested we walk over to the Covered Market for a sandwich. We bundled up and exited the library. The blue sky was dotted with white clouds, and a gentle but chilly breeze whispered through the streets. We pushed through the crowds in the Covered Market's conglomeration of different shops – from butchers to shoe shops, to cafes. After we picked up something to eat, we walked outside and found a bench under a large spreading tree.

"What do we do now?" asked Rachael.

"I haven't the foggiest," said Mr. Brooke. "I guess this was a wild goose chase anyway. The day before Ash Wednesday is only two and a half weeks away, so I'm afraid I think it's hopeless. We seem to have wasted a lot of time on what is most likely someone's idea of a good practical joke."

We sat in silence then, and I was secretly grateful. I had my fill of this nonsense and wanted to get back to my pub crawls and fun drinking friends. I was ready to meet some more girls. The challenge of courting the mysterious and attractive Rachael was exhilarating, but after last Saturday, it seemed futile to continue – or did it?

The setting sun cast a golden glow on the honey-coloured stone walls of Oxford. A lone dove was flying overhead.

"I have to get back to get ready for the service tomorrow," Mr. Brooke said finally. "Look here, why don't you both come out tomorrow for church, and then we'll go for a nice walk in the country and have a pub lunch? At least our friendship is a blessing that's come out of all this."

"That sounds lovely," said Rachael.

Before I could think of a reason to say no, I found myself agreeing to come, too.

"It's settled, then. I'll look for you at the ten o'clock service." He then left to get his car. I walked Rachael to Merton, but we said very little. I had dated lots of girls, yet I found my heart strangely heavy over my strained relationship with Rachael.

I returned to my room and took a quick shower. I began to think about where to go next this Saturday evening. I was supposed to meet Nigel, Colin and Adrian at the King's Arms, but decided I felt too weary for a night of pub crawling after all. Magdalen was rather quiet for a Saturday night, so I tried to work on my essay for the next week, but couldn't concentrate. I glanced over and saw *Mere Christianity* on my desk. What did Rachael mean about my "search"?

The Magdalen Tower bells reminded me that it was not very late. Again, I contemplated joining my friends at the pub, but vetoed that idea. I wanted some time alone. Instead, I biked down to the Cowley Road for some Indian food, and returned to my room to eat. By the time I finished eating, I was no longer hungry, but my stomach was in no shape to let me go to sleep now. I spied Lewis's book again and, with nothing better to do, picked it up. A few pages of Christian fairy tale would put anyone to sleep, I thought. I got into bed, turned on the bedside lamp, and began reading.

I realised, finally, that I was not only not getting sleepy, but I was several chapters into the book. *Mere Christianity* was not what I had expected at all. Having had many a laugh at some of the television evangelists in America, I was prepared for some silly, anti-intellectual, religious nonsense. Instead, I found an utterly readable and quite sensible book talking about God in a way I had not been exposed to. I shook my head. This was absurd! I knew Christianity, like all religions, was just a myth made up as a crutch for weak-headed folks, and I didn't want anything to do with it. I thought of Rachael: she certainly did not fit my stereotype of religious people – self-righteous, judgmental, and narrow minded. Rachael was very bright, fun and vivacious. Although she was confident, she wasn't vain or self-centred. She talked more about me, or books, or dreams of travel, than about herself. I reluctantly found now that I could not readily dismiss Lewis's book, and, if anything, I felt a compulsion to continue reading. At any rate, I rationalised, it would not be long before it all stood out as patent nonsense, and at least I could tell Rachael I had read it.

As I continued reading, Lewis seemed to be talking directly to me. I thought back to my conversation at The Bear with Nigel, Colin, and Adrian. It was as if Lewis had overheard our conversation and was writing to answer us. I read on, but stopped dead in my tracks, so to speak, when I came to Lewis's discussion of Jesus' words, and how shocking they were. I continued reading: "It was as if Lewis had overheard our conversation and was writing to us. I read on, but stopped dead in my tracks, so to speak when I came to Lewis's discussion of Jesus' words, and how shocking they were. In particular, his statement that the words of Jesus from the mouth of an ordinary man would have been considered mad and certainly not the words of a great moral teacher. And finally Lewis's exhortation to the reader to consider whether Jesus was indeed the the Son of God, or if not, perhaps a madman."

I read the entire chapter again, and felt as if I had been hit by a train. Never in my life had anyone explained God and Christianity like Lewis did. I knew now that I had to find out more before I could dismiss this out of hand.

* * *

I awoke with a start. *Mere Christianity* was lying on my chest, and my bedside lamp was still on. I looked at the clock and saw it was eight in the morning. I yawned, then leapt out of bed when I suddenly remembered that Rachael and I were going to church, and that she was picking me up at eight thirty! I flew to shower and dress.

Rachael had borrowed a car from a friend, and she stopped in front of Magdalen to pick me up, just as I rushed outside. A soupy fog forced us to go slowly as we wound through the Oxford streets and headed toward the Cotswolds. Rachael was outwardly friendly, yet the warmth I had felt earlier from her was missing.

"You look rather ragged," she said in a sardonic tone. "A late night at the pubs?"

"Well, I didn't get a lot of sleep last night."

"I thought so. You look bleary-eyed. You don't have to come today, you know."

"Actually, the reason for my lack of sleep is your fault."

Rachael cocked her head and peered at me quizzically. "Why's that?"

"I started *Mere Christianity* last night, and, frankly, I couldn't put it down. I must say that I've never read anything like it, and it puts things in ways I never considered before. It has given me a lot to think about."

"I thought you might like it if you ever started reading it." I detected a blush on her cheeks, which I hoped was due to regret at her remark about the pubs. "Lewis had an uncanny ability to explain complex matters in a way that is understandable and makes sense."

"Tell me about your friendship with Mr. Brooke," I asked, wishing to change the subject for now.

"Actually, it has been a long time since he was in Cornwall, and I was pretty young, then. I remember his enthusiasm more than I do anything else. He was always so full of life when he was in our parish, and he loved being with young people."

After we reached the village, we made our way to the church. The bells were ringing and people were beginning to arrive for the service. Most of them appeared elderly, and there were few children. The church was about a third full, and I guessed that it would hold a hundred people. The stark beauty of the building was striking, with its grey, stone walls, roughly cut wooden beams in the ceiling, and dark wooden benches. The plainness of the interior contrasted with the bright and rich purple, ruby and lapis stained-glass windows, and the gold-flamed candles on the altar.

My thoughts were interrupted when the organist began the opening hymn. A procession, consisting of one teenage acolyte, a choir of about ten middle-aged or older people, and Mr. Brooke, made its way down the aisle. He wore a black robe and white surplice with a white clerical collar. As the singing died down, Rachael picked up a Church of England Prayer Book, and she turned to a page called Order for Holy Communion. The vicar began reading that service. There was a distinct monotone both to his voice and that of the congregation.

After a tedious interval, everyone sat down, and the vicar ascended to the pulpit. He looked wearily into the crowd and gave a short sermon, basically consisting of an exhortation to follow the golden rule. It was not inspiring, to say the least, and I quickly tuned him out. After he finished, the service continued, culminating with a formal communion ceremony; I remained in my seat while Rachael went forward to join the queue.

As the congregation departed, we waited out front. The day was overcast, and a brisk March wind blew from the north. Several yellow daffodils that had emerged between the grave markers were shivering in the breeze, adding the only colour to the scenery.

"Are you ready for a brisk walk?" I heard Mr. Brooke's voice behind me.

"Sure," I replied, trying to sound more eager than I felt.

"Let's walk across the meadows to a lovely country pub I know. They have quite nice lunches on Sunday."

We set off out of the village, crossed a bridge over a clear, fast-running stream, and then walked on a narrow dirt path across a brown grassy field. There was a pungent smell of cows and sheep. The sun played hide and seek with the clouds, although it remained primarily overcast. After half an hour's walking, we arrived at an Elizabethan pub with a thatched roof. Fortunately, we found a table inside near the crackling fire, which offered welcome warmth. We ordered beers and shepherd's pies. The vicar downed his first beer quickly, and before I finished one glass, he was on his third.

Eventually, the conversation got around to the Soulbane letters. I now regretted I had ever mentioned them, and hoped this would be the last I ever heard of them.

"I guess there is nothing else we can do," said Mr. Brooke. "I've looked in so many books, I feel like a scholar of shipwrecks. It seems like a waste, though, since it's all probably just a joke."

"Yes," I said, readily agreeing, "it looks like someone wanted whoever found the letters to pursue a will-o'-the-wisp."

"But, Mr. Brooke," said Rachael, "what if they are genuine? Isn't there anything we can do?"

"I'm afraid not. Besides, Ash Wednesday is almost upon us, and we'd never be able to find it now anyway. If it is authentic, which I sincerely doubt, we'll never know. Are you ready to head back?"

The mid-afternoon sky was beginning to blacken with storm clouds, and the wind was noticeably stiffer. The leafless branches of the trees were swaying vigorously. We quickened our pace. As we approached the village, I could see the cross on top of the church steeple silhouetted against the dark, threatening sky.

When we reached the churchyard, the first bolt of lightning struck, and the rain followed immediately. We rushed inside the church for shelter. It was completely dark outside now, and a small candle to the right of the altar provided the only light inside the church. We sat on several of the benches near the back and caught our breath. The heavy rain sounded almost like the roar of the surf at the ocean.

"Rachael," said the vicar, "it's been so good to see you after all these years. I do hope you'll come and visit me again." As he spoke, a loud clap of thunder echoed throughout the church.

"Of course I will, Mr. Brooke. Cade, as soon as the storm lets up, we'd better think about returning to Oxford. I have some work to do for next week. I'm still sorry we never had any clue about the meaning of the letters. I guess it would take something like St. Paul's Damascus vision to ever figure it out now."

"What did you say?" inquired the vicar

"We need to get back."

"No, what else did you say?" he asked more emphatically.

"Just that we would need a Damascus vision now to figure this out."

The vicar was silent, and stroked his chin. Suddenly, he leapt up, startling me.

"Rachael ... Rachael, that might just be it!"

"What?" Rachael and I said simultaneously.

"The clue we've been needing. Come back to my study for a minute. I want to check something."

Despite the deluge, we went out the back of the church and ran the short distance to the vicarage. Once inside, Mr. Brooke put on the kettle, handed us a towel to dry ourselves, and turned on a space heater in the corner. As Rachael and I huddled near the heater, Mr. Brooke began running his fingers across the books on his shelves. He selected one, and began rapidly flipping pages. Neither Rachael nor I said anything, and I went over to pet old Zeke, who had awakened when we came in and was sitting in the corner of the study near the clock.

"Yes ... yes ..." said Mr. Brooke, who then kept reading.

When I could stand it no longer, I asked him, "What are you thinking?" I was irritated by this rash behaviour, not to mention getting soaked by the rain.

"Just a minute," he said quickly. Then Mr. Brooke retrieved the Bible from his desk and started paging through it. Finally, he looked at us and smiled, saying, "In Acts, not only is St. Paul's conversion at Damascus described in the ninth chapter, but also his subsequent shipwreck. The twenty-seventh and twenty-eighth chapters recount that Paul and his companion Luke were shipwrecked on an island called Malta. Here, let me read it." He read the account from his Bible of their amazing escape from a tempest.

Then, he picked up the other book he had been looking at, saying, "There's a legend on Malta that there is a certain cave where Paul lived after he was shipwrecked. It's still called the St. Paul Grotto. I've been there once, long ago ... with Anne." He paused. "There is also a legend that the St. Paul Grotto stays exactly the same size, even if stone is removed from it."

"But, what about the turncoat reference?" Rachael asked.

"Well, a devil would view Paul as a turncoat," replied Mr. Brooke. "You see, Paul was a devout Jew who persecuted the early Christians, and even participated in the stoning of Stephen. Later, he had a vision of Christ on the way to Damascus, and from that point to the end of his life, he fervently preached Christianity all over the known Greek and Roman worlds. Moreover, his writings make up much of the New Testament."

I then said, "I have a friend at Magdalen from Malta, but I must confess I don't know a lot about it."

"It's a tiny island in the Mediterranean off the coast of Italy," said Mr. Brooke. "A beautiful, historic island. It has been inhabited since pre-historic times, and because of its location in the centre of the Mediterranean, it has been part of western history for centuries. Malta has been occupied by many different countries, and is known for having once been home to the Knights of St. John. It came under British rule in the 1800s, and finally became independent in – let's see – 1964. It is primarily a Catholic country. Anne and I had a marvellous holiday there."

"I had no idea it had that much history behind it," I replied.

"Yes, it is a fascinating place. In fact, during one of his wartime speeches, Winston Churchill called Malta 'a tiny rock full of history and romance.' But, back to the point, the apostle Paul was shipwrecked there, we know that. I guess it's just wishful thinking, however, to believe we would ever find the report that Soulbane mentions. In fact, it's absurd to think we would ever find it, especially since we have so little time left."

"Yes, I guess you're right," I added, wanting to encourage everyone to give up on this.

"Maybe one of us could go," interjected Rachael. "I mean, isn't it worth a try?"

"It's such a long shot," said Mr. Brooke. "Besides, who would go and how would we get there? I have a little money saved up for my retirement, but ..."

"Then, perhaps you *should* go," interrupted Rachael. "Especially since you've been there before."

"No, I'm too old. And, even if I wanted to, well, I have problems with my heart and it wouldn't be wise."

"We need some sign or affirmation," said Rachael. "Why don't we pray and ask God to help us?"

Now, I was really wondering what I had started. This silly talk about prayer bothered me. I noticed that the vicar did not appear very warm to the idea either, despite being a man of the cloth.

"Well, I don't know," said Mr. Brooke. "How would prayer help us now?"

"Let's ask God for some sign that we are on the right track. If he wants us to find it, he will help. I feel sure of it. What have we got to lose?"

"I suppose you have a point," replied Mr. Brooke.

"Then, will you say a prayer for us?" asked Rachael.

"All right," he said. He bowed his head, as did Rachael. I was very uncomfortable, but stood there silently.

"Father ... Lord ..." he began hesitantly. "We bring before you this matter of the letters found by Cade Bryson. We ... we don't know if they are authentic or a prank, much less where we could ever find any such report. We ask, therefore, that if we are on the right track, you direct us in the way we should go. We ask this in the name of your only Son. Amen."

"Amen," said Rachael.

I had never heard a prayer like this before and thought it all rather absurd.

"I guess that's all we can do," said Mr. Brooke. "It's getting late now, and it sounds as though the storm has passed. I'll walk you to your car."

As we rode back, I finally had to ask Rachael, "Do you really believe in prayer? I mean, that someone actually hears prayers?"

"Yes ... yes, I do believe in prayer, Cade. I can't offer you proof, of course, but that is what faith is all about. It's a mystery, and yet I do believe God answers somehow, even if we don't recognise or understand the answer."

I smugly thought how naive she was, but discretion being the better part of valour, I said nothing.

* * *

Monday came quickly and, given that we were nearing the end of Hilary term, I had a good deal of work to do and quickly became absorbed with my studies. I was glad that Ash Wednesday would soon come and go, so that I could forget this entire mess. I thought about Rachael. She was so pretty and lively, and I felt a strong attraction to her, but there were other fish in the sea, I told myself. I was ready for some fun with my friends, and dropped them a note to meet me at the Head of the River pub on Tuesday night, so we could discuss plans for a cycling trip to Ireland during the Easter break.

* * *

The next week was the last of term. I had been occupied with my final essay on economic theory and with our holiday plans. Thursday night, I hurried to the Magdalen dining hall and barely made it before the line closed. The hall was half empty by the time I got my food. The dark wooden walls and benches, with the large Gothic windows and extremely tall ceiling, gave the dining hall a grandiose medieval atmosphere. In the dim light of the small lamps sprinkled down the long, wooden benches, I saw my friend, Peter Mizzi, sitting by himself, and went over to him. Peter was a plump, olive-skinned boy with dark hair and a jovial manner. We had met each other during the matriculation ceremony at the Sheldonian Theatre right after we both arrived in Oxford. Peter was a graduate student in law, and because of my interest in going to law school eventually, we found we had a few things in common. We had become friends over the last year and a half, generally seeing each other around the Magdalen dining hall or Middle Common Room.

"Mind if I join you?" I asked, glad to see Peter.

"Not at all, Cade, please do," replied Peter, who smiled cheerfully.

"What have you been up to lately?" I asked, in order to get the conversation going.

"Just the usual," he said. "I've had a busy term thanks to my law tutors! How about you?"

"The same, I guess. By the way, Peter, someone was recently telling me about Malta. You've told me a little about it before, but I'd like to know more about the country."

Peter grinned at my request and began to tell me about his island home. He talked about what it was like to live there now, and I was fascinated to learn more about the history and the people of this ancient Mediterranean country.

When he finished, he asked, "What are you doing during the upcoming term break?"

"I'm mainly going to stick around here and work, I guess. I might take a bike trip to Ireland in a couple of weeks."

"Say, why don't you come to Malta with me? My Dad works with an import-export company, and he and several colleagues are flying to London on Monday in the company plane on business. The plane is dropping them off and flying back to Malta the same day, and I'm travelling on it. There'll be some extra seats, and you could come with me. You can stay with my family. It would be great fun to show you around Malta."

I was certain my jaw had hit the floor. I sat speechless, squeezing my napkin tightly in my left hand. "I ... I ... well, thanks for the offer. But, I don't think ... It does sound ... but I couldn't impose on you."

"No imposition. I have a large family, and they would love to have you visit. Come on, Cade, we'll have a great time and you'll love Malta. Besides, Dad will be in London all week, so we can use his car to tour the island."

"Well ... but I have some work to do," I protested unconvincingly.

"Oh, Cade, come on and go. You can bring work if you want. Besides, the plane will be returning in about a week to pick Dad up, and you can fly back to London then. It won't cost you anything to fly, since the plane is coming anyway."

"But I don't speak Maltese," I objected.

"That's not a problem, Cade. Almost all Maltese people speak several languages, including English."

I tried to think of another excuse, but my mind went blank. I recalled the prayer in the vicarage on that stormy Sunday. I was dumbfounded. Somewhere deep inside, however, I knew I would be going on the plane with Peter to Malta.

"Do you really think it's okay?" I said finally. "I mean, really okay?"

"Yes, absolutely. Good, it's settled. I have to run and finish the work for my tutorial tomorrow, but I'll get together with you on Saturday about our plans. This will be brilliant fun." And with that, we shook hands and he left.

I remained sitting for a good while lost in thought, until I realised that the dons at high table were leaving. I was the only student left in the hall. I wondered if I should go and see Rachael, and found myself quickly on my feet heading to Merton.

4
History and Romance

FROM THE WINDOW of the plane, I saw three tiny sailboats bobbing along the white caps in the azure sea. Off in the distance the sun lit several golden rocks jutting out of the sparkling Mediterranean. The stark sight of these virtually treeless islands took me by surprise.

"Is that Malta over there?" I asked, pointing out the window.

"Yes, that's my home," said Peter, smiling. "The bigger island is Malta."

"What about the other islands I see?"

"There's Gozo, which is our sister island," said Peter pointing. "I'll try to take you there if we have time. The other small island you see right there is Comino."

"Where are all the trees?"

"That's what happens when people live on a small island for thousands of years," replied Peter, laughing.

The beautiful sight of these islands led me to ponder the legends associated with the Mediterranean. Odysseus came immediately to mind. I could feel my heart pounding with the anticipation of visiting such an ancient island.

Then I recalled Rachael's excitement when I told her of Peter's invitation. She had giggled and spontaneously given me a hug. She made me promise to call her at home as soon as I returned to Oxford, and we had both called Mr. Brooke. He had been virtually speechless and actually seemed a little shaken up over my news.

I looked directly down on Malta as we flew over the island. There was a large harbour surrounded by a number of imposing stone fortresses. Two ocean-going cargo ships, a cruise liner, and numerous small multicoloured skiffs were scattered about the harbour. "We're now over Grand Harbour, and that town is Valletta, which is where my family lives," added Peter, as the plane began to bank for a landing.

When we got off the plane, a burst of warm, salty air hit us. I squinted in the bright morning sun. I was reminded of our family trips to the Alabama and Florida gulf coasts and realised how much I had missed the beach and sun. I filled my lungs with the fresh Mediterranean breeze.

Peter's mother, Martha Mizzi, welcomed us at the airport. She treated me immediately as if I were one of the family, and her openness and warmth reminded me of the hospitality in my native South. The Mizzis' home was along a row of similar-looking three-storey limestone buildings just off the pavement. The only difference was the colour of each house, and theirs was a light shade of pink. The sameness of the exteriors, however, gave no hint of the lovely and comfortable interior of the Mizzi home. We entered into a large, open living area, beautifully furnished. Upstairs on the second floor, my bedroom had a picturesque view of Valletta and the Mediterranean.

"We're so glad you're here," said Mrs. Mizzi after I returned downstairs. "Peter has told us how nice you've been to him at college, and you are welcome in our home."

"You're kind to have me," I replied. "Especially for letting me come at the last minute. I'm very excited to be here and can't wait to see the island."

"You'll have a royal tour," said Peter, "but not until we have lunch."

The feast put before us was amazing, and Peter must have noticed my look of surprise at all the food.

"You see, Cade, in Malta many people come home for a big meal at lunch, and then they may have a siesta for a couple of hours. A number of shops even close for lunch, and reopen late in the afternoon for several more hours."

"I think I could get used to a siesta every day!" I said with a laugh.

After lunch, which included several glasses of wine, I was indeed in need of a siesta, but Peter insisted on showing me some of the island. We took off on foot to explore Valletta. The bright sun and brilliant blue sky invigorated me, especially after the drab English winter.

"By the way, Peter," I asked as we walked, "is there a cave on the island where St. Paul supposedly lived after he was shipwrecked?"

"Yes, the St. Paul Grotto. It's a good way from here. We can go see it tomorrow if you like."

"I'm particularly interested in seeing it," I said, trying to disguise my excitement.

The tour of Valletta was fascinating, and I began to try to soak in the history and culture of this unique island. Later that night, I was introduced to another Maltese custom when all of Peter's family and their spouses came to his mother's house for dinner. Dinner did not start until about nine o'clock and lasted for several hours and through many bottles of wine. The talk and laughter during this family gathering made the time fly by. I thought of my own family – my parents and my sister, Elizabeth. It had been a long time since the four of us had spent an entire evening together laughing over dinner. Before I realised it, midnight had arrived. No wonder they needed a siesta!

*   *   *

The next day, which was the day before Ash Wednesday, we set out in Mr. Mizzi's car for a tour of the island. A constant breeze coursed over the island, and again it was bright and sunny. Everywhere we went, people waved and smiled. There were many colourful decorations which Peter informed me were for Carnival festivities.

"Let's begin with a few nearby historical sights, and then we'll drive around some of the island," said Peter. We toured the sixteenth-century Valletta stone fortresses and the pre-historic Tarxien Temples, which reminded me of Stonehenge. Then, off we went, driving along narrow lanes. The countryside was rather barren and stony, although we saw occasional olive trees and many bushes with spear-like green leaves and pink flowers.

"Where is the cave of St. Paul?" I finally asked. I was beginning to get anxious about getting to the Grotto, yet I did not want to arouse suspicion by appearing overly eager to go there.

"It's not far from here," said Peter, and I breathed a sigh of relief. "In fact, my older brother arranged for us to get in and see it this morning. With it being Carnival today, we might have had trouble otherwise."

"That's great."

We proceeded to the Grotto, and began a tour of its underground catacombs. We had to walk carefully through the small passageways, ducking our heads to avoid the low ceilings. I tried to imagine living down there in these dark catacombs and shuddered. As we toured the caves, I frantically scanned every nook and cranny I could find in the rocks, but saw no hint of any unusual papers.

After a good while, Peter said, "I guess that's about all there is to see. Are you hungry?"

"Yes," I said, and realised there was a dejected tone in my voice. I purposely forced myself to smile and add, "Actually, I'm famished. What do you have in mind?"

"There's a nice cafe over on Marsaxlokk Bay that has really excellent food."

"Sounds good." As we left the Grotto, I cast a fleeting glance back hoping to see something, but saw only barren rock.

My heart sank. If our interpretation of the vague reference at the end of the letters was correct, this was the day Soulbane's papers were to be delivered. I felt let down and frustrated, with a tight feeling in my stomach, and I realised for the first time that I had built up some anticipation of actually finding more letters. There had certainly been no hint of any unusual papers anywhere in the Grotto. Mr. Brooke had probably been mistaken, and all three of us were guilty perhaps of letting our imaginations override our common sense. As we returned to Peter's car, however, my disappointment gave way to dismissive laughter at how silly we had been to believe such nonsense. I realised now that someone had pulled off a practical joke, and that we had allowed ourselves to get carried away. It was now time to make the most of my great opportunity to see Malta and to forget this Soulbane prank.

After lunch at a nice cafe in Marsaxlokk Bay, we struck out for the parish church in Mosta, with its huge dome. Peter told me that the natives referred to this church simply as Mosta Dome. We saw the replica of a World War II German bomb that had landed inside the church during a crowded church service without exploding. Peter then took me to the beautiful walled city of Mdina. No make-believe city could be any more enchanting and lovely. By late afternoon, as we continued our tour of the island, I was coming under the spell of this "tiny rock of history and romance."

"Oh, no!" Peter suddenly exclaimed as we were driving in the vicinity of Cirkewwa, at the northernmost tip of Malta. "I just remembered. We're supposed to be at my grandmother's house to celebrate Carnival. She's a devout Catholic, and she'll be very offended if we don't show up there. We've got to get back home now."

Peter turned the car around, and we began to head back to Valletta.

"You'll love my grandmother," said Peter. "She's eighty-five years old, but acts like she's thirty. She's also a wonderful cook and ..."

There was a loud pop, and the car suddenly jerked to the side of the road.

"Of all the rotten luck!" he yelled.

"What?" I asked, as we stopped with a jolt.

"I think we have a flat tyre. Now, we'll be late for sure. Can you help me change it?"

"Sure."

We both got out of the car. "I don't believe it!" Peter exclaimed as he opened the trunk. "There's no spare tyre in here. I'll have to walk for help. You wait here."

"Okay."

Peter began walking, and I sat back in the car. There was a church a short distance from the car. With nothing to do, I pulled out the guidebook I had purchased in the morning and began to flip through it. I found a reference to the Church: it was called Our Lady of Mellieha, and the guidebook mentioned an ancient icon of the Madonna inside the church. The book said this was one of the oldest known murals of the Virgin Mary. I decided to risk leaving the car for a few minutes so that I could walk over and see it.

After I entered the church, I immediately felt the contrast between the heat outside and its cool, dim interior.

"Have you been here before?" I turned around in the direction of the voice to see an elderly, thin, grey-headed woman, with brown, wrinkled skin and a cane. Her dark eyes blazed brightly, and she smiled warmly.

"No, this is my first time."

"This is Our Lady of Mellieha Church. Up at the altar is a shrine. You'll see there part of an old cave wall with a mural of Mary and the Christ Child. An old Maltese legend says it was painted by St. Luke while he and St. Paul were shipwrecked on the island."

I looked toward where she was pointing and started to walk forward. The old woman touched my arm, saying, "Be sure that you visit the Cave of the Madonna just outside the Church. We go to the cave to thank God and St. Mary for answering prayers. There is a statue of the Blessed Virgin at the back of the grotto. Go and see for yourself."

"I will," I replied, now in a hurry to see it and get back to the car. I walked toward the shrine at the altar, then turned to ask the woman a question, but she was not there. I went back to the entrance of the church, yet she was nowhere to be seen. I did not understand how she could have disappeared so quickly. Returning to the church, I indeed saw the painting of Mary on the wall. Candlelight flickered on her face, and I felt a sense of peace come over me. Could this painting really have been here for two thousand years? Whether or not the legend of St. Luke was true, I had an unreal sense of the passage of time, similar to the feeling I had that winter's solstice night at the Turf. I was also conscious, perhaps for the first time in my life, of being merely a traveller for a brief time in this world, as I thought of the generations of people who had preceded me on this little island.

I then walked outside and found the steep steps descending into the Cave of the Madonna. As I peered down into the cave, I saw all kinds of notes, messages, crosses, candles, and other paraphernalia on the walls. I hurried down the steps for a quick look, noting two pairs of old crutches encased in cobwebs leaning against the wall as I descended. In the back of the cave, surrounded by an iron railing and numerous small votive candles, was an ivory-white statue of the Virgin Mary holding the Christ Child.

The cave was empty and it took my eyes a few seconds to adjust to the dim light. There was no sound other than my footsteps echoing around the walls. I stood before the mute statue, which was gently lit by the burning candles.

Peter! I'd almost forgotten about the flat tyre. As I turned to leave, I glanced down and saw a packet of papers on the floor over in the corner, virtually obscured in the darkness. I instinctively went over to investigate. My heart started pounding and my palms became sweaty. I experienced a shock of deja vu when I realised that the papers were rolled up and tied tightly together with a red ribbon. I tried to untie the knot, but couldn't. Finally, I pulled on the ribbon until it broke. Hurriedly, I fumbled to open the papers with shaking, damp hands. The first page was a letter ... from Soulbane! I felt dizzy, and leaned against the wall. What should I do? I took a deep breath. I had to get back or Peter would be worried. I quickly tucked the papers under my arm and ran up the steep steps and out of the cave.

The sunlight almost blinded me as I exited. When I arrived at the car, Peter was standing already there with another man, and they were finishing changing the tyre.

"Where were you?" he asked with a note of surprised impatience.

"Oh, ah, well," I stammered between gasps. "I saw that church over there and decided to go and see it. Sorry to leave you." I managed to put the papers on the floor in the back seat without Peter noticing them.

"I was getting worried. Come on, we have to hurry. We barely have enough time to get to my house and get cleaned up, before we're due at my grandmother's."

Peter quickly paid the man some money, and we pulled back onto the road. When we arrived at his home, I hurriedly stashed the letters under the mattress of the guest bed before changing for the big party. Later, as we arrived at Peter's grandmother's house near St. Julian's Point, a full moon was rising seemingly out of the sea, casting golden glitter on the dark surface. The celebration with Peter's family was something to behold. His grandmother – a short, plump, grey-haired lady – was indeed one of the liveliest people I had ever met. We danced, feasted, and drank wine for hours. All the while, however, I kept thinking about the Soulbane papers I had just discovered. Knowing that I had a long night ahead of me, I surreptitiously emptied my glass into a nearby flowerpot. When the clock struck midnight, however, the gaiety instantly ceased, and everyone went home in virtual silence. The moon was now overhead, bathing Malta in silver light.

When I returned to my room, I immediately pulled the papers out from under my mattress. I had no way, of course, to photocopy them, but given my earlier experience, decided it would have been useless to try anyway. I pulled out my laptop, then stretched and poured water on my face. I walked to the window and observed the Mediterranean in the distance, calm in the pale moonlight. It was in striking contrast to the storm Luke described in the book of Acts. Sitting down at the wooden desk, I began typing the papers – I dared not stop and certainly dared not sleep. If I was to prevent anyone from learning that I had discovered the papers, I needed to return them to the cave at the earliest possible opportunity.

I didn't notice the sunrise until a shadow fell over my hands. I stood up and went to the window. Church bells were tolling, and people were silently making their way to a church down the street. My wristwatch said it was six thirty. I went back over to the table and picked up the Soulbane Report. I only had a few more pages to go. I was exhausted, and desperately wanted to sleep.

A hand shook my shoulder, and I started. Peter was standing there grinning, with a black ashen cross on his forehead.

"Wake up, sleepyhead. It's nine o'clock, and I've already been to Mass."

I sat bolt upright and realised I had fallen asleep at the table.

"I guess I fell asleep while working on my computer," I mumbled, not wanting to let on what I was doing. I quickly gathered the Soulbane papers together and made sure he did not see what they were.

"What do you want to do today?"

"I'm game for anything."

"How about a trip to Gozo?"

"That sounds great. First, could we go back to Mellieha and see the church and the Cave of the Madonna? I didn't have much time to see it yesterday, and I'd like a better look."

"Sure. We'll run by there first, and then see if we can catch the boat to Gozo."

I quickly typed the last several pages on my laptop, then rolled the papers back and tied them as best I could with the torn red ribbon. As I took a shower, I began to revive. My excitement at the discovery of more Soulbane papers soon made me forget my tiredness.

*   *   *

Just as we arrived in Mellieha, it began to get dark, and the wind picked up considerably.

"That's odd," remarked Peter.

"What?"

"There's no forecast for rain today. It's supposed to be clear all day. Oh well, I'm sure it will blow over quickly."

"I hope so," I added, as I looked out the car window to see huge, billowing coal-black clouds gathering quickly.

"Tell you what ... I'll let you explore the church while I go and call about the boat to Gozo."

"Okay. I won't need too long. I'll meet you back here in twenty minutes."

"Right," said Peter, as I shut the door and walked toward the church, taking care not to let him see the packet I was carrying.

I walked quickly through the church, wanting to view the mural of the Madonna again. I paused in front of the mural, wishing I could stay there and soak in the mysterious silence. I needed to return the papers, however, and get back to meet Peter.

The wind was in a fury, as I reached the steps to the cave. I heard a howling sound that must have been from the tempest, and hurried down the steps. As I neared the bottom, however, something appeared to be wrong. But what? The candles, I realised. There were no candles lit and the cave was pitch-black dark. I was about to go back into the church to retrieve a lit candle, when I heard an unworldly roar.

I stopped dead in my tracks, my heart in my mouth. That was not the wind! I heard it again – a long, loud wailing sound that sent shivers up my spine. As I stood there frozen and scared, a shrill voice started screaming, "Soulbane, you incredible imbecile! Where is the damned report? I've looked everywhere for it, yesterday and this morning. When I get my claws on you, I'll ... I'll ... damn ... my wrath is unquenchable now. You idiot! You fool! Here I am down here with a statute of the Enemy's Mother, and your damned report nowhere to be seen. You ... you ... I'm speechless with rage. It's sheer torture being near the Enemy's symbols. When I get hold of you ... damn ... If you've forgotten to leave your report, or worse, if someone else has discovered it, I'll tear you limb from limb." This was followed by an eerie, shrill laugh that echoed throughout the cave. I had never in my life heard something so chilling and otherworldly.

I was too scared to move. My whole body was trembling. I knelt down at the bottom of the steps, trying to plot an escape. Who – or what – was down here? I could see nothing in the darkness. I almost yelled after a sudden, loud clap of thunder erupted above me.

Then the voice resumed, although in a somewhat more even tone. "Calm yourself, Foulheart. You, the great and demonic Foulheart can handle this. You've been in close proximity to the Enemy before. If only I had a hellephone that worked down here, I could call that blasted Soulbane and give him a piece of my mind. If only ... if only ... hells bells! I'm surrounded by incompetence! Now, where could that report be? Foulheart, Foulheart ... think. Damn you, Soulbane! You cretin! You'll pay dearly for this." The voice began screaming again, followed by that same chilling wail.

That voice. It somehow sounded familiar. But where had I heard it before? Was that an English accent? Was this someone I knew? How maddening! I still could see nothing in this cave, and dared not reveal myself. Was this really a devil? Or, more likely, a bad – a very bad – dream. I had to get out of here. I had never truly known sheer terror until now. Suddenly, there was another piercing screech, and then the sound of something falling. "Damn you Soulbane, I'll sort you out when I catch you. You think what happened to Wormwood is bad, you'll wish I had given you such a light sentence when I'm finished with you. You little putrid, vile, gob of worthless fiend spirit ..."

There was then a loud roar, and something crashed near my head. I almost screamed and looked down to see a crutch lying at my feet. It had come within inches of my head. Had I been discovered? I held my breath, shaking violently. I pushed myself against the wall as tightly as I could.

Then, silence. I was petrified. I was about to make a run for it, when the voice resumed an incoherent wailing. I quietly placed the papers on the floor near the bottom of the steps, and then began to slink up the steps along one side of the wall, desperately hoping that I wouldn't be detected. My heart was beating so fast I could feel my temples throbbing. I was thankful that the dark clouds and howling wind from the storm concealed my presence.

When I arrived at the top of the steps, I began to run as fast as I could. The storm was in full fury, although no rain had arrived. There were numerous flashes of lightning, followed by booming thunder. Peter had not yet returned, and I sat on a bench down the street from the church, my chest heaving rapidly, my pulse racing. I was sweating profusely, and my hands were shaking.

"What's wrong?" said a voice behind me.

I screamed and jumped up.

"Cade, what's wrong?" asked Peter again. "You look as if you've seen a ghost."

"I ... I ..." I sputtered, unable to catch my breath. Then, realising it was Peter, I began to laugh uncontrollably.

"Cade, are you all right?"

"Yes, ... I'm okay," I lied. "Just a bit queasy. Maybe I overdid it at your grandmother's last night. Would you mind if we just took it easy today?"

"Of course. In fact, it's too late to try and get to Gozo today anyway, especially with this weather. Let's just go back to my house and relax. I could use a siesta myself."

I smiled, and said simply, "Thanks, Peter."

It took several glasses of wine with Mrs. Mizzi's wonderful lunch before I started to feel calm. I began to rationalise that the cave incident must have been a figment of my imagination. And yet, that voice ... it somehow sounded familiar.

5

LEGENDS AND RUINS

"OXFORD ... this is Oxford." The words blaring over the loudspeaker awakened me as the train slowed. I looked up to see the "dreaming spires," as Matthew Arnold described them. The week in Malta had been like a dream, and I had fallen in love with the place and the people. I recalled when Mr. Brooke had read from Acts, that Luke had remarked on how friendly the people of Malta were, and now I understood why. The warm welcome of the Mizzi family had ensured that the remainder of my trip had been fun and relaxing. I had had a few frightening flashbacks about the incident in the cave, but as the week wore on uneventfully it began to recede from my mind. Had I just imagined it? I wondered if I would ever know. I wasn't sure I wanted to know.

As soon as I had dropped my bag in my room, I went down to the phone booth next to the porter's lodge to call Rachael, who was visiting her mother in Cornwall.

"Rachael?" I said when the voice answered.

"Cade, is that you? Are you back from Malta? Did you have fun? Did you ... find anything?"

"Whoa, one question at a time. I had a great time."

"Don't tease me! Did you find anything? Tell me."

"Yes," I said excitedly, "I did find some more papers but not in the

56

cave we thought. You won't believe how I found them. Mr. Brooke was right about the report being in Malta!"

"No, Cade, are you serious? Did you really find something? Please don't joke with me about this."

"I'm not joking. I really did find some more papers by Soulbane. I typed them word for word on my laptop, and I'll show it all to you when you return." I had already decided never to mention the voice in the cave to anyone. I was fearful they might think I was losing my mind, and that possibility was not a little unsettling to me, too.

"Oh, I can't wait that long. Why don't you come visit me here? Mum would love it, and ... so would I."

I felt my face flush and realised I very much wanted to see Rachael. "Yes, I'll come for the weekend, if you're sure it's okay."

"Of course, I'm sure. And, you'd better bring your laptop with you."

*   *   *

As the train slowed in Plymouth, I looked out the window to see Rachael standing on tiptoe looking into the train windows. She saw me and waved.

"Hi," I said as I stepped off the train. "Can you believe my Malta find?"

"I truly can't," she said smiling. "I'm glad you've come. Mum is looking forward to meeting you, and I can't wait to read what you found."

We walked toward a small blue car, and Rachael said, "Here we are. This is my mother's car. She's made lunch for us."

As we rode in the car, I told Rachael all about my trip: the beautiful Mediterranean scenery, the hospitality of the Mizzis, and, of course, the flat tyre, the strange woman, and the Cave of the Madonna. I omitted any mention, however, of my return visit to the cave.

"Tell me about your parents," I said, trying to make conversation and get my mind off the cave.

"My mother is Irish ... She's a seamstress. She's such a dear, and I know you'll love her." She paused a moment, then added, "My father ... I barely knew him. He died when I was fairly young."

"I'm sorry."

"Not to worry, he's been gone a long time," she replied unconvincingly. We drove out into the countryside and followed the signs to Tintagel.

"Tell me more about Tintagel," I said.

"It's a lovely town near the sea," replied Rachael. "Very charming and full of legends about King Arthur. I'll take you to Tintagel Castle, which isn't really Arthur's, but its ruins still let you dream about knights of old."

Rachael pulled up in front of a small white cottage, with a navy blue door, small windows, and a red tile roof. There was a broken, wooden fence with peeling white paint around the house, and there were boxes under the windows filled with red geraniums and green ivy flowing out of them. The small, humble house in the country was somehow not what I had expected, and a picture of our two-storey, white-columned Atlanta house flashed in my mind.

"Mum, we're here," yelled Rachael as we entered the house.

A tall, stately lady came into the front room. She had dark, curly hair, and Rachael's smile and blue eyes. The resemblance was immediately obvious.

"I've heard so much about you, Cade," she said in a muted Irish lilt. "So nice to meet you. I'm Bridgett Adams."

"The pleasure's mine," I said, with more sincerity in my voice than I felt. I glanced around the room. It was sparsely furnished, and there was an electric heater in the fireplace. There were several pictures of Rachael in the room, along with a small brown sofa, and a brown and orange rug. As we walked into the kitchen, I smelled soup and bread.

"Cade, I hope you like leek soup," said Mrs. Adams.

"Sure, that's great."

After lunch, Rachael's mother went off in the car to run some errands.

"I can't wait a minute longer to see what you found," said Rachael.

We went to a room next to the kitchen that had a sewing machine, and many types and colours of fabric spread out all over the room.

Rachael pushed aside some of the materials and uncovered a brown, wooden table. She plugged in the computer, then sat down in front of the screen. I rested my hand on her shoulder as I reached over to push the buttons to retrieve the documents. Her hair gently touched my hand. Rachael turned her head slightly and smiled at me.

I took a walk outside while Rachael read the report. The back was a small area, with a vegetable garden. I fidgeted as I glanced around the garden. The fence was broken in several spots and much of the faded white paint had peeled off. The house had mould on it, and moss grew on the roof. I sat down on an old, wooden bench and distracted myself with the novel I had started on the train.

A good while later, the rusty hinges of the back door creaked as Rachael came out, and I stood up to greet her.

"Cade, I can't believe this. It's truly incredible. I can't wait to show this to Mr. Brooke. You're so wonderful to find this."

Rachael stood on tiptoe and kissed my cheek. I stepped back and smiled tensely.

"Say, why don't you show me around," I said quickly. "Are we near the castle?"

"Quite near. We can walk there. Let me get a jumper on."

We arrived at the coast after a few minutes walk. The endless Atlantic waves crashed into the towering slate-grey rocks, blasting showers of spray, while seagulls argued overhead. The overcast sky cast its gloomy outlook on land and sea.

We trudged up a steep pathway, and before us were the crumbling remains of the outline of something manmade. The weathered stones now appeared almost as part of the natural rocky landscape. It was chilly and no one else was around.

"This is Tintagel castle," said Rachael. "Can you envision King Arthur and the knights of the Round Table up on this cliff overlooking the vast sea?"

As we ambled toward the edge of the cliff, I tried to imagine knights and maidens living in this very place almost a thousand years before. These ancient ruins had their own echoes of a romantic, long-forgotten past. I put my arm around Rachael. She didn't resist. We stood silently looking at the sea. I thought of trying to kiss her, but hesitated. Rachael looked at me expectantly. Her dark hair danced in the stiff wind. Suddenly, I knelt down, picked up a rock and flung it as far into the ocean as I could. As it disappeared into the spray, the moment had passed. Rachael and I returned down the pathway. She told me more about Tintagel Castle and the Arthurian legends.

When we returned to the house, Mrs. Adams was there. The kitchen was full of wonderful cooking smells.

"I hope you like lamb," she said when we stepped into the kitchen.

"I love it," I replied.

"How long can you stay?" Mrs. Adams inquired.

"Actually, I have to go back tomorrow," I said immediately.

"Tomorrow!" exclaimed Rachael. "But why? You just got here."

"I know, but I have a lot of work to do, and I'm supposed to go on a bike trip to Ireland in a week." I knew this wasn't really the whole truth.

"Oh," was all Rachael said. Her smile disappeared.

Her mother looked at us, and her shoulders slumped slightly. After a few moments, however, she smiled and said, "Well, let's not let that keep us from celebrating your visit tonight with a good meal. Cade, do sit down and relax, while Rachael and I prepare dinner." I readily complied.

*   *   *

On the train ride back to Oxford, I thought a lot about Rachael. I had been so eager to see her, and then ... what? Maybe it was her humble home. Maybe I was, as an old girlfriend had once told me, more interested in the pursuit than the capture. Whatever the reason, I clearly had cooled our relationship.

6

SPIRITUAL BLITZKRIEG

THE VICAR SAT in his leather chair, smoking his pipe. This Friday afternoon in April was warm and sunny, and spring flowers were in bloom everywhere. He quietly put one page behind another as he read. Then, he put the papers down and began to sob. Rachael turned from the window, went over and put her arms around his shoulder.

Finally, he spoke, "I've wasted so much time. I let my faith slip away little by little, and I forgot all I learned from Lewis. We can no longer dismiss this as a joke. It has an authentic ring to it, and it is truly a miracle Cade found this. We must pray about how to handle these papers. I believe you have stumbled on to something very important, Cade."

I smiled slightly, but said nothing.

Then Rachael added, "Do you think there's more?"

"It appears so. We'll have to put our minds to it again, and we'll ask God's help again in finding the rest. We have been blessed with this, but we've also been given a real responsibility."

I wasn't laughing inside now. On the way back from Malta, I had finished reading *Mere Christianity*, and it was making a lot more sense to me now. During my visit with Rachael, she had given me *The Screwtape Letters*, which I had read with intense interest on the train back to Oxford. Had I actually heard Foulheart in Malta? I was seeing the world in a way I had never imagined, and I could not ignore the incredible events of the past several months. My mind had not yet accepted my experience in the cave, however, and I kept wondering if I would awake from some strange dream.

"We still must not tell anyone about this," said Mr. Brooke. "Not until we see if there is any more to come. We must also decide if and when to reveal what you've discovered, Cade. I've hurriedly skimmed through this. Why don't we take turns reading this aloud? I'll start off."

And he began reading aloud the Malta instalment of the Soulbane Report:

To The Most Dishonourable Foulheart,

I am pleased to present, after intensive study by myself and my fiendish associates, a full report of our investigation into the Enemy's territory – which he calls "the Church" – and into the battleground – which he calls "the World." It is clear, as detailed more fully in the following Report, that the Enemy's forces in the western world are in complete disarray and totally demoralised. The Enemy is losing ground to our Royal Hindness every day, and victory will soon be ours. (If I might add a personal note here, I can hardly wait to taste all the tender, juicy morsels that are sure to come our way.)

Our Report is divided into two major parts: the first discusses our overwhelming victories in the world at large, and the second concerns our numerous victories within the Enemy's Church itself. This instalment contains our study of the world.

As will be shown in this Report, our plans for spiritual Blitzkrieg are working to perfection: the world is becoming increasingly lost, confused, and misguided with the help of the Master's brilliant strategies. Our plans for world domination are now ahead of schedule. The Enemy is now at best despised, and at worst ignored, in the modern western world, while the values of our Hindom are becoming dominant. Soon, our Homeland and creation will be mirror images of one another.

This Report is a summary of our findings: we attempted to

highlight some of the important trends we discovered, but this is by no means an exhaustive study of our numerous victories in the world. We have extensive back-up research available at the Hindom Library, should the Base Command wish to review it. We were given excellent editorial assistance by Mushbrain and Fibspeak in paring down this Report to its summary form.

The Victory of our Royal Hindness is assured.

Your humble and ever obedient servant,

Soulbane

REPORT TO BASE COMMAND

I. THE WORLD

A. Why Mortals Can't Tell Right From Wrong

The Enemy designed these creatures with some peculiar characteristics. He gave them the ability to think, reason, feel, imagine, remember, analyse, communicate, plan, and create. Along with these gifts – which we can only vaguely comprehend – he gave them choice and free will. (Thankfully our Master learned early on to exercise his free will and depart from the Enemy.) The Enemy's plan was for mortals to expand their knowledge and experience of the world as they matured, and for education to play a key role in their development.

Our strategy has been to infiltrate every aspect of society, in order to subtly influence the lemming-like rodents away from the Enemy and toward our ends. Infiltrating their educational systems has been an integral part of that plan. This has now been accomplished. The world of education in the western world is one whose primary foundations are humanism and rationality: that is, man is the centre of the world, and all knowledge and all problems can be accessed and solved by turning to human reason. Nothing remotely spiritual such as faith or miracles is now accepted.

This infiltration was so gradual that humans never really recognised what was happening, and now it is too late. Generations of children are educated and indoctrinated into this secular humanistic viewpoint, so that it is now the accepted method of all education. The result is that the Enemy has been totally cast out of most education processes in the western world. A primary emphasis in modern schooling is to make children feel proud of themselves, to puff up their self-esteem, and to let them know that there is no such thing as right and wrong, or good and evil. The moral marshmallows turned out by this process are easy prey for our Hindom's forces. In their own words, "Garbage in, garbage out."

As a fortunate corollary to this, many parents are so busy, overworked, and preoccupied that they have virtually abandoned any attempt of teaching their children, and have left not only education, but morality, up to the schools to teach. It gives me pleasure to report our findings that there is little interest in many homes in what the urchins are being taught in school. In addition, the Church often has not taken an active role in the lives of these impressionable mortals, and thus it offers virtually no alternative viewpoint for them to consider. Thus, many children grow up fully indoctrinated into a humanistic view of the world. The results of this, of course, are easy to see: relativism and pluralism, as discussed later in the Report, are now the accepted standards by which to judge all conduct and action, which means, naturally, that there are no universal standards at all. The shifting standards of behaviour and so-called morality vary from age to age and fashion to fashion, all of which plays into our hands most satisfactorily.

As the Base Command is aware, for centuries the underlying mission of universities was the search for truth (such an ugly word!), and many of these idealistic institutions were founded on the teachings of the Enemy. This search for truth, unfortunately, meant that the Enemy could sabotage our plans by gently allowing these humans to search various paths, knowing that they would eventually lead diligent seekers to dead ends, and thus ultimately back to his own contemptible kingdom. A prime example is that vile Lewis, who went from atheism to becoming one of the Enemy's followers. Our job, of course, is to make these dead ends so attractive and enticing that the humans will stop their search, or else to give them so many different roads, that they spend their whole lives meandering in circles.

Now, however, many schools and universities are so focussed on academic "freedom" and knowledge for the sake of knowledge, with no overriding goals or values in mind, that it takes only a small push from our Forces to saturate their teaching with relativism. Our continued efforts to steer learning away from any link with a moral, much less religious, context have paid off magnificently. Now, the universities are so intent on being "politically correct," and so intent on giving credence to any set of ideas, as long as someone professes to be "sincere," that truth is a forgotten and lost goal. Combine this with a loss of absolutes, and there is simply no moral compass by which to test and analyse ideas. The world of the university is now one of our most fertile grounds, because of the splendid assumption that all ideas have equal value.

The upshot is that generations of western humans accept the precept that there is no longer any absolute right and wrong. All types of behaviour are accepted, and with each passing year, the bar of acceptable conduct is lowered. The Christian concept of sin is viewed as archaic and irrelevant in the modern world. Consequently, the Master's troops whom we interviewed reported that they hardly get excited any more about our spiritual warfare, because our battles are now so easily won. These humans hardly ever put up a fight, and even when they do, they are too ill-equipped to last long.[HN]

B. "Nuclear" Destruction of the Family

At the centre of our strategy to rule the world is the despoiling of that sickening grouping, the family. The Enemy's sentimental design for his creatures was to have a unit where husband and wife, and their

---

[HN]We noted increasing internal conflicts and fights among our Underworld forces, probably due to their increased leisure time resulting from the lack of any challenge presented in the modern world. I had to break up a fight between Bleakblab and Slobglob over who got the last bite of an admittedly sparse meal of atheist academicians.

children, could live and grow in a loving, caring, nurturing environment. A natural corollary was to have an extended family of friends and relatives to enhance the security and warmth of the home – (can you imagine anything worse?) – which would foster a society based upon the values the Enemy promotes.

The western world is now in a most satisfying crisis of untold proportions, due in large measure to family breakdown. Our Master's strategic plan has worked to perfection: quick and easy divorces are routine and widely accepted. It is no longer considered necessary for children to grow up with a mother and father married to each other. In addition, with so many irresponsible parents out there, coupled with the *perceived* economic pressures weighing on these creatures – thousands, indeed millions, of children now grow up with little guidance, discipline, or love. Child and spouse abuse is rampant. Families are divided and full of strife, and the outgrowth is a society saturated with alcohol, drugs, violence, unwanted pregnancies, suicide, depression, and crime. The Base Command should be greatly encouraged to see western society, which pays no attention to the Enemy's warnings, now disintegrating at an increasingly rapid pace.

The effects of this destruction of the family are quite evident: western society is crumbling, and the resulting chaos is a pleasure to behold. The Master's alluring principles of greed, envy, and escapism (to name only a few), are taking hold of their society. Economic and lifestyle pressures – both real and illusory – are leading to a transient, rootless society. In particular, we have worked hard to promote the notion that various expensive, materialistic lifestyles are "necessary" in the modern world. Envy has always been one of our most effective weapons! This illusion leads to a fitting treadmill for these vermin as they spend all their time worrying about financial matters, and working longer and longer hours, while taking no time to cultivate their families, much less to think about spiritual matters.

The rapidity of the demise of the family unit is breathtaking, and the collapse of western society is only a matter of time now. Based upon our in-depth investigation, it is clear that the Base Command's earlier projections of the date of this total collapse will need to be revised downward to reflect victory in a much shorter period of time than first imagined.

C. Till Something Better Doth Us Part

Another outdated concept in the modern world, and, of course, the modern Church, is marriage. Again, the Enemy seriously miscalculated: he thought these creatures could fall in love, take vows to love, honour and cherish one another, and then faithfully live the rest of their lives together. Hah! Divorce is now the norm, rather than the exception. The Church, as the Base Command is well aware, has a ceremony that includes solemn vows to the Enemy, where the couple promise to be faithful to one another "for richer for poorer, in sickness and in health." Somehow, many of these creatures seem to have forgotten about the poorer or sicker parts, and by what we observed during our undercover research, many of these humans know something about being undercover themselves, with someone other than their spouse!

Of course, the media has played nicely into our hands in this regard. Books and films portray "love" as nothing but a giddy emotion. Through the brilliance of our Master's strategies, love is now viewed solely an emotion, not an action: this distortion is a major victory for our cause. Remarkably, these gullible humans continually fall for this falsehood about human relationships. As soon as they experience this giddy emotion, they want to get married. As soon as that feeling goes away – as it inevitably does – they want to get divorced. Even while married, if someone else elicits this emotion in them, they think they are now in love with that other, and it is easy to whisper adultery in their ears. These humans ALWAYS want what they don't have, and this trait plays splendidly into our hands as we do anything and everything we can – pursuit to edict by our Royal Hindness – to launch our blitzkrieg attacks on marriages.

One of our most effective weapons is the false promise we whisper to them that the grass is always greener elsewhere. We then watch these creatures spend a lifetime in a never-ending search for happiness, based upon this ingenious deceit. "If only ..." "but when

..." and "someday I'll ..." are such effective mirages to hold out before them. They dispose of relationships as quickly and easily as possible, and they follow the numerous paths we lay before them, paved with the fool's gold of sex, money, power, prestige, and possessions, in hopes of achieving our vague promise that they will live "happily ever after." Only the Enemy can fulfil that promise, but with careful management by our armies, they never look to him.

The Enemy tried to teach these creatures that in relationships they are to seek to give to, rather than receive from, the other person. We have turned this topsy-turvy. Unselfish giving, loyalty, and self-sacrifice play no part in modern relationships, and instead, the focus is only on self-aggrandisement. This, of course, is the model for ideal behaviour that our Master has given to us, and thus is the foundation upon which all relationships in our Hindom are based. It's not surprising, then, that many of these humans feel right at home when they arrive in our dark paradise.

We have been alarmed to see how dangerous a healthy Christian marriage can be to our plans, where the couple both lean on the Enemy and on each other during good times and bad, and where they surround their children with love and support. Fortunately, such marriages are few and far between these days. The damage done to humans in unhealthy relationships, with the resulting pain to children, has been a joy to behold. It is now accepted that marriage is a temporary, rather than permanent, arrangement. Unfaithfulness is widespread, as is selfishness, abusiveness, and other destructive habits. One of the most potent weapons we have employed is that of discontentment. As couples face economic pressure – both real and imagined – we can gain a foothold by keeping them apart from one another as they work harder and harder to keep up, and we can whisper all kinds of things in their ears that are guaranteed to bring conflict and resentment into the relationship. At that stage, the marriage relationship, and even their children, always play second fiddle, and the family quickly becomes completely out of tune.

Soon, their society, with our help, will have basically "fast-food" marriages: they'll drive by one side of the registry office to get married, consume as much of the relationship as they can, as fast as they can, and then just drive by the other side to get divorced. It won't be too much of a step, then, simply to forgo silly marriage ceremonies altogether, and just move in and out with one another as it suits them. Who needs such archaic institutions as marriage and family anyway?

The Enemy appears to have known that marriage would be extremely difficult and challenging for two humans, and he told them he would help. Can you imagine if these creatures ever took their vows to the Enemy seriously? We have seen how he intervenes to help those couples who call upon him for help, and how he is at their sides instantly when they strive to keep their vows to him. Fortunately, such calls are now rare indeed.

Of course, this gives our diabolical forces several bites at the same apple. First, we destroy marriage. Then, we attack the individuals who are divorced by making them feel guilty, worthless, and unloved, not to mention angry, bitter, and disillusioned. Such wounded creatures are easy prey for us because either they angrily blame the Enemy for the divorce, or else they guiltily run from him in shame, reminiscent of our famous fig leaf triumph. We'll take either way for our purposes, because the *last* thing we want them to realise is that the Enemy apparently still loves them, even when they have stumbled. I heard our Royal Hindness lecture once on this major weakness of the Enemy – he loves these despicable creatures even when they fail, and goes out of his way to help them up again. We must at all costs continue to prevent anyone from finding this out. Fortunately, it appears we have succeeded beyond our wildest dreams.

*   *   *

I heard a faint sound that disrupted my concentration on Mr. Brooke's reading of the report. I turned and saw that Rachael was sobbing softly, her shoulders shaking.

"Rachael, are you all right?" I asked. The vicar put down the papers and walked over to where Rachael was sitting. He put his arm around her shoulders and handed her a handkerchief.

As Rachael dabbed her eyes, she said softly, "Yes, I'll be fine. It's just that what the vicar was reading brought back some sad memories."

Mr. Brooke nodded knowingly, and said, "I understand, Rachael. We can stop now, if you wish. I can ..."

"No," interrupted Rachael. "I'm better now. I just needed to have a good cry, thinking about Mum and Dad, and all. Sometimes, I think Soulbane is writing about me."

"Believe me," added Mr. Brooke, "I know how you feel. Soulbane's Report has some keen insights, and it has been rather discomforting for me, too."

The vicar stood up and put on the kettle for some tea. Rachael had stopped crying and was petting Zeke. She smiled as Mr. Brooke handed her a cup of tea. His hands were noticeably shaking, and he spilled some on Rachael.

"Oh dear, I'm so sorry, Rachael," exclaimed Mr. Brooke, as Rachael used his handkerchief to wipe her lap.

"Not to worry, Mr. Brooke," said Rachael, who was almost laughing. Meanwhile, Zeke was eagerly eating the shortbread that Mr. Brooke had dropped on the floor, and we all began to laugh. I welcomed this break in the tension I had felt as Mr. Brooke had been reading this first report. I did not want to let on how troubling I found some of the things Soulbane reported.

"By the way, Rachael and Cade, I think we've had enough of formalities. My name is James ... no more Mr. Brooke, please."

"I'm better, really, Mr. Brooke ... I mean ... James," said Rachael, smiling. "I truly want to continue. In fact, I'd like to read the report for awhile."

As Rachael went over and picked up the reports, I looked at her pretty, tear-stained face, and wondered what exactly had gone wrong in her family.

7

THE HEART OF THE MATTER

As we settled ourselves back in our chairs, I saw that James had surreptitiously poured himself a glass of Scotch. Rachael appeared not to have noticed, and she began reading where James had left off:

D. The Wizardry of Technology

Perhaps the area of greatest advancement for our Royal Hindness's cause in the modern world – and our own greatest hope for the future – is in technology. These humans are real suckers for technology, and it provides tremendous opportunities for us. While supposedly advancing their civilisation, technology also provides a means of escape: escape from the world and from life, and escape from interaction with other humans, not to mention, escape from the Enemy. Plus, and most wonderfully, technology often results in mindless scripts and images being written into their all-too-impressionable minds. Humans somehow thought that technology would make life easier and give them more freedom. Instead, just the reverse has occurred: as technology advances, they are expected to do more in less time, they are overwhelmed with information, and their lives are in fact becoming increasingly frantic. Of course, this is important to our strategy, because guess who gets squeezed out in

71

their frenzied lives?

Television is the most obvious example of this. As our Master has taught us, the greater the power for good, the corresponding greater the power for harm. The proliferation of television, and its widening scope with cable, satellites, and videos, has worked wonders for our plans. In the early days, the best service we could expect from television and films was to anaesthetise their brains, wasting their time and leaving them somewhat listless. Although the content was not particularly bad or evil, we were nevertheless satisfied with the way television cut off productive time humans used to spend reading, writing, exploring and talking. As time went on, however, the content became much more to our liking – sex, violence, adultery, greed, lust, anger and many other of our virtues – increased ever so gradually that they soon were not only commonplace, but *expected*! The damage done to their children in the all-important formative years has been incalculable (despite our careful record keeping). Not only have moral absolutes been replaced with relativism and murky value systems, but sex and violence have become a major part of their viewing culture. Literally thousands of hours of their lives have been flitted away in front of the television screen, with at least mindless entertainment, and at best, a script of our values onto their subconscious minds.

In addition, the wretches spend so much time watching television, that they spend little time talking with each other and building relationships, all of which the Master is able to use to his good advantage. Whether these humans are merely anaesthetised, or else programmed with all sorts of ideas, our Royal Hindness can use these avenues to promote the hellish values we prize so much. Not that these humans are very bright in the first place, but as their minds have turned to mush, we have so many opportunities to encourage them to waste their lives away on their couches, or else to whisper suggestions of lust, violence, anger, resentment, selfishness, greed, and envy into their ears as they watch hour after hour of television and videos. Our own hellevision could learn some programming lessons from these humans.

Not that our victory is limited just to the screen. Music has been a most fruitful source for us, because the Enemy designed them to have a subconscious mind that often hears and retains messages they are not even aware of. Thus, the words of their songs can help reinforce our Master's values as they listen to the spellbinding music. Some of their songs are, pardon the pun, pure music to our ears: they glorify murder, suicide, rape, violence, greed, drug abuse, and lust, our favourite themes.

Another magnificent tool for our purposes is the computer. As these humans become more reliant on technology, they do not have the time or the inclination to trust anything to their unseen Creator. Not only that, but the computer is becoming now what the television was for the last fifty years: a means by which we cut off human contact. People now spend hundreds of hours in front of the computer screen. We monitored various so-called "chat rooms" and were delighted to see the countless wasted hours, often in meaningless or even perverse "conversations," many times with false identities. They have access to so much information at their fingertips, that they are both mesmerised and overwhelmed by the volume and variety. It is so easy to infiltrate things like the Internet to further our diabolical purposes, and the little computer nerds never know what hit them as they pass their time "surfing the net."

Computer games, many of which depict violence and dark forces, particularly caught our attention and provided us with a delightful diversion from our undercover investigations. Plus, for many mortals, computers are seriously habit-forming, and you know how we thrive on human addiction! Our goal, of course, is to make the computer screen another means to create mush-brains, as we have done with much of the television viewing. Moreover, the subtle messages we can send through the computer, which they really never think about, serve the Master's purposes quite well.

We had an opportunity to surf the net ourselves during our research, and what a joy ride it was! It was like we were back home enjoying the Base Command's wonderful programming on our hellevision. The depth of depravity we saw was more delicious than we ever imagined, and the delightful perversions depicted on our computer screens had us drooling. Of course, as our Royal Hindness has so wisely known, the human heart not only is corruptible, but it has not changed in thousands of years. That is why we have been so successful, because our strategies (with some refinements) continue to work from generation to generation. These stupid creatures never learn – they fall for our same old tricks over and over again. This is one reason we remain forever puzzled about what the Enemy is up to, because we will never understand why he can possibly care for these morons.

It is truly wonderful to see their cultural suicide at work – in their art, books, magazines, music, television, and films. It is so rare now to see these things promote the Enemy's values (in fact, several of the TV evangelists may have done as much harm to the Enemy as good), and our values are being increasingly promoted. Just let someone raise a question about the content of their art (in whatever form), and the hue and cry raised by those who are profiting by these things deafens the voice of those who lament the content of these various art mediums. The rallying call is "freedom of speech and thought." Of course, they are so hung up on their freedoms, that the corresponding value of personal responsibility has been tossed aside. Plus, with no permanent value system in place any more, they have no basis (or desire) to judge content on any moral basis.

Even Scrunchmouth and Baldface expressed surprise at the level of degradation we saw: the more bizarre or perverse – the more likely it is to be highlighted. These humans have been told so many times by those becoming wealthy from the media that the public *demands* sex, violence and perversity, and that "wholesome" values will not sell, the gullible population now accepts this premise as a given. Thus, like cattle, they just follow wherever the television, films, or rock groups lead them. In conjunction with our attacks on moral absolutes, this has had such a great effect on the lifestyles and culture of the western world, that the Enemy's influence decreases daily. It is not hard to envision our Master's total victory in the near future. It will not be long now before the accepted view is that everyone can choose whatever lifestyle pleases them, and with the absence of any moral compass, who is to tell them otherwise? "Love thyself" is the new commandment for the western world. Besides, the minds of these creatures are becoming so programmed – not to mention so weak and spongy – that we will have our way with them whenever we want.

Rachael turned the page thoughtfully, and cleared her throat. James stood up and retrieved a glass of water, handing it to Rachael. She smiled, took a sip, and began again to read:

E. Road Kill on the Information Superhighway

The last chapter noted the wonderful impact technology is having on the spiritual lives of these humans. A related aspect of this modern society is the information overload these morons now experience. They equate sheer knowledge and information with "advancement." Of course, even the Enemy recognises that knowledge without wisdom is folly, but fortunately, the humans have no such recognition.

For centuries these humans had a limited amount to occupy their minds, because their world was smaller, and their knowledge not far advanced. Now, however, their knowledge is increasing exponentially, and this is in no small part due to the technological revolution they are undergoing. It is not unlike their industrial revolution, where we saw so many opportunities presented to us. Foulheart still talks about the banquets he enjoyed as they spent their energies moving from agriculture to industry, and of the delightful ways in which people were exploited in factories and lost their sense of community.

At this time, two factors are coinciding so that we are presented with a virtually unprecedented opportunity to steal their souls: the explosion of information and the global communications network. Their feeble minds are inundated all day long with information and events and places, much more than they could ever absorb. Moreover, their knowledge is changing so quickly that they can no longer even keep up with the current state of knowledge and by the time they try to learn it, it has changed. The result is that many of them have simply shut their minds off (not to imply that many of them ever had them on in the first place!), while others try vainly to keep up only to be forever frustrated. This information explosion has done wonders to them psychologically: they feel quite inadequate and ignorant, and they question their place in the world. Plus, we have been able to promote pluralism so much more easily. Now, there are so many choices offered to them – new cultures, new religions, new lifestyles, and literally millions of different viewpoints and ideas – that they are completely overwhelmed. Their inborn curiosity makes them want to try it all, and their lack of any moral compass means they have no means to differentiate between various – and often conflicting – ideas and philosophies.

The global communications network has meant that our job is virtually done for us. Their media, that thrives on sensationalism, bizarre events, and the destruction of any right to privacy, has aided our cause greatly. The Enemy is rarely mentioned, and usually when he is, it is with scorn and derision. However, if a famous person burps in public, the whole world now knows about it in a matter of minutes. In their homes, all of this information can be continuously thrown at them through radio, telephone, television and computers. With instant world-wide communications, the modern western society is one of instant sensual and material gratification. The Enemy's so-called virtues of patience, perseverance and sacrifice have disappeared from their culture. They want everything they see, and they want it now.

Parallel to this is that modern western society is the society of the sound bite. Weak-brained mortals have no patience to hear or read about anything beyond the most superficial headlines. Thus, fifteen- or thirty-second clips of news are about all they can take in. More and more, every aspect of their lives – not just news, but work, books, relationships, and even prayer to the Enemy – is nothing more than quick clips with little substance. Because they have no real attention spans, even momentous current events gain their attention for just a few days before passing into history. This sound bite, film clip society, has made our battle so much easier: they hardly even notice the decline now, while our Royal Hindness is in his ascendancy. When we achieve our final victory, that will probably only get a short mention on the five o'clock news. Little will they realise it's too late ... until it's too late.

The icing on the devil's food cake of all this is that these humans are now faced with an incredible array of options and choices – more than ever before in history. This bombardment of information, made possible by their technological advances, brings thousands of facts, ideas, philosophies, lifestyles, cultures, places, and events into their homes each day. The vermin are deluged with information and options, and it is so much easier for our tempter fiends to zip in and keep them filled with ideas of always wanting to explore different options, and to overwhelm their pea brains with information (the more useless and trivial the better, naturally). Our job is to keep them busy, with no quality time for contemplation that might allow them to think about the Enemy, or, Hell forbid, to pray to him. Of course, envy is such a useful tool for us in this, because we can always entice them with golden carrots of glamorous and wealthy people and lifestyles that fan the flames in their hearts of greed, envy, and lust. The delicious result is that now it is we who are faced with so many options, as we try and decide from which of the numerous different appetisers and desserts of these lost human souls to choose.

F. We're Number 1!

We have also been able to capitalise on the obsession in western culture with being first or best. Being number one at all costs is so destructive to the psychology of millions of the vermin, yet they persist in pursuing this illusion. We have easily infiltrated such thinking and promoted it whenever possible. Everywhere – in sports, in business, in schools, and in their social lives – the pervasive desire to be *numero uno* is evident. To explain fully this phenomenon would take more space than this Report can allow. Just watch their business tactics to see how obsessed they are with finishing first, including, of course, being the richest, and it is wonderful to watch the imbeciles use some of our devilish logic in justifying any means if it results in finishing first. This win-at-all-costs attitude exists in all aspects of their society. Their posters and bumper stickers mirror this obsession: "Whoever has the most toys wins." And, "Winning is not the best thing, it's the only thing." Long forgotten in the real world is that mumbo jumbo they like to *pretend* to observe: "It's not whether you win or lose, but how you play the game." What hogwash!

The damage done by this obsession with winning has been incalculable. Because these stupid creatures are continuously in competition, they constantly feel they are worthless (which our Father Below wants them to believe). Therefore, they seek other avenues to find value in their lives, including alcohol, drugs, new age philosophy, materialism, astrology, and spiritualists. How satisfying for us to watch them finally give up the race because they don't perceive themselves as "the best," and to see them collapse on the roadside of life in depression, self pity, and despair. The Enemy is losing many of his creatures every day to this phenomenon. For some reason we have yet to understand, he wants all of them to know they each have infinite value because they are his children, and that external things are temporal and of little eternal value. Thank badness the humans are oblivious to this flaw in the Enemy.

This desire to be first blinds these humans to the Enemy's values. Even those who achieve worldly success are never satisfied. They always want more. The only exceptions we found are people who depend on the Enemy for contentment, but we are doing our best to force them into extinction. For our purposes, it doesn't matter which dead-end road these humans take in trying to find self-worth, as long as it takes them away from the one who showed them the way to find eternal life. We do not comprehend why the Enemy thinks eternity with him is worthwhile. Even our Royal Hindness quickly saw the horror of spending eternity with the Enemy. Yet, the Enemy actually expects his stupid children to sacrifice the earthly things that get in the way of "heaven." Fortunately, these humans can't see past their own noses. It is their motto to live only for today and for themselves, which means our loading docks have become increasingly crowded of late. The only truly important game is the eternal one, and on many playing fields we are winning that game hands down.

G. Eat, Drink, and Be Merry

Parallel to the desire to be first, is the mortals' myopic focus on youth, beauty, power, fame, sex and wealth. Humans have been led to believe that only those with beautiful bodies, or huge bank accounts, or worldly power, or glamorous fame are truly worthwhile people. We thought the ancient Romans were narcissistic, but they didn't hold a candle to the culture currently under study. Humans in modern-day culture all strive for the fountain of youth, while ignoring the only thing that truly matters: the condition of their hearts and souls. We observe the high irony of the fact that they seek eternal youth in this world, and thus miss the true fountain of youth in the Enemy's eternal spiritual realm. The Enemy's Son clearly taught over and over that such things as superficial beauty, wealth, power, prestige, or social status mean nothing in the Enemy's Kingdom, yet his words go virtually unheeded today. It doesn't take a lot of effort on our part to make millions of these humans think themselves miserable and worthless, because they believe they are not as good looking as a supermodel, as athletic as a sports star, or as rich as an international jet-setter. It has been wonderful to observe during our undercover research how truly miserable these people make themselves, and how few turn nowadays to the Enemy for comfort. Their entire self-esteem is based upon superficial and transitory matters, yet they can't or won't see it, and this makes our job increasingly easy.

The focus of humans in western culture is on themselves. They never really get beyond looking at their own reflections or fulfilling their own needs. This focus inward means, of course, they have no time for the Enemy or their fellow humans. "I" and "me" are their favourite topics of conversation. The Enemy tried to tell them that they must lose their life to gain it, but we have convinced them otherwise.

Modern western culture is obsessed with sex. It is on their minds constantly and it pervades all aspects of society. It is their occupation and preoccupation. Of course, the Enemy invented man and woman and sex. But, instead of following the Enemy's rules about the proper use of his invention, these humans have instead taken our advice and perverted it. You know how we love perversion! Portions of the Church hardly whimper about this, and thus offer no real voice in the matter. Plus, their sex drives are so overstimulated, that our job of temptation is quite easy, and we have turned many a human's attention away from the Enemy and toward the lusts of the flesh. During our undercover work, we found that the world and the flesh are at the apex of the pyramid of values in the western world, which means, of course, that the base of the pyramid of western society is our Royal Hindness.

We also have a dual strategy for those who, in the world's eyes, do possess some humanly desirable beauty or wealth or social status first, it is easier if they go through their lives so focussed on themselves and these temporal values that they never consider any other options. Vanity and wealth have always been two of our most successful strategies in this regard. Second, if they do start in any way looking at the Enemy as an option, it usually only takes a gentle nudge or a "well-meaning" friend to get them back to themselves. Third, if they finally wake up before it is too late, then we can often make them think they are no longer of any value now that they have aged, or we can throw some calamity their way so that they lose their wealth or status and become outsiders. We can then usually send them the path of alcoholism or drug addiction or some never-ending search for meaning or vague spirituality that runs them in circles. The end result, for our purposes, is the same: another juicy morsel.

Finally, we face the challenge that these humans are programmed with an inner spiritual longing. The Enemy is the only one who can satisfy that hunger, but fortunately the little darlings never seem to catch on. In their desperate search for inner peace, they try all these worldly lures, never realising that, as ends in themselves, such transitory things are merely our bait for reeling them in. Thank badness the imbeciles never figure out what the Enemy's peace is all about, and the western world is a fisherman's paradise for Our Royal Hindness.

H. The Sledgehammer Approach

While we've had numerous victories in the Church and the World, we've managed to win even when it appears on the surface that we are losing ground: where some of these followers of the Enemy try to force their view on everyone through the political process. While supposedly espousing the Enemy's values, the self-proclaimed religious political groups adopt every worldly and Machiavellian technique possible to stomp its opposition. The result is that they in fact send a message of hatred, division, and intolerance as they try to pound their values on others through the lawmaking and political process. At first we were fearful of these groups, but no longer. There is, of course, a real danger if the Enemy's followers were to get involved in the political process and use the Son's methods of operation. Many in the political movements, however, have lost sight of the Son's own teachings. He railed against the lawmakers and hypocrites, and he taught that what must change is the human heart. We are so fortunate, however, that in the political arena, the effort by the so-called religious political groups is spent primarily on external matters – for if this same time and effort were spent in sacrificial love to their fellow humans, we would be in trouble. Instead, they ignore the human heart and focus their efforts on trying to sledgehammer people with their values. Can you imagine what would happen to our efforts if they were to spend their time in prayer to their Creator, and loving their neighbours, instead?

One of our primary strategies, which has worked to perfection for centuries, is to confuse church and state. Our first line of defence is to promote the establishment of a state church, or failing that, to at least muddle the lines between politics and religion. It's then so easy to create a watered-down version of Christianity, because it reduces the dynamics of a relationship with the Enemy down to a matter of ritual, formality, and patriotism. Nothing takes the life and spirit out of his church faster than allowing Caesar to be made pre-eminent.

Mind you, this is entirely different from having his followers get involved in the political process and attempt to promote his virtues by changing the minds and hearts of people through eloquent argument and personal example. Our plans have been greatly interfered with when such people work with the Enemy to effect social change, such as, for instance, the abolition of slavery and the recognition of equality among people. This type of involvement we must avoid at all costs.

Therefore, whenever possible, we must continue to encourage humans to involve Caesar in the Enemy's matters. As long as we can keep people focused on trying to force values externally, instead of changing hearts internally, our strategy for world domination is in no real danger.

I. "Are There No Prisons?"

Likewise, because these humans ignore or ridicule any spiritual aspect to life, they have failed miserably at dealing with crime. It is often a matter of the human heart, which even the Enemy's Book says is desperately wicked. The breakdown of families, the loss of the concept of human worth, economic deprivation, drugs, and alcohol are destroying western society. The failure by society to instil moral behaviour in their children, to educate and care for the underprivileged in society, to give any economic hope to the poor, or to treat the spiritual causes of crime, has resulted in overflowing prisons and a criminal justice system that is bursting at the seams. Their answer? Treat the symptoms by building more prisons. Scrooge would be proud.

Consistent with the sledgehammer approach discussed above, these humans try to impose justice and punishment from the outside, without trying to deal with the inner spiritual sickness, and the moral and economic depravity, that is often the root cause of crime.

Our work during this study was so arduous, that we took several holidays to relax and refresh ourselves. We tried visiting orphanages, brothels, and drug dens, each of which had their own charm. The most wonderful resorts for us, however, were their prisons. These are bastions of hopelessness, despair, abandonment, and depravity, saturated with drugs, alcohol, pornography and weapons. The inmates are on a first name basis with our Royal Hindness, who is the king of prisons. There is little real attempt at rehabilitation, and we found the prisons to be a delightful place of recreation. If prisoners are not totally depraved before they enter prison, they are after being in prison. Again, as long as society ignores the human heart in dealing with crime, and treats the complex underlying causes of crime with a sticking plaster, we'll continue to have many earthly prison paradises to visit when we get homesick.

J. It's My Right

Our Master has ingeniously turned one of the human race's potential advances to our own purposes: namely, so-called human rights. As we have known for centuries, extremes of any type (except extreme devotion to the Enemy), are most useful for our purposes. For centuries we have enjoyed watching while a relatively few number of people oppress a very large number. It was delightful, seeing the disgrace associated with one group of humans enslaving other groups. The little snits actually thought they were "worthy" of being masters over other humans, little recognising that our Royal Hindness is the only true master they have. To see humans made to live in squalor simply because of the colour of their skin or their perceived social status or class – of course, by no choice of themselves – is a delight of untold proportions to our Underworld. Human misery is one of our greatest recreations, second only to seeing them destroyed because of the sins they chose as their ultimate masters.

While it is evident that our Forces suffered some setbacks after the Enemy's Son came into the world, we hope his influence is on the wane in several quarters and soon to be extinct. Gradually, over many centuries, his teachings (so repugnant to us) that *every* human being is of enormous value to their Father, and that it is not the external appearance, but the heart and soul, that truly matters, made some inroads into our plans. We watched in agony as slavery became outlawed, and as the poor and oppressed of the world began to gain freedoms they had never known before. Then, just when it appeared we might have to enter a full retreat, the Master ingeniously realised that human rights were a great way to divide, instead of unite, people.

What the Enemy had worked for – the recognition of the incalculable worth of all humans – became a powerful instrument of divisiveness in our hands. The Master and our Forces began to whisper to these vermin that they all had "rights." It did not take long for these gullible creatures each to start believing in their own individual "rights," and to begin asserting those rights vigorously, to the exclusion of the "rights" of others. The important point in this is that the "common good" is no longer a consideration. Whenever we can elevate individual, exclusive rights and eliminate actions done for the common good, we are closer to paralleling the behaviour in our beloved Hindom.

Now, instead of bringing people together, the clamour for individual rights has driven a further wedge into the bedrock of their society. Everyone is so intent on asserting their individual rights, or the rights of their particular group, that they have become angry, distrustful, and jealous of others who disagree with those rights. Although the establishment of these rights have caused us temporary setbacks, our Master has, in his inimitable way, turned these rights to our advantage. With the increased focus of western society on self, concern for their fellow man and the common good has been extinguished. In addition, our Forces have helped to create a culture of blame: someone else is always at fault when evil happens. Accountability is a word that will soon be eliminated from their dictionaries and relegated to a dusty tome of archaic concepts. These humans are so busy pointing fingers of blame at others or at society or, most suitably of all, at the Enemy himself, that forgiveness and selfless love will also soon be forgotten.

Parallel to the assertion of individual rights, however, has been the failure of the human community to take responsibility for the poor, the sick, and the needy. Of course we enjoy seeing them remain in poverty, both materially, physically, and spiritually. At the same time, the needy have, with our Master's help, come to think it is their right to be helped, that society is totally to blame for their problems, and that they bear no responsibility for their choices or to better their conditions. This has resulted in a glorious tennis match between individuals and society: each puts the ball in the other's court. Without a recognition on both sides of the net that there is plenty of blame and responsibility to go around, the match proceeds *ad infinitum* without resolution. We just sit on the sidelines ... cheering.

The Enemy had a grand vision for his beloved ...

A rapid-fire pounding on the door jolted me out of my trance-like state as I listened to Rachael's melodious voice reading the report. James stood up, his face clouded over, and I glanced up to see that it was almost ten-thirty at night.

Before the vicar could reach the door, however, a man flung it open, shouting, "Quick! Mrs. Comely's house is on fire. We need help." And, with that, he ran off.

8

LOCKED GATES

WE LOOKED OVER at James, who said quickly, "She's a widow who lives just down from the vicarage. You two go see what you can do, and I'll be there right after you."

Rachael and I leapt up and quickly headed out the door. As I glanced back, I saw James swig the glass of Scotch. There were orange flames coming out of a window in a small, stone cottage. A crowd was gathered around, with a lot of confusion and shouting. As we arrived at the cottage, someone handed me a hosepipe, yelling, "Take this down next to the well just below the church and attach it." I ran in the direction he pointed.

I wasn't sure how long we worked to put out the fire in the kitchen of the cottage. Mrs. Comely, an elderly woman in a long pink nightgown stood outside, fretfully pacing. After we had worked frantically for a good while, a fire truck came to a screeching halt in front of the cottage. Soon thereafter the fire was completely put out, leaving only some smoke and a thick smell of burned wood and plastic in the air. I then looked around to find my friends. Rachael was kneeling down next to the elderly lady, who was now seated on a bench in front of the cottage across the street, and was handing the woman a mug to drink. At first I could not find the vicar. I finally spied him sitting down in the street, gasping for breath.

"Mr. Brooke ... James," I screamed, running over to him. "Are you okay?"

He looked up at me and nodded affirmatively, but said nothing. He continued to breathe heavily. Finally, he said between gasps, "Yes ... I'm fine ... just a little faint ... but I'll be all right." He started to stand up and began to fall. I reached down instinctively and caught him.

"Can you ... help me back to the vicarage?" he asked after a few moments. I put his arm around my shoulder and helped him to his feet. We then walked, slowly and unsteadily, back to the vicarage. I helped him inside, and he sat in his big leather chair.

"Thanks, Cade," he said after a few moments. "Do you mind looking in the loo and bringing me my heart medicine? It's in a green bottle."

I complied and brought him the bottle. He took out several tablets and motioned toward a glass, saying simply, "Water." After I filled the glass, he swallowed the pills, sat back in the chair, and closed his eyes with a sigh.

"Are you sure you're all right?" I inquired again, worried. "Should I call a doctor?"

"No need to call a doctor. My heart is a bit weak, and these pills will take care of it. I'll be fine if I can just sit for a bit. Where's Rachael?"

"I think she's ..."

Just then Rachael came in, her face black with soot.

"I was trying to help calm Mrs. Comely," she said before we could say anything. "James, are you all right?" Rachael then rushed over to his chair.

"Yes, my dear. I got a little faint, but Cade brought me my heart medicine, and I'll be fine."

Rachael gently stroked his head, and James smiled, saying, "How is Mrs. Comely?"

"She's understandably a bit shaken. She apparently had gone to bed and a neighbour saw the flames and woke her up and got her out of the house. Mrs. Comely's daughter turned up a while ago and is taking her mother home with her tonight."

Just then, the clock struck the half hour, and I realised that it was now twelve-thirty.

"I had planned to drive you back tonight," said James. "I'm afraid, however, I'm not in any shape to do that now. You're welcome to stay here. Rachael, there's a guest room, and Cade, I have a couch to offer you. I'm sorry it's so late. You two must be exhausted."

"What about the rest of Soulbane?" asked Rachael, as she wiped the soot off her face with a towel.

"I'm too spent to read any more tonight, much as I want to," said James after a momentary pause. "Besides, I have to conduct a funeral tomorrow, and then I must prepare for the church service on Sunday. In fact, why don't you take my car back to Oxford? I'll get it later."

"I'm really not tired now, with all this excitement," I admitted. "Rachael, do you want to stay at the vicarage, or go back?"

"I do need to get back," said Rachael apologetically. "But how will you get your car?"

"I tell you what," said James. "I want to read the rest of the report, and you've mentioned the mysterious comment at the end. Why don't I take the bus into Oxford on Tuesday, and meet you at the Student Union at half past two? I believe we can find a quiet place to discuss this report there. Then perhaps we can do some research on this new mystery."

"Sounds good," Rachael replied.

James retrieved his car key, and Rachael gave him a hug as we started to leave.

"Are you sure you'll be all right?" I asked again. Some colour had returned to his cheeks, but he still appeared unsteady.

"I'm fine. I just need to get some rest. I'll see you on Tuesday and will get my car back then."

I volunteered to drive and Rachael did not argue. We talked about the excitement of the fire and how fortunate Mrs. Comely had been that her neighbour had seen the blaze. Then, we both fell quiet, and I began to think about the portions of Soulbane we had read and wondered what had made Rachael so upset. I thought about asking her, but realised the issue was moot when I glanced over and discovered she was fast asleep.

When I pulled the car up in front of Merton, I gently shook Rachael, who awakened and smiled groggily.

"We're at Merton. Let me walk you to your room."

"I'm ... I'm fine," she said quietly. "Just let me get ... oh, no, I don't have my key to get into the College."

Merton, like most Oxford Colleges, locked its doors at midnight, going back to traditions established centuries before. Students used to have to climb over walls and fences to get in after midnight, and there were many tales told of such student misadventures. Now, Oxford students were generally given keys to get in some side door. My key, for instance, allowed me to get into a small door facing Longwall Street, and I had made good use of it.

"What do you suggest?" I finally said. I was very tired myself and wanted to crawl into bed.

Suddenly Rachael grinned impishly, saying, "Are you game for a little fence climbing?"

"Of course!" I said immediately, not wanting to turn down such a challenge, and trying to mask my reluctance.

"Come on, then," she replied, as she got out of the car. Rachael led me along Merton Street, one of the few in Oxford still made of cobblestones, and in the light from the street lamps, this scene could have been hundreds of years earlier. The sky was cloudy, and the evening was cool, but very still. Several Oxford bells simultaneously announced it was two-thirty in the morning. We came to a large iron gate at least twelve feet tall that led to a pathway beside Merton and back to the Christ Church Meadows. I had walked down this lovely path called Grove Lane many times during the day, but had never faced the closed gate before.

As I was trying to figure out how we would scale the gate, Rachael said, "Here, give me a step up."

I cupped my hands, and Rachael stepped nimbly in them and grabbed hold of the iron gate. She quickly pulled herself up and was soon over the gate. I heard a gentle thud as she landed on the other side.

"Do you want to try?" she asked, laughing.

"You bet," I said, hoping I would not embarrass myself.

"Well, are you coming tonight or waiting until the gate opens in the morning?"

"I'm fixing to," I said as I looked for the best place to grab hold of the gate.

"Fixing to? You Americans have the oddest expressions!"

By this time I had hoisted myself halfway up the gate, and soon found a place to gingerly pull myself over, avoiding the sharp points that threatened my future existence. I almost lost my balance as I crossed the top, however, and slid ungracefully down the other side, desperately trying to remain upright. I almost succeeded but lost my grip and fell the last few feet.

Rachael was laughing again as she reached down to pull me up. I ignored her hand and leapt to my feet, brushing the sand and dirt off my trousers.

As we walked down the path, the only sound was the crunching of our feet. We arrived at the back of Merton, with the expansive Meadows before us.

"Want to walk down to the river?" whispered Rachael.

"Sure." The exertion of climbing the gate had reinvigorated me.

We walked down to the Thames, which gently lapped against the wall separating the Meadows from the river. Without a word, we began to pick our way along the path beside the river. The moon, which was about three-quarters full, peered between the clouds that were breaking up, casting its silvery light on a sleeping Oxford. I glanced at Rachael, wondering what she was thinking.

As if reading my mind, Rachael began speaking softly, saying, "Cade, I know this doesn't matter to you, but just so you know, the reason I was crying earlier this evening ..."

She paused, and I stopped walking and looked at her, wondering what she was about to divulge. "Rachael, of course I care."

She resumed walking thoughtfully. "Cade, I could see your sudden change of heart when you visited me in Tintagel. I knew then I wasn't what you wanted. But I wanted to explain why I was so upset. You

see, my father left us – that is, Mum and me, when I was around ten.
I had just come in one evening from playing at Tintagel Castle, and
my parents were having a terrible quarrel. My father had been
drinking, and he was hitting my mother. She was screaming. I ... I
didn't know what to do. I went to stop him, and he hit me. I ran
outside and without knowing where to go, for some reason I ran to
our parish church. We never even went there, except maybe at
Christmas, but something led me there. The vicar and Mrs. Brooke
were working inside the church, and I ran in there. After I told them
what happened, James went down to the house, while Mrs. Brooke
stayed with me. I was so upset, and couldn't stop crying. That was the
first time my father had ever hit me, although I had seen bruises on
Mum before and wondered where she got them. She always had some
kind of excuse. I knew my father drank a great deal, but I was so
young, I didn't understand it. Mrs. Brooke took me to her house, and
made me some hot chocolate. Later, James came back with my
mother. Mum and I spent the night in their house, and James stayed
up all night with me. I was too scared and upset to sleep. Although I
hardly knew him, he was so kind and gentle. I never saw my father
again after that night."

She paused and took a deep breath, then continued, "Soon after
that, I rebelled. I was angry and hurt inside, and said hateful things to
my mother. We had dreadful arguments. I thought she had got my
father to leave ... I loved him despite his faults. I was too young to
understand everything then – his alcoholism, his violent temper, and
how irresponsible he was with money. I began to eat everything in
sight and gained a lot of weight. That compounded my problems, and
then the Brookes moved to the Cotswolds, and I lost someone who
had become a real father figure for me. I began to entertain thoughts
of suicide ... I was so unhappy. My mother and I fought all the time.
I started hanging around a group of kids who smoked marijuana and
seemed to be constantly in trouble. I was truly lost, with no one to
turn to."

"Rachael, I ..." I began, and started to put my arm around her.

"No, it's all right." she said, stepping back. "It was around this time, however, that I saw my mother change. She became more peaceful, and began reading the Bible. She had started going to James's church every Sunday, just before they moved to the Cotswolds. I didn't want to have a thing to do with church then. I thought it was a bunch of hypocrites and fools. Yet, I couldn't get over the change in my mother. In fact, although I kept picking fights, she wouldn't fight back. Do you know how maddening that is?"

"Yes," I replied, just to fill in the silence. "Rachael, you don't have to tell me anything you don't want to."

"I'm OK, Cade. Anyway, I almost dropped out of school then, and was really bewildered. I was so hurt that my father had left us, and I'm not sure I ever got over his striking me. I was very angry and bitter and didn't know where to turn. I certainly didn't understand my mother's change, and I decided to watch for awhile and see if it was temporary or not. Then, about a year or so after he'd gone to the Cotswolds, James and his wife stopped by one day. They were visiting Tintagel and wanted to see how we were doing. Mum was not home, but we ended up visiting for several hours. The long and short of it is that they began to tell me about Christianity and explained how God was ready to help if I would only ask. They even prayed with me, and I had never prayed with anyone before. That afternoon began a long journey of faith for me – a journey that I'm still on. I was so insecure, and in many ways still am. It took me a long time to even try to forgive my father for the pain he caused us. I don't know where I would be now without God. He gave me a security I've never had before. Plus, my mother is now my best friend in the world."

Rachael stopped walking and smiled faintly. She then continued, "Anyway, Cade, it's good for me to get this off my chest. I guess we'd better get back now and try and get some sleep."

I realised we'd walked well past the village of Iffley. As we quietly retraced our steps along the river toward Merton, the dawn began to break. Before us was a panoramic outline of the Oxford spires and colleges, accentuated by the pink rays of the sun shining through the clouds. The new day was welcomed by a chorus of birds perched in trees along the river. I was stunned at Rachael's revelation. I would never have guessed her childhood had been so troubling. I wondered about her father – how could anyone have been so irresponsible and abusive?

I felt I need to say something, but what? Finally, I blurted out, "Rachael, I'm so sorry for you and your mother. I ... I, well, is there anything I can do?"

"No, no," she replied gently. "Just letting me talk about it was a help. That's all in the past now."

We finally arrived at Merton, but it was unnecessary to climb over the wall into the College. The porter would have the front door open by now, so we walked around to the main entrance of the College.

"Thanks for listening, Cade." said Rachael smiling. "I'm fine, now. Really."

"Good," I said, not really knowing what to say. "I'll see you on Tuesday." I impulsively kissed her on the cheek, then waved as she walked into the College. As I got into the car, I was tired and puzzled. Rachael was much more complex than I had imagined, and yet her personal story had, in some odd way I couldn't explain, attracted me to her. She had unlocked a gate in her heart and made herself so vulnerable ... so human. I felt embarrassed that she had seen how fickle I was, and wondered if my first assessment of Rachael was rash and shallow. She still talked about God in a strange way, as if he made some tangible difference in her life. It was all very puzzling, but I was too weary to try and work it out now, and instead could think only of finding my bed.

9

FOOL'S GOLD AND RIDDLES

THE FOLLOWING Tuesday, we met at the Oxford Union. James said, "I arrived here early and bagged a quiet spot where nobody would disturb us."

"Let me find where we left off the other night before the fire interrupted us," I said as I thumbed through the pages. I cleared my throat and began to read:

The Enemy had a grand vision for his beloved minions. He foolishly thought that, being made in his image, they would be able to love one another unselfishly. Instead, these humans have devised more ways to divide themselves into groups than even the Base Command could conceive. Not only is there division based upon obvious differences like skin colour, language, ethnic background, or culture, but they also divide themselves by wealth, perceived social status, education, physical appearance, family heritage, political and religious beliefs, and a thousand other categories. A myriad of labels is used to classify, and thus place a value on, other people, and racism is alive and well. There are sub-groups within sub-groups within groups, all thinking their own particular group is exclusive and correct, and none willing to listen to, much less accept unconditionally, other groups.

How the Enemy could have possibly thought that these two-legged animals would be capable of finding intrinsic value in the gift of life, and of valuing the hearts and souls of people, rather than focusing on temporal external matters, is a mystery to us. He planned for his children to live as a global family, and to use their diversity as a strength; instead, this diversity is an inherent weakness that is destroying peace and community. War, violence, hatred, and incivility have been great assets in our strategic plan for world domination. Each passing year sees our job grow easier and easier as the animosity and division among these creatures intensifies, and hordes of lost souls are crowding into our Hindom Gateway, dazed and confused.

K. Our Beloved Earthly Twins: Relativism and Pluralism

Two of our favourite world domination strategies have come into full bloom in the western world. The first, relativism, is now firmly in place in their thought and culture. The Enemy is by his very nature a moral absolute – an abhorrent concept to us. One reason for our Master's revolt was that our Royal Hindness could not stand to be with a Being that was pure truth, light, and love. (Our Homeland fortunately knows nothing of such distasteful matters.) Because of the natural human tendency towards folly and selfishness, the Enemy had to give them Ten Commandments to make certain they knew the rules to live by. Our undercover research has confirmed that almost no one even knows these Commandments any more, and that even where they are known of, they are viewed as nothing more than the Ten Suggestions (and bad ones at that I might add). Finally, out of complete desperation and because our Master was winning every battle, the Enemy resorted to sending his own heir to attempt a last-ditch rescue mission. Although our efforts to destroy him by torture backfired on us, it appears that this extreme measure has had no lasting effect on these humans.

Slowly and patiently over the centuries, the Base Command continued to chip away at these absolutes and to put relativism in their place, and the fruits of these labours are now quite evident. Relativism is now the dominant religion for these humans, which means, of course, that all philosophies, religions, and viewpoints are equally valid. Because there is no longer any standard by which to judge ideas or conduct, the floodgates are open to any sort of religion, philosophy, or lifestyle. The cardinal "sin" of relativism is intolerance. In our efforts at subversion, we find that without the counterbalance of truth and responsibility, tolerance alone makes the Enemy's minions weak and defenceless. On the other hand, naked intolerance, unmitigated by love and empathy, divides them by hatred and prejudice. Both cause us to triumph. Of course, our ultimate goal is to replace all human passions with indifference, which is our Hindom's only genuine emotion.

A natural result of all this is the death of conscience in the western world. Thanks to our multitude of strategies, many mortals no longer recognise right from wrong, personal responsibility, or shame, and the Enemy's gentle whispers to their conscience now fall on deaf ears.

With this basic tenet of relativism in place, it will not be long before even human life is just another relative concept with no transcendent value at all. Then, everything goes: murder, euthanasia, war, and the rest of our Hindom virtues will become prevalent and acceptable, justified only by whoever is in power. After all, without any ultimate standards by which to judge conduct, what's wrong with a little Holocaust now and then? The ultimate judge now is power and money, not intangible virtues and ethics. Relativism has been our most successful strategy and has ensured that our loading dock workers are having to work extra shifts to keep things moving. Of course, with the victory of relativism, Christianity has been relegated to just one of thousands of "options," which means that soon – despite some worrying evidence to the contrary – we hope it will be just another minor religion practised by a few demented fools.

The twin brother to relativism is pluralism. These philosophies go hand in glove. Once relativism is accepted, then it is only natural that any so-called religion or philosophy or idea is considered valid and on equal footing with any other. We observed tremendous successes (not to mention downright fun) experienced by our Forces throughout the western world as all sorts of philosophies, life forces, and spirits are dreamt up and promoted. The more amorphous and impersonal, the better.

It would be impossible in this Report to detail the many different religions these humans have devised, some with our help, and some the little darlings have dreamt up all by themselves. The important point, from our perspective, is that they channel their thoughts and energies away from the Enemy, and instead toward some dead-end street. Of course, one of our greatest victories is the notion, gaining widespread acceptance – and soon to be universal – that it really doesn't matter what you believe, as long as you are "sincere" (what a marshmallow word). I have often heard Foulheart gleefully tell about the many wonderful morsels he has tasted of such "sincere" humans, who chose to live their lives only for themselves and apart from the Enemy.

In this regard, we have finally achieved one of the Master's greatest goals: humans either no longer believe in "the Devil" at all, or else they worship him. Either way is fine. Of course, ultimately, we would like for all to see the darkness and worship our Master as we do. Nevertheless, it suits our purposes just as well if they don't believe in us at all. This means our subtle attacks work marvellously (although Wormwood's blunder of letting Lewis discover those damned letters he published did cause us some problems). Often, if they don't believe in us, they don't believe in evil either, which helps immensely. Now that the world has become so "civilised" and "technologically advanced" and "educated," it is no longer in vogue to believe in such ignorant myths as devils or spirits or evil or sin. Of course, the corollary to this is that there is no need to believe in the Enemy either, much less in outdated concepts like redemption and atonement.

Unfortunately, he apparently designed these stupid creatures with an inner longing for himself – something we fiends naturally find abhorrent, but which our research has confirmed. Our job for centuries has been to get them to ignore these longings altogether, or else to fill that void with something appealing and temporal, and thus fool them into thinking that is all there is. Of course, there are always the reliable subterfuges, such as affluence, power, and materialism, which do the trick almost every time. Increasingly, however, as many humans have become aware that civilisation and modern advances have not provided all the answers they seek, these *wunderkind* have turned to any number of forms of religion or spiritualism, much too numerous to go into in this Report. More and more people are trying to fill these inevitable voids by turning to spiritualism, astrology, numerology, superstition, new age, or an amorphous life force for insight and direction. Obviously, whenever possible, it is our job to promote any and all murky and ill-defined spirits.

Frankly, we had not expected such an upsurge in this, but it has been most gratifying. Our Royal Hindness is often able to control or direct them toward fuzzy-headed notions of forces "out there," and sometimes toward such dead-end avenues as devil worship, witchcraft, drugs, violence, hatred, and even murder. As we continue to destroy the Enemy's influence wherever possible, we expect even more followers. They will never learn that "all that glisters is not gold." Centuries of our triumphs with all types of fool's gold have proved that.

L. The Garden of Eden: Round Two

Round One in the Garden of Eden resulted in a RESOUNDING victory for our Master. We still celebrate Our Father Below's masterful achievement, where he tricked Adam and Eve and forever corrupted their descendants. We are on the verge of yet another major victory for our dark world: to destroy, not only the Enemy's creatures, but also the larger garden they call "Mother Earth." These humans have used their chance at stewardship of their earthly home to destroy and deface their Creator's art work. He thought they would be his gardeners and work in partnership with him, but starting with the first couple, our Master prevailed. It has been downhill for the Enemy ever since.

This legacy has been handed down to all generations of these fallen children, and they have shown little regard for the world they were given. Just look at the way they have, in their lust for money and power, eliminated forever thousands of the living animals and plants made by the Enemy; they have polluted the air, water and land to mirror their own spiritual pollution; and they have defaced the natural beauty the Enemy thought so highly of when he created this world. We now are pleased to document a damaged and ugly world so different from the Earthly Paradise the Enemy had envisioned at the beginning. Not that they have yet achieved the dark, stark beauty of our Hindom, but that will come in time.[HN]

Of course, of even greater delight to us is the hunger, poverty, starvation, sickness, want, and despair so many of these humans experience every day. How wonderful it was for Baldface, Scrunchmouth, Bleakblab, Slobglob, and me to walk the streets of their ghettos and observe squalor, deprivation, drug and alcohol addiction, violence and hopelessness, even in the midst of the so-called richest countries in the world. In fact, we had to tear ourselves away from watching the intense suffering of so many millions of his creatures.

Meanwhile, they spend so much of their resources for their own material comforts, as well as in arming themselves to attack and defend against the other creatures they distrust so much, that they don't have time to care for their fellow man. We used to fret that as they became more technologically advanced, humans might finally attempt to eliminate the poverty and disease of their fellow creatures, but we no longer waste our time with such silly thoughts. They already have the ability to feed the hungry and heal many sick and starving children, but instead they put their time and resources into trying to make themselves more powerful and wealthy. We've always relished the poverty and starvation of past generations, but that was not nearly so gratifying as it is now that the vermin could actually do something about it ... but won't.

M. I'll be Suing You

This Report has outlined some of the wonderful changes in western culture which have helped our plans come to fruition, including the

[HN]I understand from Foulheart that the Base Command has worked diligently to start a nuclear war, but that the Enemy has thus far prevented such an event from occurring.

insistence on individual rights to the exclusion of the good of society as a whole, and the elimination of personal responsibility. A tangible example of the fruits of our labours is how litigious westerners have become. They will sue anybody, anytime, for anything. They talk about justice and fairness, but they want *money* and *power*. We have been able to use this mind-set to great advantage.

As part of our research, we attempted to interview that special species of vermin they call lawyers. Badness knows, there are enough of them down here! (Even our Royal Hindness can't stand to be around them for very long.) It is clear that the goal of lawyers in their trials is not justice, but winning. We tried to get a group of them to explain to us why there is so much litigation in western society, and why society is so distrustful of the legal system, so that we could clarify the matter for this Report, but all they did was argue, and we never got a straight answer. Later, several even tried to send us a bill for their time!

The lawsuit mania has been most useful. While the Enemy has stressed over and over to his children to be so crass as to turn the other cheek, love their neighbours, and act without self-interest (can you imagine Hell with such revolting behaviour?), these humans adore controversy, division, competition, and winning. Now, they sue each other at the drop of a hat. Even followers of the Enemy, who espouse some of his despicable ideas (on Sundays at least), don't hesitate to sue one another any time they feel their "rights" have been infringed. Western society is a culture of blame. Hell forbid if they ever tried to put any of the Son's teachings into practice in their daily lives: a lot of lawyers would be out of business. Fortunately, there is no real danger of that.

N. The Spinning Top of Life
One of the great characteristics of the western world is that it is in such a hurry. Busyness is the trademark of these people: not that they know what they're trying to accomplish, just so long as they are busy. We used to have a great deal of trouble when people took the time to relax, read, or engage in deep, meaningful relationships, and thereby

contemplate the world and the meaning of life. The Enemy has the upper hand in such situations, because when people take the time to look around them, they start realising there MUST be something more than just the material world. And, as they spend time getting to really know other people, all too often they develop bonds of friendship and caring. Such a disgusting trait among these humans! Our research disclosed that as humans examined their hearts, they apparently felt a longing for something – often they did not know what – that only he could fill. (Why that is so remains a mystery to our Hindom.) Furthermore, time to contemplate often led humans to that mysterious, despicable practice the Enemy adores called prayer.

Our research indicates that he allows anyone to pray to him anytime, anywhere. As the Base Command is aware, we are able to monitor prayer traffic to the Enemy, although we have not yet broken the code in order to know what these humans are saying to him. We have, however, confirmed a direct correlation between prayers directed to him and intervention by the Enemy. It's one of his most dangerous weapons, and one in which we have yet to find an adequate mode of attack

But such contemplation is no longer the case. Their society is now so fast-paced, they have little time for serious thought of any meaningful sort. The humans we observed have an obsession with being busy, even if the tasks are meaningless. They are like toy tops: as long as they're spinning, that is all that matters to them, even if they're not going anywhere. The result, of course, is that we can easily fill their days and nights with work, or events, or entertainment, or almost anything. It seems that the more trivial we make it, the easier it is to keep them occupied. Not only do they not have time for serious contemplation, they make no time for any serious prayer or reading of the Enemy's Book. Moreover, they have no time to visit or help one another, because they are so focused on their own busy lives. This has done wonders for our cause, not to mention the added benefits of seeing the physical and mental health of these creatures devastated by the stress and strain of modern-day life.

The proverbial "rat race," as they call it, has snared thousands, indeed millions, of these imbeciles. Workaholism is rampant throughout their society: they work harder and harder and accomplish less and less. The stupid creatures can't seem to figure out that quantity does not mean quality. This is a two-edged sword for us: while this means that our banquets of late have been overflowing with food, the taste of these shallow humans leaves something to be desired.

It is now quite easy either to keep them occupied totally with work or activities, or when they finally do run out of steam, to fill their time with mindless television, frivolous novels and magazines, forays onto the Internet, or our age-old standby, sleep. Anything, as long as it is not aimed toward developing a relationship with the Enemy. Of course, these dullards aren't as much fun when they reach our shores, but no matter, as long as they do, of course, end up in the Hindom of Our Father Below.

O. Honesty is the Worst Policy

It would be impossible to comment on every social and cultural quirk in the western world. We have attempted to distil some of the more important trends and outline them in this Report. One such trend we found so wonderful is that these humans are liars and cheats (a trademark of our society we so dearly cherish) as a matter of routine. The hogwash they mouth about honesty, integrity, and ethics is nothing but hot-air balloons: pretty, yet empty, words. This is a culture that prides itself on dishonesty and on seeing how much they can get away with.

There are big lies and small lies, but lies all the same.[HN] Our undercover research allowed us to have a unique insight into their daily lives, and what we found made us ravenous. This is a society that abhors truth and adores falsehood. They lie about anything and everything: they fib about their taxes, they cheat on their spouses, they steal from their employers, they put up false fronts to their neighbours, they stab their friends in the back, and the list goes on and on. Their main preoccupation now is not to get caught, and if for some reason they do get caught, then their propensity to shift blame takes over. They point fingers and blame everyone but themselves.

Because shame is no longer a recognised emotion in western society, and personal responsibility is an outdated, irrelevant concept, no one is held accountable for lying anymore. This accepted practice is one more notch in the belt of our Royal Hindness, who has been rightfully called "the father of lies."

P. Ashes to Ashes
Thanks to the brilliant work of our Master in the Enemy's garden, our accomplice death was introduced into the world. To observe modern society, however, you would think death no longer exists. It is only rarely written or spoken about, and our Forces have found it easy to keep these vermin from contemplating death and what might happen beyond. Death has been put out of their common experience and pushed away from their conscious thoughts.

These creatures, remarkably, act as if they are ignorant about the reality of death, even though it happens to every single one of them. They all somehow block out this inevitability and live their lives in denial. As one of these human writers said just before he died, "Everybody has got to die, but I have always believed an exception would be made in my case. Now what?" If we can keep them from thinking about death, then they never get around to thinking about whether there is anything beyond death, much less ever doing anything about it. One of our greatest pleasures is seeing the looks on

HNWhile we're on the subject of lies, a special victory is due to be mentioned. One of our greatest triumphs is that, within a mere fifty years, some neo-Nazis are actually claiming that the Jewish Holocaust never happened! As you know, our Master Plan called for us to work toward this result, but never in our wildest imaginations did we think we could get as far as we have in such a short time. To think that this is being debated in some circles, within the lifetime of participants in, and survivors of, the Holocaust, is a victory almost without parallel. In fact, we hereby recommend that Shamoath, who headed up this operation, be given the Medal of Dishonour for this. This is an especially great victory, not only because of the swiftness with which it was accomplished, but also because, in a virtually unprecedented move by his Royal Hindness, several of the regions in our subterranean Homeland had already been renamed to commemorate these great victories for our forces, including Auschwitz, Dachau, and Buchenwald, to name a few.

their faces when we greet them at the loading docks, and they suddenly realise for the first time that death is real. How we sneer when they arrive at our gate saying, "Now what?"!

One would think that since death comes to all of them, they would try to understand it better and at least figure out if that is the end or not. But, death is not a pleasant subject, and it is either avoided completely, denied, or treated abstractly. For, above all, they want to dwell on pleasant things. Thank badness so many of them never take time to learn about the dreadful occasion when the Enemy overcame death, burst open our gates, and brought that blinding light to our darkened realm – all in order to give them eternal life.

Q. The Great Garbage Disposal

One of the largest hurdles the Base Command has had to overcome was the influence the Enemy had in western culture concerning the value of each human life. After all, he made them in his ghastly image. His horrendous Ten Commandments, his Scripture, and the teachings of his Son, all point to the enormous value the Enemy assigns to each of these vermin. This was a primary basis for many of the terrible reforms we observed, such as the abolition of slavery, or the enactment of child labour laws, or the recognition of equality in the civil rights movement, and it was a basic tenet of their civilisation, even for those who did not recognise the Enemy. Of course, the hideous event when he became one of them also shows the mysterious worth he assigns to these creatures.

Now, however, human life is often not viewed as being anything special. You need only look at the widespread use of drugs and alcohol, the poverty and despair, and the hopelessness in many lives, to see this. It is also quite evident in their rise in crime. Violence and incivility are pervasive in western culture. For many, human life has no real value; children are commandeered as soldiers, and rape, murder, abortion, suicide, and euthanasia are on the increase. Creating life in laboratories and genetic tampering have made them believe they are the creators. The human soul is a completely forgotten concept. The main point, from our perspective, is that now their culture is headed toward a dark sunset, where human life is not viewed as unique. The results will be enormously satisfying for our Royal Hindness, for once the wonder of the Enemy's free gift of human life has been lost, then the whole concept of soul becomes meaningless. At that point, the Enemy's eternal values will fall by the wayside as meaningless and irrelevant.

Modern western society is the "consume and dispose" society. All things – goods, services, and relationships – merely exist to be consumed. The centre of the universe is the self, and the goal of the self is to consume for personal satisfaction. If something is broken, the idea is not to repair it, but instead to throw it away. Once something has been consumed, it is just discarded as useless. Given the hectic pace of life, and with materialism as their god, these humans would rather toss out anything that doesn't work and just buy something new. How we love consumption!

Of course, for our purposes, it is not the consumption and disposal of goods we care about (except to the extent it destroys the environment), but the consumption and disposal of values and relationships. Our focus is to ensure that all so-called virtues, if they are thought of at all, are viewed as transitory and replaceable, rather than permanent and enduring. In this, our Forces have succeeded beyond our wildest dreams. Now, all ideas and virtues being relative, they are easily cast aside. Because philosophy, religion, and other concepts are all viewed as being on equal footing, they can be adopted and tossed aside whenever convenient, and certainly whenever they begin to produce the least bit of unpleasantness or anything resembling a pang of conscience. Thus, the Enemy's invention of virtues has been cast aside in the modern world. Such loathsome concepts as loyalty, honour, integrity and truth are merely conveniences, not non-negotiable values. Besides, certain other of the Enemy's virtues have likewise been abolished, including humility, perseverance, and unselfishness, meaning that the disposal of anything that proves too difficult or challenging is the only option considered.

A natural result of the disposal of values is the discarding of relationships whenever they become difficult, unpleasant, or inconvenient. Once we can direct these humans away from such crass virtues as self-sacrifice, forgiveness, unselfish giving, loyalty, and perseverance, and couple this with the Master's brilliant strategy of eliminating personal responsibility, then we can easily lead them away from their relationships with other humans. Thus, instead of sticking by one another and working out differences – whether between husband and wife, parent and child, employer and employee, or neighbours – these creatures quickly exit such relationships at the first sign of trouble. Furthermore, we are always holding before them the mirage that the grass is greener elsewhere: they fall for our oldest and most reliable deception almost every time.

The Enemy designed these vermin to live in community, and gave them a longing for lasting friendships and love. Of course, because our Royal Hindness has caused them to live in a fallen world, no relationship will ever be without problems and difficulties, and the closer the relationship, the greater the likelihood for pain. Because the modern world has abandoned such relationships, however, these humans spend their lives desperately seeking permanence, yet avoiding it whenever it is within their grasp. This notion carries over to their religion, too, such that they go from religion to religion, philosophy to philosophy, lifestyle to lifestyle – always desiring what they think they don't have, and readily discarding what they do have as soon as they have consumed what they can, or as soon as there is the least sign of difficulty.

Our ultimate goal, of course, is well within sight: these humans are far down the road to creating the notion of a disposable race. With human life thus viewed as expendable, it won't be hard to push them to simply discard humans who are viewed as worthless or broken – the sick, the poor, the aged. The next step is to get them to view the merely non-productive or the non-conforming as disposable, and voila! Victory is ours. Our Royal Hindness will then become the greatest garbage disposal of all time, as their useless, discardable souls get flushed down the spiritual sewer to our Cimmerian Homeland.

R. The Great Escape

A final aspect of western society needs to be mentioned: drugs and alcohol. These two marvellous opiates are destroying millions of lives, with little more than a whimper from the western world. With our hellish values of despair, depression, and hopelessness pervading their society from top to bottom, it has been a cakewalk for our Forces to foist drugs of all types upon them. The millions of addicts who are destroying their lives and those of their friends and families made our research very pleasurable.

Substance abuse has destroyed their minds and bodies, wreaked havoc in their relationships, and caused a descending domino effect of crime and destruction. In fact, we hereby recommend that the Base Command issue a special commendation to DAMN – our Drug Addiction Misery Network – for the multitude of ways in which they have aided in the utter destruction of millions of these humans. Our calculations show conclusively that addictions are escalating dramatically; long may it continue.

S. The Black Hole of Life

The culmination of all that we studied about the western world leads us to believe is that it is in its spiritual twilight, much like the death of a star. Despite the material riches and technological advances they possess, there is a tremendous emptiness in their lives. It is like a doctor treating an illness by making a wrong diagnosis and prescribing the wrong medicine: these humans have a spiritual need, but they try to satisfy it with material and temporal things. This leads to despair, hopelessness, emptiness, boredom, violence, envy, and loneliness. Our research found tremendous unhappiness in western society. They search desperately for meaning, in all the right places: right for us, that is.

The beauty of all this is that western culture has, in effect, created a black hole which is drawing all spiritual life out of these humans. As they travel further away from the Enemy and his teachings, the vacuum gets larger and more powerful. Our Master has long planned for this eventuality: this black hole will finally swallow up all of these humans in a deep, dark, spiritual void from which they will never escape. When that occurs, the war will be over, and we will be victorious. During the time between when we started our research and when we finalised this Report, we monitored this black void with the help of the Base Command's sophisticated tracking techniques. What we learned is that the spiritual emptiness that is being created, with the masterful strategies of our Royal Hindness behind them, is growing at an increasingly rapid rate. We compared the Base Command's projections about the end of the spiritual war with our own calculations, and we are confident the Base Command's projections are too conservative and need to be shortened considerably. We look forward to the day when the Enemy's earthly paradise and our Homeland become swallowed up together into one gigantic black hole, with our Royal Hindness as the ruler of this dark, cold universe.

This concludes Part I of our Report. Part II will be delivered on All Hallows' Eve at the high Southern Cross.

> Respectfully submitted,
> Soulbane
> Captain, Junior Devil Corps

*   *   *

When I finished reading, I glanced at my watch to see that it was late in the afternoon. My throat was dry and I felt profoundly unsettled by these grim predictions. There was silence in the room, and we looked at one another quizzically.

"Do.you really think this is authentic?" Rachael asked finally.

"I don't know," said James. "It is hard to fathom, yet the unbelievable circumstances surrounding Cade's discoveries, make me feel these are really Soulbane's words. Besides, this description of the world hits all too close to home, at least for me."

"It describes many of the outlooks and attitudes I've come to accept," I replied.

"What do you think, Rachael?" asked James.

"Ever since I first saw the letters, I've had a feeling that they were real. It was too incredible to believe, really, and yet I had this ... well, this intuition about them. For me, the confirmation came, not when Cade found this new report, but when he received the invitation out of the blue to go to Malta. That was an answer to my prayers in an unmistakable way, and I believe these frightening reports truly are from a devilish source."

"The Malta trip was an incredible coincidence," I added.

"Well," said James, "an English cleric, Archbishop William Temple, when asked by some sceptics to prove that prayer works, once said, 'When I pray, coincidences happen, and when I don't pray, they don't.' That's a good way to put it, and thanks to Rachael and her faith, we've had some 'coincidences' ourselves."

"One thing I've wondered," I said, "is why the report would be left in a cave that is arguably a Christian symbol?"

"Yes," said James, "that's an interesting question. Then again, if a devil wanted to hide a report where it was least likely to be discovered, what better place to put it? Maybe they're somehow attracted to Christian sites – like a death wish, so to speak. Or possibly some act of sabotage is planned. Look at the dates of your discoveries – the winter's solstice and Mardi Gras, both pagan celebrations; which fits, too, with this reference to Halloween."

"What do we do now?" Rachael inquired.

"First, we need to see if we can find Part Two that is mentioned," said James. "As I cautioned you before, we still must tell no one, until we see what else there is. In the wrong hands, these papers could be trouble. If we still think these are legitimate, then we need to figure out the best way to make them public. Look what C.S. Lewis accomplished with his publication of *The Screwtape Letters*."

When I said good night to Rachael in front of Merton, I awkwardly shuffled my feet. I still wasn't sure what to make of our recent walk in the Meadows, and for once, I found myself speechless. I was beginning to regret the cold shoulder I had given her in Tintagel, yet still found myself waffling over making any type of commitment. For her part, Rachael seemed pleasant, yet quite distant, and I did nothing to change that. As I walked back to Magdalen, I impulsively turned to run back and give her a hug, but she had disappeared into the college. Instead, I continued on to Magdalen, still puzzling over the many bizarre turns my life was taking.

10

THROUGH A GLASS, DARKLY

"WHERE HAVE YOU BEEN, Cade?" said Nigel. "We haven't seen much of you this term."

"I guess I've been pretty busy lately," I replied evasively.

The beautiful June afternoon was a perfect time to be sitting outside at the Perch pub. The weeping willows shuddered in the gentle breeze, and the puffy white clouds floated effortlessly in the sky.

"Aren't these English summer days wonderful?" asked Colin. "It's our payback for the dreary winter."

"Cade, are you seeing Rachael Adams these days?" interjected Adrian.

"A little," I said. Actually, I had only seen her briefly twice since we had read the report with James. I had been very busy with my work, and ever since my trip to Tintagel, Rachael had kept a certain distance.

"Well," said Colin, "just don't get too serious with us." I didn't feel the need to tell them that I had cooled the relationship.

"Cade," said Nigel, "I don't want to burst your bubble, but word around Merton is that Rachael has a boyfriend."

I unexpectedly felt a shock through my body.

"Are you sure?" I finally asked.

"I haven't wanted to say anything," said Nigel. "But I have seen her with a chap at Univ ... name's Charles, I think."

Adrian put his hand on my shoulder, and said, "What are your plans for the summer vac, Cade?"

"I plan to spend most of it in Oxford, and then take off with a Eurail pass for my grand tour of Europe," I replied, without thinking. My mind was racing and my heart pounding over this unexpected revelation about Rachael. For the first time, I realised that I felt more than a passing fancy for her. How could I have been so shortsighted? Was it that the proverbial chase was more exciting than the capture? I hadn't ever thought of the possibility she would find someone else, but until this moment, I also hadn't realised I cared for her so much. I somehow simply thought Rachael would always be there if I ever changed my mind.

"Say, why don't we run into London tonight, and try to pick up some women?" asked Colin." "I know several bars we can go to."

"Sounds great!" said Nigel. "How about it, Cade?"

"Uh, well ... I already have plans ... uh ... I don't know," I answered, hesitantly. I wasn't about to tell them I had agreed to go to church with Rachael the next day. Over a month ago, James had called and asked us both to come see him on this particular Sunday, which was the only reason for Rachael and me to see one another. Now, I wished I'd never agreed to go.

"Oh, come on," said Colin. "You're only young once, and we'll have a great time."

I was in two minds about what to do. My head told me I should stay in Oxford, but an adventure with my friends had a strong appeal.

"All right, let's go," I said finally. The news about Rachael had now made me angry, and I was ready to let off steam.

"Good, mate," said Adrian. "I knew we could count on you. Let's see if we can find some girls in London and have some fun."

* * *

We took the late afternoon train into London and headed for several pubs. Colin was very familiar with the City, having grown up there. I understood we now had the unspoken male challenge of seeing how much we could drink before someone gave in. I vowed to myself that I would not be the first. After a few beers, any apprehensions that may have lingered about our trip into London or any thoughts about Rachael were long forgotten. As the night wore on, I felt better and better. We were having a grand time of it.

"I know a great place we can go to dance and meet some girls," said Colin finally.

"All I can say is enough talk, let's see some action," replied Adrian.

By this time Nigel could barely speak. I knew how drunk he was when he began trying to quote Shakespeare and instead out came a bungled Yeats. We were all quite amused at this point. I felt invincible and was ready to storm the Tower of London.

Colin led us to a large, smoke-filled bar with bright, flashing lights and incredibly loud music. There were plenty of good-looking women, and I could tell that Adrian's Australian sense of adventure was in full gear. We grabbed some more beers, then went on an exploratory expedition of the place.

I saw a tall, shapely girl with long bleached-blonde hair standing near the dance floor, and when she smiled in my direction, I took that as an invitation to come over. I tried to talk, but it was virtually impossible over the music.

"Would you like to dance?" I finally yelled at her.

"What?" she yelled back.

"I said, would you like to dance?" I repeated, pointing toward the dance floor.

"Sure, handsome," she said, as she took my hand and pulled me toward the middle of the dancing people.

I smiled broadly.

We danced for a good while, and I was thoroughly enjoying myself. She wore a tight fitting blouse, dark trousers, and boots. I felt a tap on my shoulder and turned around to see a shorter chap with an earring pointing at the blonde woman and saying something about "his girl." I was fortified enough by the beer to launch the Norman Conquest, and seeing this guy made my blood boil. Remembering my lacrosse days – that the best defence is a good offence – before I knew it I swung my left fist, and he doubled over as I hit him in the stomach. I marvelled at my own fighting prowess. Within seconds, however, he was upright and quickly landed several hard blows to my face and stomach. I was momentarily stunned. My anger was raging now, and I swung wildly. He ducked and my right fist landed squarely on the woman's cheek, knocking her down. She was on the ground screaming and crying. I tried to help her up to explain it was an accident, but several people grabbed my arms and pulled me away.

"You bastard," she shouted as I was being pulled away. She was sobbing and holding her face. A huge man, who must have been the bouncer, stepped up and grabbed my arm. His muscular, tattooed arms were enormous. Before I could protest, he pulled me through the crowd and threw me out the door.

"You're lucky I'm not phoning the police," he yelled. "Now, get the hell out of here and don't ever come back."

I felt something moist, and touched my nose to find it was bleeding profusely.

Adrian and Colin ran out.

"Cade, are you all right?" asked Colin, catching his breath.

"I ... I think so," I replied, not really sure. I had blood all over my shirt.

"Bloody hell," said Adrian. "Who did this, mate? Let me go back in after the bugger."

"No!" I found myself yelling. "Let's not make it worse than it already is. Let's go. Where's Nigel?"

"I don't know," said Colin. "I'll go and find him."

A few minutes later, Colin emerged with a singing Nigel, who could barely stand up.

"Nigel's too drunk to get back to Oxford," said Colin. "Let's take him to my house. It's not far from here, and I have a key to get in. My folks are off on holiday. We can also get Cade cleaned up. Let's all go there and crash."

"Fine with me," said Adrian. "It's time we got the hell out of here."

When I heard the phrase, "It's time ..." my mind thought back to the past winter's solstice at the Turf. What was I doing here, drunk and bloody?

"Thanks, but I'll take that late train back," I said stubbornly.

"Oh, come on with us," protested Colin. "You're in no shape to ride the train."

"I'm okay, really," I said, jerking my arm away from Colin. "I just want to be left alone." I had no intention of staying.

"Suit yourself," said Colin. "Let's go." He and Adrian got on either side of Nigel, and the three of them staggered off, as Nigel serenaded them with rugby songs.

* * *

The last train back to Oxford from Paddington stopped in every station, and the ride seemed interminable. My head was splitting from the alcohol and my new nose job. I could tell that the few others on the train were looking at me and wondering about my bloody nose. A dark-suited older man, his face buried in *The Times*, muttered audibly, "Lord, what fools these mortals be." I winced at these words of a sanctimonious Puck. One drunk was singing softly, and I thought he made a pathetic sight. Shortly thereafter, when I went to the toilet cubicle, another pathetic sight greeted me in the mirror. My left eye was swollen and bruised. I hadn't even realised I had a black eye. My nose still had blood on it, although the bleeding had stopped, and there was blood all over my shirt. It wasn't pretty.

As I sobered up during the train ride, my anger subsided and was replaced with embarrassment and remorse. My right hand was still red from the blow I had landed on the girl. I could not get out of my mind the sight of her sitting on the floor stunned and crying. I shuddered with disgust at myself.

The train finally pulled into the Oxford station, and I found my bike and rode home. I was sober now, but also tired and hurting. It was almost three o'clock when I arrived at Magdalen. I remembered, then, that I was supposed to go with Rachael to James's church in a few hours. How would I ever get up? How would I ever face Rachael and explain my eye? I wanted to crawl in a hole.

When I got to my room, I found a note on the door:

Cade, something has come up. I'll try to meet you either at

the service or for lunch, if I can. You can take the 8:40 bus.
Please tell James I got tied up. – Rachael

I was too tired to wonder what could have come up. I washed my face and fell into bed without setting an alarm.

"*You bastard!*" I bolted upright in my bed, sweating. It was a dream, no, a nightmare. I was aware of a shooting pain in my eye. I glanced at the clock and saw it was only six-thirty. Oxford was very still. I got up and looked in the mirror. My left eye was even more swollen and black, and I held a cloth soaked in cold water on it. My head was pounding, and my stomach was like a small boat in a raging tempest. I couldn't ever remember feeling this bad. Ever. The previous evening was hazy, to say the least. As the events in London began to come back, however, I felt sick. I was haunted by the image of the girl on the floor crying after I had hit her. "*You bastard!*" screamed in my head over and over. How could I have done that? The black eye I saw in the mirror was indicative of what I felt inside. How could I face James and Rachael? Yet, hung-over and embarrassed, I nevertheless decided to go to James's church, for reasons I could not articulate.

*   *   *

The communion service began in the same monotone fashion, although I detected something different in James's voice. I couldn't see Rachael, so I sat near the back in the corner. Shortly thereafter, James mounted the pulpit for the sermon. He looked back to where I was sitting, smiled, and began to speak:

"Friends, I have been your vicar for almost nine years. You are my friends and my family now. You were here when my lovely wife, Anne, died of cancer six years ago. But I come before you today to say that I have let you down, Anne down, and, yes, I have let God down. I have a responsibility to you to preach the gospel, and the power of the word of God. In that, I fear that I have failed."

I could hear a few people muttering in the congregation, as James continued. I felt embarrassed by the personal nature of his sermon.

"I must ask you and God to forgive me. I should have preached Christ to you – Christ crucified and Christ risen from the grave. That's the good news. God, the creator of the universe, made each of us and knows each of us. Moreover, he loves each of us so much he allowed his only, dear Son to suffer a most horrible death for our sake."

James began to choke up, and I could see tears welling in his eyes. He took a drink of water, wiped his forehead, and continued, "I have been in a fog these past six years. I was angry at God for taking Anne, angry that he never gave us children, and gradually my faith slipped away until there was little left. Two young friends have helped to rekindle the flame I once had for God, and I thank them dearly. C.S. Lewis, whom I knew, helped me as a young man with my struggles over doubt. I have let him down, too."

People were shifting in their seats and looking at each other with puzzled faces. James continued on for several more minutes, and then concluded: "There is much I want to say today, much I will say in the future. Thanks be to God. Amen."

I really don't remember much about the rest of the service. Afterwards, as people left the church, some greeted James warmly, and one woman even broke down in tears and hugged him. One or two people avoided greeting him at all and slipped out the door quickly.

After everyone had left, James came over to me, saying, "What happened to you?"

"It's a long story," I replied sheepishly. "I'll tell you about it at lunch. Do you know where Rachael is? She left me a note saying she was tied up but would try to be here."

"No, she phoned me yesterday to say something had come up. Well, how about you and I going for a nice lunch?"

"Sounds good."

On the walk through the same meadows, I told James what had happened the previous evening. I still felt mortified at my actions, but I felt an almost cathartic release by telling him about it. He listened to my whole story before saying anything.

"I can tell you feel very badly about this. We often do things we later regret. I've had my share of mistakes, I can assure you. The important thing, Cade, is what you learn from this. We can't undo the past, but we can learn from it. You know, man is a funny animal. St.

Paul himself once wrote something to the effect of, 'Why do I do the things I should not do, and fail to do the things I should do.' I can relate to that. That's why forgiveness is so central to the Christian faith."

I was comforted by his words and non-judgemental tone. I had berated myself all morning, and I thought James could sense that.

We had a leisurely pub lunch in the same country pub. I noticed James seemed more relaxed in his general manner and slowly nursed the one beer he had ordered without quite finishing it. Personally, I felt too queasy still to even think about beer and instead had lemonade. Our conversation centred round trying to find the next instalment of the Soulbane Report, but I could not get the events of last night off my mind.

"I must confess," I interjected, "that I'm mystified about how the Malta trip came about. It truly dropped in my lap. What a coincidence that I ended up eating with Peter that night."

"That's the mystery of prayer," said James. "We'll never understand the ways of God or the mysterious way in which prayer works in our lives. Remember what I told you about coincidences?"

"Yes, but how does this fit in with the rest of what you were saying?"

"God works through human circumstances, and he is interested in the details of our lives. One of the things that motivated me to become a Christian as a young man was studying some of the stories in the Bible. I was deeply impressed by a prophecy in the book of Micah, which was written about seven hundred years before the birth of Jesus. It predicts that the tiny town of Bethlehem will be the birthplace of the Messiah. This is why when the wise men saw the bright star and came seeking a new-born king, they were directed to Bethlehem."

"What's so amazing about all that?"

"Well, look what had to happen for Jesus to be born in Bethlehem. Seven hundred years after this prophecy, a poor peasant girl, living in a small city called Nazareth, is engaged to be married and becomes pregnant. Instead of casting her out, as would be his right, Joseph still agrees to marry Mary and raise this child as his own. Then, at this very time, Caesar Augustus requires a census of the Roman world be taken, and this means that Joseph, who is from the family of David, has to travel to his ancestral home of Bethlehem. All of this takes place just in time for Joseph and Mary to travel there and have the baby. Not to mention, of course, that although the universe was already millions of years old, several stars or planets converged at this exact same time to form the Star of Bethlehem. None of these events, viewed in isolation perhaps, is particularly incredible. But, taken all together, they can only be described as truly miraculous. They fulfil events prophesied hundreds of years before they occurred. And, that's only one of a number of prophecies fulfilled by Jesus. If you study the Messianic prophesies, it is truly amazing how many were fulfilled by the life of Christ."

I was beginning to get the idea. I had never heard of this before, and wished I knew something about the Bible. I knew nothing about it except some stories I had heard as a child, the few times I had been to Sunday school with a friend.

"I wonder how we can find the next part of this report?" I said, changing the subject.

"The only suggestion I have is for us to meet again at the Bodleian next Thursday and undertake another search. This reference to the Southern Cross is baffling. Of course, there's the famous constellation, and there are crosses all over the world. I don't see how we can find this, but we'll try. I never thought we would find the first instalment either."

After lunch, we agreed to take a long walk in the Cotswold countryside and enjoy the beautiful afternoon. It was warm and sunny, with a soft breeze. There was not a cloud in the sky. As we walked, I realised that I missed Rachael very much. I wondered about her boyfriend. What was he like? Did she really care for him? I wanted to go and see her as soon as I got back to Oxford. But what would she think of my black eye?

"James," I suddenly said as we walked, "do you really believe Christianity is true?" I had not intended to tackle this subject, but after the events of the previous evening, I was in inner turmoil. With Rachael absent, I felt more comfortable talking to a priest.

"Yes, Cade, I do. I haven't lived my faith since Anne died, but your discovery of Soulbane has brought me back to God. I can't give you any easy answers, however. Rachael tells me you've read *Mere Christianity*, and that's about the best defence of Christianity I know of. First, of course, you have to deal with the issue of whether there is a God, and for me, in looking at the universe, I have to believe there is a designer behind creation. I believe we humans all have a spiritual void that can only be filled by God. As the French philosopher Pierre Teilhard de Chardin once said, 'We are not human beings having a spiritual experience. We are spiritual beings having a human experience.' That's why this Soulbane Report is so important, because it shows we all try to fill that void with something, and Soulbane's job is to make sure it's anything but God."

"Why do you think there's a God?"

"For lots of reasons. I just can't believe that this world, our solar system, and the whole of life are just random. I see behind all that a Creator. It's just as when you look at, say, old St. Michael's church at the Northgate. You see a building, but no architect. And yet, you know there was an architect. In the same way, I look at all of creation, including the natural laws of physics, the way mathematical formulae can precisely describe physical components of the universe, our sense of morality and conscience, and this beautiful, complex world of nature, and I see an architect behind that."

For some reason, I thought of the faceless voice in the Malta cave and wondered if that had been real or imagined. I didn't dare mention it to James, fearful he would think I had a screw loose somewhere.

"But, do you really believe in angels and devils, and all that?"

"I think there is a spiritual world which is just another dimension of reality that is not observable by humans. I believe the Scriptures when they speak of the existence of spiritual beings."

"I'm just not sure I buy that. I mean, how can you believe in something you can't see?"

"Well, I just came across an analogy the other day in a book called

The Solitaire Mystery. In fact, I happen to have a copy of these particular pages in my coat pocket, because I looked at them last night as I prepared my sermon. Here, let me read it:

A Russian cosmonaut and a Russian brain surgeon were once discussing Christianity. The brain surgeon was Christian, but the cosmonaut wasn't. "I have been in outer space many times," bragged the cosmonaut, "but I have never seen any angels." The brain surgeon stared in amazement, but then he said, "And I have operated on many intelligent brains, but I have never seen a single thought."*

When James finished reading, I stopped walking. Finally, I said, "Hmmm. I never thought of it that way."

"You see, we have words to describe emotions, and yet you can't objectively show them to me. I can sometimes observe their manifestation, say if someone is angry or happy, but I can't see the actual anger or happiness or love. Just so, our thoughts are very real to us, yet not to anyone else."

"So, how do you get from God to Christianity?" I finally asked, now very much wanting to continue our discussion.

"Well, Christianity is different from other religions, in that it claims not only that there is a God, but that God is personal, and, astonishingly, that God once walked this earth as a human being. I love the beautiful opening of John's Gospel, where he says, 'In the beginning was the Word, and the Word was with God, and the Word was God. The same was in the beginning with God. All things were made by Him: and without Him was not anything made that was made. In Him was life; and the life was the light of men ... And the Word was made flesh and dwelt among us, full of grace and truth.'"

"That's a nice, lyrical passage, but I guess I'm still pretty confused by all this."

"I don't blame you. It's a truly mind-boggling idea. Christianity, Cade, rises and falls on the person of Jesus. If he was not God, then

---

*Jostein Gaarder, *The Solitaire Mystery* (New York: Farrar, Straus and Giroux, 1996), pp. 155-156.

there is no Christianity. If Jesus was not a real person who died and rose from the grave three days later, then as St. Paul says, Christians are the people most to be pitied, because their religion is a lie. On the other hand, if it is true, then we have hold of something marvellous."

"But ... do you really think Jesus was God?"

"Yes, I do. All through history, people have acknowledged his uniqueness, even those of other faiths. This itinerant preacher has had an incredible impact on the history of the world, and his life and words are startling. I remember a story from the Victorian era, when Auguste Comte, a French philosopher, told Thomas Carlyle that Comte thought he would start a new religion. Carlyle said, 'Splendid. All you have to do is to speak as no man ever spoke, to live as no man ever lived, to be crucified, rise again the third day, and get the world to believe you are still alive. Then your religion will have some chance of success.' That sums it up pretty well."

"It's all so hard for me to grasp."

"Cade, I just don't think Christianity is something that someone made up. It's too complex and paradoxical. In fact, I believe that if you study the life of Christ seriously, it takes more faith *not* to believe that he is God incarnate!" James began to chuckle.

"Tell me something about the Bible. I don't know much about it, but have always assumed it was mainly myth."

"The Bible speaks on the fundamental issues of life: How did the world and universe get here? Why are we here? And, what happens after death? These are, arguably, the most important questions any human being ever asks. Let me say this, the Bible describes the world and human nature just as I have experienced it. It doesn't sugar coat life; human sin is there for all to see. You spoke to me about your anger last night and the terrible result. Well, we're all far from perfect. Many of the great figures of the Bible are shown failing in every conceivable way: Moses and David did terrible things. Peter denied Jesus twice the same night he told Jesus he would never desert him. The good news is that God loves us despite our human failings, but, at the same time, he took sin seriously enough to send his Son to the Cross. Without knowing that God is suffering with and for us, I would find it hard to have faith, given the pain and suffering in the world."

"That was the next thing I was going to ask," I said. "How can a supposedly good God allow suffering?"

"That's the million pound question. I can't pretend to understand it all, but let me say that God created a rich and diverse world, where our choices have consequences. With free will, comes the possibility of evil choices. A Christian writer who had enormous influence on Lewis was George MacDonald. He once said that 'Only God understands evil and hates it.' Ultimately, you have to trust that God knows what he's doing. Christianity, unlike some other religions, deals head on with suffering and evil, because its whole foundation is the belief that God suffered an agonising death by crucifixion to atone for our sinfulness. God never promises us we won't have difficulties in life, but he does promise us he will be with us. We are never alone, and that, to me, is incredibly comforting."

"Well, why doesn't God simply prevent suffering?"

"That's the ancient paradox: that given the suffering in the world, supposedly God is either not all powerful or he's not all good. Let me just say what I once heard attributed to Saint Augustine: 'Without God, we cannot. Without us, God will not.' In other words, we are stewards of this world, or if you like, we are in partnership with God. He gives us real responsibility to act in the world, and also to pray. From our human perspective, life is not fair or just. Yet, where does our sense of fairness and justice come from, unless there is a moral Being behind creation? You know, despite all our struggles and doubts in this life, I believe God has a loving purpose which we will fully understand one day. St. Paul said, 'For now we see through a glass, darkly; but then face to face: now I know in part; but then shall I know even as also I am known.' That is our Christian hope."

As we arrived back at the church, James paused at the fence surrounding the churchyard. He leaned on the rail, staring at the grave markers, and said, "Cade, there is one fact no one can escape."

"What's that?"

"One day, all of us will die. Death is the great leveller, of rich and poor, prince and pauper, healthy and sick. Have you ever read Thomas Gray's *Elegy Written in a Country Churchyard?*"

"Yes, in a college course, but it's been a while," I replied, vaguely recalling the poem.

"It's one of my favourite poems," continued James. "I memorised it years ago, and it is almost a part of me now. At any rate, one of the stanzas goes like this:

'The Boast of Heraldry, the Pomp of Pow'r,
And all that Beauty, all that Wealth e'er gave,
Awaits alike th'inevitable Hour.
The Paths of Glory lead but to the Grave.'

If death's the end, things would look bleak for us. Jesus, however, told us it's not, and that he is preparing a wonderful place for all the faithful."

"I guess I've never really thought about death. It seems so remote." I looked at the crumbling tombstones and shuddered.

"You're right, death often is the one thing we try not to think about, yet it's the one and only fact about our lives we can count on with absolute certainty. I look upon this life as a pilgrimage to another world we can't see or imagine, but we can somehow yearn for. Lewis called it 'joy.'"

We walked into the vicarage. "Will you help me learn more about all this?" I asked James, as we entered his study. Zeke got up from the corner and came over to James, licking the vicar's hand. The room seemed to have been tidied up, and although the crystal decanter of sherry stood on a table in the corner, the bottle of whisky was no longer in evidence.

"Of course, I'll be delighted to. In fact, I've got something for you." He walked over to his desk, picked up a large burgundy book, and handed it to me. The gold lettering embossed on the cover read *The Holy Bible.*

"Cade, everyone has to read this for themselves and see if they believe it's the Word of God. No amount of argument can ultimately persuade people of this. It still comes down to faith. You, too, need to read it and decide for yourself."

"Thanks." I felt funny holding a Bible, but was nevertheless touched by the gift. We said our goodbyes, and agreed to meet at the Bodleian in a couple of weeks to see if we could solve the mystery of the Southern Cross.

As I stepped on the bus, I self-consciously hid the Bible so no one would see me carrying it. I sat down in the back and looked inside the front cover. It was inscribed: "*To Cade Bryson, With Kindest Regards, James Brooke.*" I turned to Genesis and began to read with great interest.

*   *   *

When the bus dropped me off in the centre of town, it was becoming dusk. I walked down the High toward Magdalen. As I neared Uni, Rachael suddenly stepped out of the entrance, a few yards in front of me. My heart skipped a beat, and I instinctively started to run up to her. Then, a man stepped out behind her, and put his arm around Rachael. I stopped dead in my tracks. Before I could turn away, however, we were face to face.

"Hi, ah, Rachael," I said. Rachael's hair was dishevelled, and she had dark circles under her eyes. I was nervous and jittery and wondered what she'd been up to.

"Cade ... oh, hello, a ..." she stammered. "I'm sorry I didn't make it to church today. Oh, excuse me, Cade, this is Charles Matthews. Charles, this is Cade Bryson."

"Pleased to meet you," said Charles, who was a medium height, thin student with long fine brown hair. He was rather sullen looking with sad brown eyes.

"And you," I said, trying to sound civil.

"Cade, what happened?" asked Rachael suddenly. She was obviously looking at my eye.

"Oh ... that ... well ...," I stammered.

"You weren't fighting, were you?" she asked.

"Actually, my face did seem to get in the way of a fist," I said with a weak laugh, trying to make light of it.

Rachael just shook her head, and turned to Charles, "Come on,

Charles, I need to get back to Merton."

"So long, Cade," she said icily as they began walking up High Street.

"Goodbye, Rachael," I murmured as I watched her and Charles walk arm in arm up the street. My heart seemed to sink within me.

As I walked on down High Street, Magdalen Tower came into full view. Pausing to look at the magnificent structure, I felt a twinge in my right hand, where I had hit the girl the previous night. The repercussions of the taste of the forbidden fruit were still alive and well in Cade Bryson, I mused sombrely.

II

Now the serpent was more crafty
than any other wild animal that
the Lord God had made.

Genesis 3:1

11

TOWERS AND FAITH

SEVERAL WEEKS LATER, I met James at the Bodleian. We talked about the Southern Cross and bandied about ideas, but came to no conclusions. Rachael was working in London for the summer, and I hadn't seen her since that afternoon in front of University College.

"Well, we have the summer to work on this," said James finally. "Cade, will you be around?"

"Yes, I plan to be here most of the summer, except maybe for a train trip to Europe."

"Jolly good. We'll have some time then to study this mystery. Now, how about some lunch."

"Sounds great."

We picked up some sandwiches, walked to the Magdalen cloisters quad, and sat down on the grass. James was wearing a black shirt and a clerical collar, and it was the first time I had seen him wear such clothing except on Sundays. The cloudy day was cool. The windows of the dining hall and chapel overlooked one side of the quad, which was surrounded by a medieval arched passageway. The stony gazes of the gargoyles were fixed on us.

"James, can I ask you something?"

"Certainly." I noticed that his hands no longer shook, nor was his nose the crimson red it had been when I first met him.

"I've read parts of the Bible you gave me. I find some of its words are very powerful and moving."

James smiled, saying, "Yes, Cade, it is an incredible book. A former Master of Balliol College, Benjamin Jowett, once said that you might begin 'reading the Bible as if it were any other book. You will soon find out that it is not like any other book.'"

"I still don't understand faith, though. I mean, if God's really there, why not just show himself to everyone?"

"Let's see, how can I put it? If we were to see God now, in his full glory, we would be overwhelmed. For some reason, in his wisdom, he saw that our faith had to be developed in steps and without coercion. In Hebrews it says, 'Now faith is the substance of things hoped for, the evidence of things not seen.'"

"What if someone doesn't have any faith?"

"Cade, we all have faith in something. It's part of human nature to trust in something, whether it's our own intellect, our possessions, our money, our job, our social standing, or another person. Go over to Keble College sometime and look at a painting there by Holman Hunt called 'The Light of the World.' It shows Christ knocking on a door, and it's based on Revelation 3:20, where it says, 'Behold, I stand at the door, and knock: if any man hear my voice and open the door, I will come in to him, and will sup with him, and he with me.' Jesus patiently knocks on our hearts, but he doesn't force the door open. He wants us to love him freely. I heard the knock when I was about your age and opened the door, and I've never regretted it. Take a look sometime at Lewis's intriguing book, *The Great Divorce*, which illustrates God's risk in letting us choose, and our responsibility to make right choices."

"I don't know how God can take risks when he's safely sitting up on a throne somewhere in heaven."

James smiled thoughtfully. He plucked a blade of grass, examined it, and then said, "It's Jesus' life on Earth that shows the humility of God, and the way he made himself vulnerable for us. The creator of the universe was born as a baby in a stable and placed in an animal's feeding trough. St. Paul puts it like this in the second chapter of

Philippians. 'Let this mind be in you, which was also in Christ Jesus: who, being in the form of God, thought it not robbery to be equal with God: but made himself of no reputation, and took upon him the form of a servant, and was made in the likeness of men: and being found in fashion as a man, he humbled himself, and became obedient unto death, even the death of the cross.'"

As I offered James an apple, I asked, "Hmm. Well, where does the resurrection fit in to all this?"

"Ultimately, Cade, the proof in terms of human verification that Jesus was God comes from the resurrection. The Bible makes it clear that Jesus returned in bodily form, albeit a different type of body, and that the nail marks in his hands and feet were visible. Jesus spoke to the disciples, knew who they were, and answered questions. He even ate a fish in their presence. No other religion makes such a claim: their founders all died and were buried. Again, the first question is whether that event is a historical event, or just a made-up story. A marvellous book you might want to pick up is called *Who Moved the Stone?* Written by Frank Morison. He actually set out to write a book to disprove the resurrection and show it was just a myth. When he examined all the evidence carefully, however, he came to just the opposite conclusion – that the resurrection was an actual, historical event."

"But what is the significance of the resurrection?"

"That's where I'm coming to." He pulled out a small, dog-eared paperback from his battered briefcase. "Here's a book by Michael Green, who was a rector of St. Aldate's Church here in Oxford, called *Man Alive!* You're welcome to keep it. Let me read you his summary of the importance of the resurrection:

The most compelling argument for the existence of God is Jesus Christ. By his incarnation, his teaching, his death and resurrection he has shown us what God is like. He shows us that God is personal. He shows us that God is holy. He shows us that God is love. He shows us that God forgives – at infinite personal cost. He shows us, by the resurrection, that evil will not have the last word in God's universe.

In the risen Christ we have the answer to our doubts about God. That is why the resurrection matters.*

I sat pondering this synopsis, quite moved by it. I then stood up to stretch, saying, "That's very thought-provoking. But, James, I'm still not sure what to make of Christianity. In some ways it is so appealing, and yet there are things that don't make sense or that I don't really like about it, I guess. All this talk about sin, for instance."

I noticed James was smiling, and wondered if he was laughing at me. "Let's take a walk," he said suddenly.

James extended me his hand, and I helped him up. "Why don't we take the path back to Addison's," he said as he pointed toward the passageway leading to New Buildings. We walked through the passageway and faced the beautiful Georgian facade. Just to the right was a lush herbacious border, in full bloom this summer's day with richly coloured flowers set off by hostas and other foliage plants. This garden provided the invitation to enter the gates into Addison's Walk. We turned left onto the dirt path, and began to walk around the circular pathway. As we came to the next turn to the right, I looked down the long pathway, which was encircled by trees. The green leaves formed almost a magical, fairy-tale tunnel through which to walk.

"The reason I was smiling a minute ago, Cade, was because you sounded almost like virtually a tape recording of a conversation I had many years ago with C.S. Lewis," said James finally, breaking our silence. "I had many of the same thoughts you have. Was Christianity really true? What if it didn't suit me personally? Some of it just didn't make sense. What about all the unanswered questions I still had?"

I nodded, in full understanding of these thoughts.

"One afternoon in May, I came to see Mr. Lewis in New Buildings. He asked me to take a walk with him, and we walked along this same path. We stopped about right here." James stopped then, almost at the next turn in the path. There was a clearing in the trees to our right,

*Michael Green, *Man Alive!* (Leicester: Inter-Varsity Press, 1967, reprinted 1976), pp. 59-60.

and through the small portal I could see the large meadow, with tall, lush green grass, interspersed with airy wildflowers playfully dancing in the gentle breeze. At the far end, framed by the window in the trees, stood Magdalen Tower. I had walked here several times, but never before noticed this beautiful view of the meadow and Tower.

"I remember it as if it were yesterday," continued James. "When we were standing here, this field was completely covered with buttercups, as if someone had laid a yellow blanket across the meadow."

I tried to envision the sight he was describing.

As we resumed our walk, James then said, "Lewis turned to me and referred to the Magdalen Tower being like the Christian faith: it is there whether or not one has actually seen it, or whether or not one likes the way it is designed. In the same way that one views the world from the tower, so one stands upon faith to view reality. Lewis went through a period when he thought Christianity was nothing but one of the world's great myths. Later, he came to see it as the Truth, in the sense that Christ was an actual, historic figure who was resurrected from death – God in the flesh. He thought that the Bible may not answer all our questions, but that it starts us on the right path to understanding this world and human nature.'"

I stared at Magdalen Tower, letting these words sink in.

"Cade, I don't know if you find that makes sense, but it was enormously helpful to me at the time."

"Yes, that is very helpful. I wish I could have met C.S. Lewis."

"He was a remarkable person. Such a brilliant mind, and yet, in many ways, he was so humble. I still miss him very much."

By now we had completed the circuit around Addison's Walk. Suddenly it began to rain, and we quickly gathered our things and ran for shelter under the Cloisters. We stood there peering through the arches as the rain came down in sheets.

"James," I asked suddenly, "how did you know Anne was the one for you?"

He smiled, saying, "That's a good question. She was full of life, and she made me feel wonderful whenever I was with her. She became my best friend, and then one day, I realised it didn't matter where I was or what I was doing, as long as Anne was with me. That's when I knew I was in love. Why do you ask?"

"I don't know. It's just that ... "

"Rachael?"

"Well, no ... yes ... I don't know. I've never met anyone like her, and I often think of her, and yet, I'm not sure. I don't understand women."

"Don't even try," he laughed. "They are mysterious creatures. Rachael is quite a girl. You see, her father was an alcoholic, and she and Bridgett had a terrible time of it when Rachael was young."

"Yes, I know," I said quietly.

"Rachael has as much character as anyone I've ever known. Her father drank up what money they had, and he ran through a small inheritance he received. He finally got sacked from his job at the bank, and one day, he took what little money was left and disappeared. That's when I was their parish priest. Bridgett was devastated, because despite everything, she loved him, as did Rachael. They made the best of things, and Bridgett became a seamstress. I think she believed that one day her husband would get sorted out and come back. Then, they heard he had been killed, possibly murdered. They never really found out what happened."

"I can't believe Rachael had it so tough."

"Yes, she had a very rough go of it for a while, but thankfully she weathered her storms. Everyone in the parish loved her, and they all gave her odd jobs so she could earn a little money. I could see that quiet dignity of her mother in Rachael that first time you and she came to see me. I still thought of Rachael as a young girl, and I marvelled at what a beautiful woman she has become."

"How did she get to Oxford?"

"She's got a brilliant mind, and did very well in her exams. She received a grant and her parish at home pitched in to help her some, too. And, as you've seen, her mother makes beautiful clothes, and thus Bridgett also has some income. Rachael has overcome a lot of obstacles in her life."

"I'll say. You would never know it, however. She never dwells on her difficulties."

"That's the mark of real character. That's what I saw in my Anne, too. She was poor as a church mouse, but she was rich beyond measure in character and wisdom. That's something you can't buy."

I felt a twinge at that remark. I realised that I often looked only at superficial things or outward appearances in women.

The rain let up after a few more minutes, and James said, "I'd better be going. I'm almost late for a meeting at Christ Church Cathedral. I'll be praying for you. Let me know how I can help. I value your friendship, Cade."

"And I yours," I said sincerely.

After James left the College, I walked into the Magdalen Chapel and sat down. The beautiful white marble statues of the apostles seemed to stare at me. I studied the large painting above the altar of Christ carrying a cross. Was it really relevant to me, I wondered? I thought of Rachael, too, and longed to see her. I began to realise that she had often been on my mind this summer. Then my spirits sank as I recalled our visit to the sea in Cornwall, and our encounter in front of University College: I doubted seriously that Rachael wanted to see me.

12

TIME, PLEASE

THE SUMMER was a pleasant one. I loved the long, quiet Oxford
days, and found it a fruitful time to read, study, and relax. I
decided to postpone my trip to Europe, because I really did not want
to travel alone.

One afternoon in late July, I returned to Magdalen from the
Radcliffe Camera. I had thought a great deal about God lately, but
could not bring myself to make any kind of decision. My deeply felt
prejudice against Christianity was difficult to dislodge, and the
thought of commitment made me queasy. As I passed through the
porter's lodge, I saw Mr. Thompson.

"Hello, Mr. Thompson, how are you today?"

"Very well, Mr. Bryson."

"Tell me, did you ever know C.S. Lewis?"

"Yes, I did. In fact, I was his scout for a time."

"No kidding! Tell me about that."

"I was a young lad training to be a scout, after working in the
Magdalen kitchen. Mr. Lewis's scout got ill for several weeks, and
they had me fill in. He was ever so kind and, well sir, I think he took
a liking to me. Even after I stopped being his scout, he would ask me
'round for tea occasionally and we would chat. He even came to the
christenings of my children. When my two boys were born, he gave

me a hundred quid each time, which was a fortune to me. He knew without asking that it was tough going for me and my wife. I was almost too embarrassed to take such a large sum, and all he would say was, 'Just think of it as a gift from God.' Well, sir, he didn't have to do that. I would have done anything for him."

"I'd like to know more about Mr. Lewis."

"I'll be glad to tell you. He was a real prince of a man. Unfortunately, I'm on duty until late tonight. Perhaps we can meet one afternoon, say, next week?"

"I'd like that."

"Good. Tell you what, I'll meet you at one of Mr. Lewis's favourite pubs, the Eagle and the Child, at half past five a week from today."

"Great. See you then."

*   *   *

At the appointed time the following week, I arrived at the pub affectionately known as "The Bird and the Baby" by the locals. Mr. Thompson came in about five minutes later, smiling broadly as usual.

"Sorry I'm late," he said.

"No problem," I replied. "I just got here myself."

"Let me buy you a beer. What'll it be?"

"Lager, please."

Over several beers, Mr. Thompson talked to me about C.S. Lewis. He told me how Lewis had befriended his family, and in the process shaped Mr. Thompson's Christian faith.

"Mr. Lewis was like a second father to my boys. They loved him. I'm a blessed man, Mr. Bryson. Do you know about this pub's connection with Lewis?"

"No, I'm afraid not."

"Lewis and some others, including J.R.R. Tolkein, had a group called the Inklings. Sometimes Mr. Lewis's brother, Warnie, joined them, too. They would meet to discuss life, literature, Christianity, and God knows what else, and they often came here to chat. In fact, there's a small placard over there that mentions the Inklings," he said proudly, pointing toward a wall.

"I think I'd like to learn more about Lewis's life."

"Funny you should say that. I almost forgot to give you this." He reached into his bag, pulled out a book, and handed it to me.

The title read, *Surprised by Joy*, by C.S. Lewis; it was an autobiography.

"You're welcome to keep it as long as you wish," said Mr. Thompson. "I would like it back though."

I looked then inside the cover to see a now familiar handwriting, "To my dear friend, Robert, with much affection, Jack Lewis."

Mr. Thompson's face was momentarily clouded, as if he was intensely sad, then he smiled again, saying, "I'd better get along home. I've enjoyed our visit."

"Me, too. And thanks for the beers."

I gripped the book tightly when we exited the pub, and waved goodbye to Mr. Thompson as he rode up the street on his bicycle.

It was about seven in the evening, so there were still several hours of daylight left. I began to walk back to Magdalen, meandering past Balliol and Lincoln Colleges, and then on to High Street. Sitting in nearly the same spot next to the wall of All Souls just across from the church of St. Mary the Virgin was the homeless man I had almost run into that cold February afternoon. I instinctively veered away from him.

"Can you help a poor man?" he asked as I was about to pass by. He had on a blue sweater with holes in it, faded blue jeans, and old army boots. He stared at me with vacant brown eyes. I averted my eyes and began to pass. Then, I heard him begin sobbing.

I turned around and stooped down beside him. "What's your name?"

"Newt. Me mum named me Newton, after the scientist, but me friends call me Newt."

He never blinked. I moved my hand in front of his face, but his eyes did not follow. He stared blankly ahead.

"Why are you crying, Newt?"

"I'm so hungry," he replied, his voice quivering.

"I'll be right back."

I leapt to my feet and went up the street to the Turl Pub. I ordered a steak and kidney pie and some cheese, and brought it back to him.

"Thank you, sir," said Newt, who began to devour the food.

I got up to leave, and he turned his head in my direction.

"I can tell you're American. I used to train with Americans when I was in the British Army. What's your name?"

"Cade ... Cade Bryson."

He extended his dirty hand with long, blackened fingernails, saying, "Pleased to meet you."

I didn't want to take his hand, but did. He had a firm grip.

"How long have you been blind?"

"Since the Falklands War. A shell went off near me. I haven't been much good since. Me wife left me, and I have no family." He started sobbing again.

"Where are you staying?"

"There's a night shelter where I sleep. Some mates bring me here sometimes, and they'll be along about eight to pick me up."

"Can I do anything for you?"

"Just be me friend," was all he said, staring at me.

"I am, Newt." I got up to go, and reached in my pocket. There was a ten pound note there. I pulled it out and clasped it in Newt's hand.

He smiled, then said, "Bless you ... bless you, Mister."

I walked thoughtfully down the High toward Magdalen, no longer worried that I was too late for the dining hall this evening.

*   *   *

In mid-August, I finally read *Surprised by Joy*. I was fascinated by Lewis's account of his early years and his thoughts about God. Yet it was his description of joy that positively blew me away. Wasn't that the same feeling I had that Solstice night at the Turf, and again in Malta? I began to realise that I had to decide whether to let God in, or keep him out and move on. Either way, I knew I was coming to the divergence of roads described in Robert Frost's famous poem. Which road should I choose?

One cool, sunny August afternoon, with an absolutely spectacular clear, blue sky, I took a walk up High Street to Cornmarket, and then down to St. Giles' Street. I paused at Martyr's Memorial. In a nearby spot almost four hundred years ago, Bishops Latimer, Cranmer, and Ridley, had been burned at the stake for their Protestant faith. That much I knew, though I knew little else, except I recalled that Archbishop Cranmer had compiled the first Book of Common Prayer for the Church of England. What would make these men willing to suffer such a hideous death? What could possibly be *that* important? Was there anything in my life so meaningful? I didn't really want to think about it, because I knew the answer.

As I stood looking at Martyr's Memorial, I heard what others have called a "still, small voice" repeating something. But what? It came again. "Time, please." What did it mean? Whose voice was it? I shook myself out of this reverie and quickened my pace toward Waterstone's to engage in my favourite pastime: book browsing. I needed to get my mind busy on something else, and thought I could find something to distract me on one of its capacious floors. On my way to Waterstone's, I tried to avoid looking at the cross marked with cobblestones in the road in front of Balliol that identified the actual spot of the burnings.

After restlessly spending some time in the bookshop, I remembered that James had mentioned a painting at Keble, so I found my way to Keble College Chapel. The painting by Holman Hunt showed Christ in a white robe with a crown, holding a lamp, and knocking on a door. The rustic door was overgrown with vines, and it was latched from the inside. As I stood there looking at this vivid painting, I seemed to hear those quiet, yet persistent words again, "Time, please." What did it mean? Who was calling me and why?

As I walked back to Magdalen, I recalled that I needed to return Mr. Thompson's book to him. I didn't want anything to happen to such an obviously important memento. After I had retrieved the book from my room, I headed toward the porter's lodge.

"Hi, Mr. Thompson," I said cheerfully, as I entered the lodge. "I wanted to return the book to you."

"Did you enjoy it, sir?"

"Yes, it was intriguing. Now that I've read it, maybe you could tell me more about him sometime."

"I'd love to. What are you doing right now?"

"Well, nothing, actually."

"Good. I'm just finished with work. Why don't you come up to my house for a spot of tea? I'd like you to meet my wife and son."

"Thanks. That would be nice," I said, feeling somewhat doubtful, but not wanting to hurt his feelings either.

"It's settled then. Go 'round and get your bike and meet me here in ten minutes. I live in the village of Iffley."

As we rode up past the Iffley turn off, I noted how many people waved to Mr. Thompson and called him by name. He had a kind word for everyone, and we stopped once to chat with a man in a tweed jacket walking his English sheepdog.

"'ello, Ralph," said Mr. Thompson, as he pulled his bike up on the pavement to talk to the man.

"Evening, Robert," the man said. "How is Rose?"

"Very well, thanks. Oh, I almost forgot myself. Ralph Mitchell, this is my friend, Cade Bryson."

"Pleased to meet you, Mr. Mitchell," I said, extending my hand.

"The pleasure is mine," said Mr. Mitchell as he shook my hand. "I take it you're an American, but can't guess your accent."

"I'm from Georgia, sir. Guess I talk a little slower than some Americans."

"It's a lovely accent, Cade," said Mr. Thompson, slapping me on the back.

"And, Robert, how is Clive?" asked Mr. Mitchell.

"Doing magnificently," said Mr. Thompson.

"Jolly good," said Mr. Mitchell. "All the best."

With that he waved good-bye, and we resumed our ride up the road.

"Who is Clive?" I asked.

"Oh, he's one of my sons. I have two lovely boys, well, men now, Clive and David. David teaches at a school in Cambridge, but Clive works here in Oxford. You'll meet him shortly."

I had rarely met anyone like Robert Thompson. He seemed forever cheerful, as if he didn't have a care in the world. I could not recall ever having seen him cross or melancholy. His broad smile and friendly banter greeted everyone who entered the Magdalen Lodge.

I was beginning to puff a little as we headed up the hill towards Iffley. Mr. Thompson, although much older and larger, kept up a good pace on his bicycle.

"Let's stop here," he said suddenly. "I need to pick up some milk and cheese for our little tea."

I was thankful for the rest, reminding myself how I needed to get back on my exercise programme. I had slipped from my lacrosse days. Back on our bikes, we arrived in the village, which had rows of small, well-kept houses, nestled along narrow streets. It was very still this summer afternoon.

"Before we go home, let me show you around," said Mr. Thompson. He took me along several small, quaint streets. Then, as we went up one street, I saw in front of us a magnificent stone Norman church. He stopped and got off his bike. We walked around the church to the huge, carved wooden doors at the back of the church and stepped inside. The afternoon sun sparkled through multi-coloured stained-glass windows. I was struck by the echoing series of arched stone passages, with unique ornate ribbed designs carved over the apex of each.

"This is St. Mary's," he said. "It was built in the late twelfth century. This is where my lads were baptised."

I spotted the baptismal font. "By the way," I said with a sudden thought, "doesn't the 'C' in C.S. Lewis stand for Clive?"

Mr. Thompson grinned and nodded, saying, "You're right. My son is named after Mr. Lewis. Speaking of Clive, let's get on home. I could use a cup of tea myself."

We stopped in front of the red door of a small terraced cottage on the main road. "Good afternoon, Mr. Thompson," said an old woman across the street road watering her window box filled with petunias.

"A lovely day, isn't it, Mrs. Jones," he said to her, waving a greeting as well.

Immediately inside the house was a small, but inviting, room with a well-worn sofa and comfortable-looking chairs. There were various pictures of people around the room.

"Robert, is that you?" said a female voice from somewhere else in the house.

"Yes, my dear," he replied, adding, "I've brought a guest." He winked at me, smiling.

A plump, grey-haired woman entered the room, wearing a plain blue dress with a white apron. Mr. Thompson gave her a kiss on the cheek, then turned to me.

"Rose, dear, this is Cade Bryson. He's an American up at the College."

"So nice to meet you," she said smiling. "Has Robert made you ride all the way here? You look like you could use some biscuits."

"It's nice to meet you, Mrs. Thompson," I said. I liked her immediately. I also had been in England long enough to know she was offering cookies, not southern biscuits, as I would have originally thought.

"Where's Clive?" asked Mr. Thompson.

"He's out in the garden, since it's such a lovely day. You two go on out there and enjoy the sunshine, and I'll make us a pot of tea."

We walked out to the back garden. It was enclosed by tall, red brick walls. There was lush, green grass in the oval centre of the yard, surrounded by a blur of colours from the many different flowers.

"It's lovely back here ... and so peaceful," I remarked.

"I like to garden. It's my way to get close to God and to forget the cares of the world."

I noticed, then, that someone was sitting on a wooden bench under a pear tree at the other end of the garden.

"Come meet Clive," said Mr. Thompson, walking toward the bench.

As we got closer, the man looked up and smiled. He was short and dumpy, with fat fingers. He had straight red hair that was combed down into bangs on his forehead. He had a crooked smile and eyes that did not both appear to focus.

"Hello, Clive. What are you doing?"

"Hi, Dad," said Clive in a lisping voice. "I'm repairing the hoe."

He had a metal hoe in his lap and was wrapping some wire around the hoe and the wooden handle. I simultaneously realised that Clive was mentally handicapped and had to make a conscious effort not to show surprise.

"Let me see, Clive," said Mr. Thompson, and he bent over to look at the hoe. "You're doing a splendid job, son. Thank you."

"You're welcome, Dad," replied Clive, smiling.

"Clive, this is Cade. Cade, my son Clive."

"Nice to see you, Clive," I said immediately, trying to be gracious despite my feelings of discomfort.

Clive looked at me, broke out into a grin, and said, "Would you like to see our garden?"

"Yes, I would like that." Clive then took me around the garden, walking with a slight limp. "What's that spicy smell?" I asked him.

"Those are pinks," he said confidently and I recognised the sweet fragrance of cloves in the silky red and white petals. He proceeded to point out clematis, sweet peas, and cornflowers as we strolled about, impressing me with how much he knew. Clive was so nice, in his simple way, that I soon overcame my embarrassment about his handicap.

The long, summer evening was very pleasant, as we sat out in the garden and talked. Mrs. Thompson brought out shortbread and some cucumber sandwiches with the tea. She sat knitting while we visited. The love this family felt for one another was tangible. I thought of my own family: so well-educated and well off materially, yet it had been a long time since I could remember all of us just spending an afternoon enjoying each other's company.

"Tell me more about C.S. Lewis," I finally asked Mr. Thompson, as he poured out more tea.

"As I told you before," began Mr. Thompson, "I was working in the kitchen at Magdalen. One day the bursar came to me and asked if I would like to become a scout. I jumped at the chance. Anything to get out of peeling potatoes. I began as an assistant, working with an older scout named Michael. He had been at Magdalen since 1922, after being in the Great War. He was a lovely man and took me under his wing. At any rate, one day Mr. Lewis's scout became ill, and they asked me to look after that scout's staircase. That's how I came to know Mr. Lewis."

"When was this?"

"It would have been in about 1947, when I was seventeen."

"You must have been quite young when you started working, then."

"Yes, but you see, the Second World War had just ended and my father had been killed in France. We lived on a small farm outside Oxford, but it wasn't enough to support us. I dropped out of school and went to work. I found a job at Magdalen, and was happy, because I could make some money and still be close to my family. My mother didn't want to see me leave, but she knew we had no choice. My older sister and her husband helped on the farm and it wasn't large enough for me to work there, too. Anyway, I loved it at the college and before I knew it, well, here I am a lifetime later. In fact, I retired a year or so ago, but missed the students so much Magdalen let me come back to work. I have a lovely life, you see."

Clive pulled up a chair next to his mother. He handed her some flowers he had just picked in the garden. She put down her knitting and held the flowers, saying, "Thank you, Clive. They are ever so pretty." Clive smiled.

Mr. Thompson continued, "Mr. Lewis took a liking to me, I think. I was scared to death of him at first, but he was most kind to me. One day I walked in on him while he was praying. I was about to go out quietly when he called me to come on in. Mother had always taken us to church at home, but I hadn't gone since I'd started to work at Oxford. Mr. Lewis asked me if I would like to pray with him, and I said I would. From that day forward, he would talk to me about books and God and other things that I had never learned before. A few years later, I met Rose and fell in love."

I looked over at Mrs. Thompson, and could see her smile and blush.

"We got married, and a couple of years later had David," he

continued. "Then, we had Clive. He was a happy little boy, and we named him after Mr. Lewis. Mr. Lewis had gone to Cambridge by then, but he wrote to us from time to time and came by to visit sometimes when he was in Oxford. He had a home not far from here called the Kilns, where he spent many weekends and summers. He knew we didn't have a lot of money, and sometimes I would find some money left for us in an envelope in the lodge. It never had a note with it, but I knew who it was from."

The sinking sun at the end of the garden was now a large orange ball, and it cast long shadows toward us. I took Mrs. Thompson's offer of some more shortbread.

"Why don't we go inside now," said Mrs. Thompson. "I think it's getting a little cool for Clive."

"I probably should be going," I said.

"We're enjoying your company," said Mrs. Thompson. "Won't you stay for a little supper?"

Before I could protest, Mr. Thompson said, "Splendid idea, my dear. Let's go in for a sherry."

We retreated to the living room, and Mr. Thompson soon had a glass of sherry in my hand. He then said, "I'm afraid I'm boring you with all this talk about us."

"Not at all," I assured him. "I want to hear more about you and Mr. Lewis." I could hear Mrs. Thompson and Clive pottering around in the kitchen, talking and laughing.

"Would you like to see a picture of him?" asked Mr. Thompson.

"Sure!"

He walked over to the mantel, picked up a framed picture, and handed it to me. It showed a much younger Robert Thompson with an older, balding gentleman in a tweed coat.

"This looks like Addison's Walk," I said.

"It is. Mr. Lewis loved to go walking in Addison's, especially since it was right next to his rooms in New Buildings."

"When was this taken?"

"Oh, about 1949, I should think. Let's see, where was I? Oh yes, by the time Clive was about one, we knew something wasn't quite right. He wasn't developing like David had. It was then we found out that he was slow. It was devastating at first to us. In fact, the day after we learned it from the doctor, almost as if he knew already, Mr. Lewis came by the house. We both had a good cry about the news, but Mr. Lewis began to help me get over my anger at God. He helped me see that all life is a gift. Now, of course, I know what a special blessing Clive has been. I've never known a more loving person than Clive. He has brought us immense joy. I thank God every day for him."

I was amazed by this. I kept thinking about the difficulties of having a handicapped child, now an adult, and I marvelled at someone who could say he thanked God for him. We talked for another hour or so, over a delicious supper of vegetable soup, fresh baked bread, cheddar cheese and apples. Mr. Thompson told me more about C.S. Lewis, including his marriage to Joy Davidman Gresham and her subsequent death from cancer.

"I never saw Mr. Lewis more down than after she died," said Mr. Thompson."

"When was that?"

"In 1960. Mr. Lewis was crushed. He wrote a book about it, but he used a pen name, so no one knew it was his until later."

"Oh ... what book was that?"

"*A Grief Observed*. There's another book and movie about Mr. and Mrs. Lewis, too, called *Shadowlands*. There are two films, actually, and both were set in part at Magdalen. I watched them do the filming and even met the actors who played Mr. Lewis, first Josh Ackland and later, Anthony Hopkins. I also met Claire Bloom and Debra Winger, who both played Mrs. Lewis. They're lovely ladies."
He smiled and winked as he mentioned these two actresses.

"So when did Mr. Lewis die?"

"November 22, 1963. I'll always remember it, because I lost a true friend that day. You know, Mr. Lewis wasn't any highbrow, intellectual snob like some people think. No sir, he was so kind to common people, like me and Rose. I never knew a more godly person than C.S. Lewis."

We went back to the living room and talked for a good while.

When I heard the clock strike ten, I stood up to leave, saying, "Thank you for a wonderful afternoon and for dinner, too. This is one of the nicest days I've spent in Oxford," I added sincerely. I hoped I had not overstayed my welcome with such delightful people.

"Please come back anytime," said Mrs. Thompson, allaying my fears as we bid one another goodnight.

*   *   *

As I rode my bike back to Oxford, my mind went over the images of this day: martyred bishops, Christ knocking on doors, and a family that, in humble and even difficult circumstances, showed joy and thankfulness. I thought about that snowy December night when I had first discovered the strange letters. So many incredible events had happened since that night.

Like that winter's solstice night, Magdalen was again quiet and deserted. For some reason, I walked over to the base of Magdalen Tower and tried the door. I don't know why, since the door was always locked. To my surprise, however, the huge door creaked and slowly began to open when I tugged hard on it. There was one light bulb lit near the first landing of the stairs, but otherwise it was pitch black dark inside the Tower. I retrieved my bicycle lamp, and ascended the steps. The thud of my feet on the metal steps resounded inside the Tower. It was eerie climbing up the Tower in the dark, with my lamp as the only source of light, and spooky shadows everywhere. I was gasping for breath by the time I reached the doorway at the top.

A refreshing blast of cool air riffled through my shirt as I opened the door and stepped onto the roof. The night sky, moonless and cloudless, brilliantly displayed the Milky Way. The only sound I heard was the breeze coursing through the turrets. I looked at each of the four spires in the corners of the Tower, with bronze flags on them, remembering how they blazed like torches when reflecting the afternoon sun. I almost jumped out of my skin at a sudden, deafening boom, before realising that it was the Magdalen bells. I thought of Falstaff in *Henry IV, Part 2*: "We have heard the chimes at midnight, Master Shallow."

I walked around and gazed over the sides of the Tower at the shadowed buildings of Oxford. Standing on this Tower and looking down at Magdalen's Cloister quad, both of which were built in the late 1400s, evoked a feeling of awe. I looked up High Street toward Queens and All Souls, and beyond to the Radcliffe Camera and St. Mary the Virgin Church, then over toward Christ Church and its famous Tom Tower, then to Merton and the Christ Church Meadows. The perspective from the Tower caused me to reflect on the choices before me with a fresh sense of clarity and urgency. Oxford was hushed and still now, as I soaked in the view of its ancient spires reaching up to the limitless heavens. I remembered the line from Matthew Arnold about Oxford: "And yet, steeped in sentiment as she lies, spreading her gardens to the moonlight, and whispering from her towers the last enchantments of the Middle Age ..." That same feeling of timelessness and pilgrimage came over me again.

I thought again of that winter's solstice night in the library, of Rachael, James, the cave in Malta, the Thompsons, and C.S. Lewis. Something else was whispering to me on top of Magdalen Tower ... "Time, please." Now, I knew that voice. I knew it instinctively. It was God. The Holman Hunt painting flashed in my mind. Then, Martyr's Memorial. I knew it *was* time. Lewis's books had given me a totally new perspective on faith, and the compelling words of the Bible which James gave me had touched me somewhere deep within. I still wanted to run and hide, but realised that was not the answer. I understood that faith meant stepping out into the unknown. Not "blind" faith with no rational basis, yet, at the same time, I had to put my trust in something – Someone – I could not tangibly see or empirically prove, any more than I could prove a thought. "Time, please," said the voice again softly.

I leant on the cold stone, and truly prayed for the first time in my life. As I asked God to come into my life, I half-expected in this magical setting to hear choirs of angels and see supernatural sights in the night sky. Instead, the stars stared back silently, and the only choir I heard was the tolling of the Magdalen bells. I felt no blinding flash of inspiration, but I knew I had made a decision: I had taken a fork in the road.

On my way home from the Turf last December, I would never have imagined myself on the summit of Magdalen Tower praying – not in a million years. I looked down at the Magdalen New Buildings, (new, that is, in 1733) where according to Mr. Thompson and James, C.S. Lewis had rooms for lodging and teaching for over thirty years. It reminded me of a passage in *Surprised by Joy** that I had read and re-read, where Lewis talked of being in his Magdalen rooms feeling "the steady, unrelenting approach of Him whom I so earnestly desired not to meet." Lewis said that in 1929, he finally surrendered and prayed, adding that he was "perhaps, that night, the most dejected and reluctant convert in all England."*

Tonight, I understood *exactly* how Lewis must have felt. Nevertheless, in some unexplainable, yet comforting way, I sensed that I had finally come home.

*C. S. Lewis, *Surprised by Joy: The Shape of My Early Life* (New York: Harcourt Brace & Company, 1955), pp. 228-29.

13

CALM BEFORE STORM

I RELUCTANTLY SAID GOODBYE to the mild Oxford summer. The long, pleasant days almost made up for the bleak winter. The comfortable weather extended into early October, and as the new term began, I still found myself in a summer mode. This was due, I was sure, to having stayed in Oxford, while most students had left for other places. During the summer, I had discovered the pleasures of studying in the Duke Humfrey room, which is one of the oldest parts of the Bodleian library. The bright painted ceiling is one of Oxford's priceless treasures. It was a quiet, inspiring place to study.

Rachael spent most of the summer working in London, and we had bumped into each other only once on a July afternoon in Oxford, about a week after my lunch in the Cloisters with James. Rachael and I had talked briefly about the Soulbane papers, and I filled her in on our dead ends. I had been very glad to see her, and she had been pleasant, yet still distant. I suspected she must still be seeing Charles, and I tried to act nonchalantly. Nevertheless, after that chance meeting with Rachael, I found myself thinking of her even more often.

James and I had met in Oxford several other times during the summer. I had also attended his church most Sundays since the night on top of Magdalen Tower, and had visited several Oxford churches as well. We were becoming close friends, and I found him to be a fountain of information about matters of faith. We searched diligently for an answer to the Southern Cross mystery, but could not unlock the secret of that oblique reference. Finally, just after term began, we met one last time in early October.

"I'm afraid we're out of luck," said James over tea and scones one day. We were sitting in the Old Mint Cafe, part of a Baptist church built next to the site where Charles I had coins minted during the English Civil War. "I've looked into every book I can think of, but can't figure this one out. I guess the second instalment, if there is one, will forever remain undiscovered."

"It's a shame we didn't find it. But, at least we have one part of it," I replied, trying to be optimistic.

"Yes, we should be thankful for that. Now, we'll have to decide what to do with it. Anyway, I know that with term starting you'll be very busy."

As we parted, James put his hand on my shoulder and said, "Thank you, Cade, for your help in this. It means a lot."

"Well, I appreciate your friendship more than you know."

"Blessings to you," he said as he got in his car and sped off. I stood there until he was out of sight.

*   *   *

Oxford was again bustling with activity. There was a tangible exhilaration in the autumn air. I eagerly immersed myself again in my PPE studies, continuing my summer ritual of studying in the Duke Humphrey Room. Near the end of the first week of term, I was working on my first essay of the term. I thought of visiting Rachael but feared it would be awkward. What would I say to her, and supposing Charles was there? What excuse could I use to go see her? I was restless and couldn't concentrate. It was after one, and I was getting hungry. I often grabbed a quick lunch at the King's Arms because it was close to the Bodleian, so I decided to go there. I was sitting at a table in the front corner, when Rachael and another girl walked through from the back room. My heart started racing. I didn't know whether to wave or not. I felt paralysed to act. What if she was with Charles?

"Cade, hello," I heard her say. Did I dream it? Rachael smiled and waved, and I stood up. I hit my coffee cup and it spilled on the floor. My face burned crimson.

"Hi, Rachael," I said as she came over. "Will you join me?"

"Actually ..." she started, then paused, and I was about to fill in that she was waiting for Charles.

"... that would be lovely," she said. "Cade, this is my friend, Julia."

"Hello, nice to meet you," I said, with as much friendliness as I could muster.

"And you," she replied. "Rachael, I've got to get back to Merton for my tutorial. I'll catch up with you later."

"All right, Julia," said Rachael cheerfully. "I'll see you at dinner tonight."

Rachael sat down, and we both started to speak, then both stopped, then both laughed.

"You first," I said.

"I was just going to ask about your summer," she replied.

We talked as I finished my lunch. We both had coffee, and more coffee. I finally realised it was about three, and we were the only patrons remaining. Rachael looked radiant.

"Would you like to go with me to Blackwell's?" Rachael asked. "I've got to get some books for term."

"Sure," I said, oblivious to the work I had left in the Duke Humfrey room.

After we finished at Blackwell's, we stood on the sidewalk, looking across at the Sheldonian Theatre. The sculptured heads stared back at us blankly.

"Well," said Rachael, "I guess I'd better get back to Merton." Did I detect a blush on her cheeks?

"Say, have you ever seen 'The Light of the World'?" I asked impulsively.

"No, I haven't, though I've always meant to."

"Come on, I'll show you." We walked to Keble, and I showed Rachael the Holman Hunt painting.

"It's lovely," she said, after looking at it for several minutes. "Do you know the symbolism?"

"Some of it," I said and proceeded to parrot the things James had told me about it.

"That's very impressive, Cade."

"I wish I could take credit, but, actually, James explained it to me."

"It's getting late. I'd better let you get back to your work."

"Let me walk you back to Merton."

"All right," she said, and smiled just as I remembered from that first night in the Trout. My heart was melting. "I promised Julia I'd meet her for dinner. She's a fresher and doesn't know her way around well yet. Why don't you join us?"

"Well ... are you sure?" I said. Rachael wasn't having to twist my arm.

"That is, of course, if you have time."

"Yes, yes, I have time," I replied, perhaps too eagerly. The last thing I wanted to do now was go back to studying.

The Merton dining hall had the dark, rich atmosphere of many of the old colleges. We had a festive time at dinner, talking about the upcoming term. Several times our eyes met and locked briefly, before one of us turned away.

As we said goodnight, I asked, "Rachael, would you like to go with me to the Oxford Union on Saturday night? I hear there's going to be a lively debate." I dug my fingernails into my hand waiting for the rejection.

"That would be wonderful," she said and smiled. "I'll see you then."

It was too late to return to the Bodleian. I took a long way back, going under the Bridge of Sighs and down New College Lane. I thought of popping into the Turf for a quick pint, but decided instead to return to my room and write a long overdue letter to my parents. I whistled softly to myself as I walked, something I hadn't done in months.

*   *   *

Rachael and I saw each other several times over the next week or two. We talked about Soulbane and lamented our inability to solve the puzzle of the second part of the report. We talked about many different things, and I found myself wanting to share everything with her. One morning in mid-October, I dropped Rachael a note on a whim to see if she wanted to go punting the next afternoon, and was excited when she sent a note back agreeing to go.

We met at the dock just under the Magdalen bridge. The afternoon was crisp and sunny, and the few white clouds accentuated the deep blue sky. We lazily punted down the River Cherwell. The bright yellow and red leaves on the tall trees in Christ Church Meadows reflected in the calm water. Rachael sat in the front facing me, as I stood in the back pushing the long wooden pole in the river's bottom. She had her dark hair tied back, and she was wearing a hunter green turtleneck sweater. Our eyes met briefly, before she turned away. As we glided on the glassy water, we talked and laughed.

"Rachael, I never found out why you couldn't go to James's church last June," I finally asked the question to which I had been dreading to hear the answer, because I figured she and Charles were seeing each other. I gripped the pole tightly, fearing the worst.

"Oh, yes, I was helping at a battered women's shelter that weekend. A mother came in crying and distraught, and I stayed up all night with her and her little girl."

At the mention of that, I recalled how I had spent that same night, and my stomach tightened. I decided I had nothing to lose, so I added, "I thought maybe you had a boyfriend … that guy I saw you with in front of Univ?"

She looked down, then said, "Oh, you mean Charles? He helps with the women's mission, and we'd gone to college to talk with one of the dons there who also works with the shelter. I was so tired that afternoon … I hadn't slept in about thirty-six hours. Charles literally had to hold me up to walk back to Merton." She paused, then added, "Yes, we were seeing each other for a while. But … there was someone else I could not get out of my mind." She looked up at me and smiled coyly. She was definitely blushing.

"Now, tell me about your black eye."

I felt a churning in my stomach. I had hoped never to have to tell anyone else, especially Rachael, about that dreadful night. I had done all I could to forget it. Rachael was looking directly at me, however, so I took a deep breath and told her the whole story. When I finished, there was a lump in my throat, and I wondered if Rachael would even speak to me again.

After a few seconds of silence, which seemed like an eternity to me, Rachael smiled slightly and said, "Cade, we all make mistakes. I've made more than my share. The important thing is whether we learn from them or repeat them. I know you well enough to understand that's not the Cade standing here on this punt."

I couldn't believe Rachael's gentleness and understanding. I had done everything to avoid telling her about that night in London, yet by doing so I felt freed of some heavy burden. And, I felt even closer to Rachael. As I looked into her blue eyes, I wanted to shout with joy. I pushed the pole again and turned back to see Magdalen Tower through the trees, its reflection shimmering in the water. I thought of the lovely garden in University College, with the inscription from Ben Jonson, "In small proportions we just beauties see, and in short measures life may perfect be."

"Watch out, Cade!" Rachael screamed, intruding on my thoughts.

I looked up quickly to see Rachael ducking as our punt drifted under an overhanging tree. Just then a branch hit me in the stomach. I held onto the branch as the boat and Rachael continued downstream. Rachael was laughing so hard tears were streaming down her face. I tried to salvage my dignity, but quickly burst out laughing, too.

"Well," I yelled, dangling over the river, "are you going to just leave me here?"

"I'll have to think about it," she said, still laughing, as she picked up the floating pole and brought the punt around to get me.

We punted for another hour or so. Rachael picked up *Alice in Wonderland*, saying, "I've been told that Lewis Carroll used to take young Alice punting here. He began to tell her stories, and voila, he wrote a book." Rachael began reading some passages from the book. Spending this beautiful fall afternoon floating alongside Christ

Church Meadows with Rachael made me feel as if I were in Wonderland, too.

We finally went back toward the landing near the base of Magdalen Tower. As we reached the shore, Rachael stumbled into my arms trying to get off the punt. The sudden embrace surprised us, and we found ourselves holding each other tightly. Without a word, we kissed. I held her more tightly, then lost my balance. We both toppled over into the river. As we bobbed up to the surface, Rachael sputtered and laughed, saying, "Cade, I see you haven't lost your touch."

I was embarrassed, but tried to act unruffled. "Well, Miss Adams, I rather like your drenched look."

She laughed again and shook her head impishly, flinging water everywhere. We pulled ourselves out of the river and borrowed a towel from the boat proprietor.

I walked Rachael back to Merton, and kissed her again. I think I floated all the way back to Magdalen.

When I entered the Magdalen Lodge, Mr. Thompson greeted me.

"Might I enquire, Mr. Bryson, what you have been up to?" he said, grinning. I realised my clothes were still wet and clinging to me. "By the way, the other porter left a message here for you."

He handed me an envelope, and I tore it open. *Who could it be from?* I stood there, forgetting my appearance, as I read: "To Cade Bryson – We received a telephone call from America to say that your mother has been in an accident. Your father asks you to ring home urgently."

"Is everything all right?" I vaguely heard Mr. Thompson asking me. I was numb.

"I ... I uh, well, no actually," I stammered, handing him the message.

"Cade," said Mr. Thompson as he read the message, "come back here and use the lodge phone."

I came back into the porter's office. He handed me a phone and went back out, leaving me alone to make the call. I realised that it was probably about eleven in the morning in Atlanta, as my shaking hands dialled the number.

"Hello," said the voice on the other end.

"Hi, uh, this is Cade, who is this?"

"Oh, Cade, this is Ruth Jenks, your next door neighbour. I've been waiting for you to call. Your mother's in critical condition at the hospital."

"What happened?" I asked, wanting to scream.

"She was in a car accident this morning. A hit and run, we think. Your father is at the hospital with her. I have the number, and he said for you to call as soon as possible."

I immediately phoned my father. It was the first time I had ever heard him really shaken. Mom had been hurt badly and had been in surgery for five hours. She had some broken bones and cuts, and was unconscious. It was still uncertain whether she had sustained any permanent spinal or brain damage. Could I come home?

When I hung up, I just sat there. Mr. Thompson came back in, and his face showed concern. At the sight of him, I broke down and began to sob.

"Cade, what can I do to help?"

"I ... I don't know. I can't think. I need to get home to Atlanta right away."

"I'll help you get a plane ticket. I can borrow Ralph Mitchell's car and take you to the airport. Don't worry, I'll see that you get off all right."

The relief I felt at those words was inexpressible. This wonderful man was so concerned about me, and I knew it was genuine. We made reservations for a plane for the next morning, and I went back to my room to pack. I then walked over to Merton to find Rachael.

"Oh, Cade, I'm so sorry," whispered Rachael sympathetically.

"How can this happen now? How can God let this happen?"

"I don't know," said Rachael. "It's a complicated world. I do know he cares."

"That's not good enough. If this is how he treats people, I'm not sure I want anything to do with him."

"I understand how you feel."

I was surprised by this comment. I had expected some trite defence of God. We talked for a good while, and Rachael was very sensitive to my anger and confusion.

"I'd better go finish packing," I said finally.

"Your family needs you right now. I'll do anything I can to help, and you and your family will be in my prayers. Cade, I was going to give you this to you for your birthday in a couple of weeks, but maybe you can use them now." She went over to her desk, picked up a wrapped package, and handed it to me.

I opened the wrapping and found a boxed set of C.S. Lewis books. I looked at the titles: *The Abolition of Man, The Great Divorce, Miracles, The Weight of Glory, The Problem of Pain,* and *The Four Loves.*

"Rachael, how did ..."

"James said you might like them," she replied, with a faint smile.

I realised, then, that over the course of the summer during our talks, James at one time or another had recommended each of these books.

"Thanks, Rachael." My mind really wasn't on C.S. Lewis now, but I knew this was a gift from her heart.

When I got to her door, she came over and hugged me. I wanted to remain locked in her arms and forever put off facing my family's crisis.

*   *   *

As I walked out of the Merton gate, the ubiquitous Oxford mist had returned. I had no raincoat or umbrella and hoped I could get back to Magdalen before it began to rain. I shivered in the cool air. The wet, brown cobblestones on Merton Street glistened from the reflection of the street lights. Tom Tower began its nightly ritual of tolling one hundred and one times. Each peal reverberated down the quiet lane. My mind was racing: I had a million things to do, including getting money and packing for the trip. Mr. Thompson was picking me up at four in the morning to get me to Heathrow in time for my plane. I hurried my pace, wishing I had my bike with me. As I reached High Street, Colin Greene was coming in the opposite direction a few yards in front of me.

"Oh, Colin, hi," I said quietly, extending my hand.

"Hey, Cade," he replied, shaking my hand. "It's been a long time. How are you?"

"Actually, not too well at the moment. I've just learned that my mother has been badly injured in a car accident, and I'm flying back to the States tomorrow."

"I'm sorry to hear that." He appeared to look past me in embarrassment when he said it. "Let me buy you a drink. That always helps me when I'm down."

"No, no thanks," I said impatiently. "I've got to go and finish packing."

"Well, good luck and I hope your mother's all right," said Colin. He shuffled his feet awkwardly, then gave a brief wave and continued walking up the High Street.

"Thanks," I muttered under my breath glumly.

It was beginning to rain harder. Under a light across the street between St. Mary's and All Soul's, I saw a familiar figure curled up and seemingly clutching the wall. I was in such a hurry, and Newt would never know I had not stopped. I had not seen him since the summer. Yet, for some unexplainable reason, I crossed the street anyway.

"Newt, it's me, Cade." He was dressed in the same faded blue jeans and old blue sweater. His beard was longer, and his greasy hair dishevelled.

"Cade, Cade Bryson, the American?" He appeared disoriented.

"Yes, it's me. Are you all right?"

"I don't want to trouble you with me problems."

"No, tell me."

"Well, you see … it's me leg. I broke me ankle a week ago and can't hardly walk. Me mates were supposed to get me over an hour ago, but I'm afraid they're either drunk or have forgotten."

"Where do you need to go?"

"Back to the night shelter just past Cornmarket Street." The bells in St. Mary's tolled quarter past nine. I needed desperately to get back to my room to pack.

"Let's go then," I said.

At that point, Newt started crying, his shoulders heaving. I knelt down, took his hand, and said, "Why are you crying, Newt?"

"It's just that . . . I was sitting here, with me broke ankle ... and ..." He began sobbing again, and I patted him on the shoulder. He then continued, saying, "... Looks like me friends forgot me ... I thought I was left here for the night, and I started praying and asking God to help me. I was about to give up when you came along."

I thought about how close I had come to not checking on Newt and shivered. I then reached my arms under Newt, saying, "All right, Newt, let's get you back to the shelter." As I picked him up, I almost threw him over my shoulder and realised that I had greatly overestimated his weight. His clothes masked his thin, bony limbs. His pungent body odour reminded me of our locker room after a hot day's lacrosse game. I carried Newt up High Street, stopping several times to rest. We were both getting soaked by the steady, chilling rain, and we tried to distract ourselves by telling each other a little more about our lives. He directed me past Cornmarket to the correct side street, and I found the shelter. There were haggard, dirty men huddled in groups of three or four under an awning, smoking cigarettes. One smiled, revealing yellow teeth with a front tooth missing.

"Just put old Newt over there ... that's his spot," said the man, pointing to a corner just inside the door. I walked inside and laid him gently down.

"Bless you, Cade," said Newt. "I'll never forget this."

"I'm just glad I came along. Can I do anything else?"

"No, I'll be fine now. Me friend, Jimmy, will take care of me." The man who had told me where to put Newt smiled and nodded in agreement.

As I walked away from the shelter, the men all stared at me with sullen, hopeless eyes. It was now close to ten at night, and I hadn't eaten since lunch, nor even begun to pack. Somehow, it just didn't seem to matter. I hardly noticed the rain any more as I walked back to Magdalen.

14

THE MOUNTAIN

I THOUGHT MY PLANE would never touch ground. I was terribly anxious about my mother and had fidgeted the entire flight, unable to sleep. I brought along several of Lewis's books and read *The Great Divorce*. Despite my exhaustion it struck a chord with its discussion of the dual nature of free will and personal responsibility, and the choices we all have to make.

My father met me in the Atlanta airport. His unshaven face was gaunt and pale, and there were dark circles under his eyes. I had never seen him so haggard-looking before. He told me more about the accident, and that my mother had been upgraded to stable condition. Apparently, Mom remembered nothing of the accident, and so far no one had been apprehended. We drove straight to Grady Hospital.

As we entered the room, it was very bright inside, because the sun was shining directly into the windows. I gasped involuntarily when I saw my mother lying in the bed connected to several tubes. As I got closer, I saw she was thin and very pale. Her head and arms were heavily bandaged. I felt queasy.

"Is she conscious?" I asked Dad.

"Sometimes. She became somewhat alert late yesterday. She sleeps most of the time, but she knows who I am. The doctor says that's an excellent sign."

I went over to my mother's bedside, and held her hand. Her eyes opened. She appeared to be focussing, as if confused, and then she smiled.

"Cade," she whispered hoarsely, "I'm glad to see you."

"I love you, Mom," I said immediately.

"I love you, too, son," she whispered. We had never really said that to each other since I had been a young child. I felt a huge lump in my throat.

I stayed a good while, although Mom slept most of the time. When the nurse came in to check on her, Dad took me home to sleep.

During the next week I saw a few friends, but mainly spent time with my family at the hospital. My younger sister, Elizabeth, had come home from college, too. Dad was more reserved than usual. As a seasoned trial lawyer, he usually appeared supremely confident and self-assured. Now, however, he was much more quiet and contemplative.

After the first week, it was clear that Mom was out of danger and would be all right. She had no permanent neurological damage, but would still anticipate a long recovery time. I began to think about Oxford. Rachael had been on my mind often, and I found myself longing to see and talk to her.

"Son, maybe you should get on back to Oxford," Dad said one night at dinner.

"Yes, I've been thinking the same thing," I replied.

"Why don't you take Elizabeth to Sewanee tomorrow, and then you can return to Oxford in a few days."

* * *

Elizabeth was in college at The University of the South, in Sewanee, Tennessee. I had never been there, so I welcomed the chance to see it. We drove up a winding mountain road, as the trees put on a spectacular display of autumn colour. Just as our car passed between two tall, stone columns marking the entrance to the university, Elizabeth put her index finger to the roof of the car.

"Why did you do that?" I asked.

"It's sort of a Sewanee tradition that we have a guardian angel here.

When we leave the Domain, we take the angel with us, and we drop her off when we return to campus."

I laughed at this quaint custom.

When we arrived in Sewanee, I was struck by the beauty of the campus. The brown stone buildings were all built in a Gothic style. Despite the fact that I had never set foot here before, it seemed somehow familiar.

"Does this remind you of anything?" Elizabeth asked as we stopped the car in the middle of the campus. To the left was a tall, dark clock tower, while in the middle of the quadrangle was a large stone building with an observatory on top. To the right was a stately Gothic-looking stone church, with huge stained-glass windows and a tall tower behind it.

"Actually, it does somehow remind me of Oxford."

"It should. Sewanee has a lot of connections with Oxford and Cambridge, including the architecture and the black academic gowns."

"I wondered why some people were wearing gowns. Tell me more about Sewanee."

"Well, let's see. The town of Sewanee gets its name from a tribe of American Indians. The university was founded just before the Civil War by the Episcopal Church. That's why you see the lovely church over there, called All Saints' Chapel. The school has about ten thousand acres up here on what we call 'The Mountain.' Union troops blew up the original cornerstone during the Civil War, and Sewanee started over again after the War. Actually, Oxford University gave Sewanee a number of books to start its library."

I felt a vague sense of deja vu, although I couldn't put my finger on it. "What's that tower?" I asked Elizabeth, pointing to the stone tower with the clock, which was framed by tall maple trees splashed with bright yellow leaves.

"It's Breslin Tower. If it looks familiar to you, it should: it's modelled after Magdalen Tower in Oxford." We then walked into a peaceful grassy courtyard surrounded by tall, brownstone buildings. "This is Guerry Garth," added Elizabeth. "It's one of my favourite spots on campus."

As Elizabeth spoke, the bells in the Tower tolled four, and the sound transported me back momentarily to Oxford. I was looking forward to returning there and realised how fond I had become of that ancient city and university.

"It's a beautiful place," I remarked.

"Yes, Cade, I love it here. Let's drop my bags off at the dorm, and I'll show you around."

"Sure, let's go."

As we walked around campus, I saw several jack-o-lanterns. I had completely forgotten that today was Halloween.

"Before it gets dark, how about a long walk?" asked Elizabeth. "It's such a nice afternoon."

"That's fine with me." We began walking away from campus and down a long road. We talked about Mom, and exchanged stories of our childhood. I looked at my sister: she was no longer the little girl with ponytails and braces on her teeth. She was becoming a woman, and I thought how pretty she was with her curly brown hair and large brown eyes. The road undulated through silent woods filled with the yellows, reds, and oranges of autumn. The air was completely still, as if in reverence for nature's colourful wake. A deer stopped about twenty feet in front of us, looked at us quizzically, then bounded into the woods.

As we reached the top of one of the hills, I stopped dumbstruck. About two hundred yards ahead of us stood a huge white cross, rising before the purple and orange sky, and framed by golden leaves.

"Isn't it beautiful?" inquired Elizabeth. "We just call it 'the Cross'. You should see it at night, all lit up standing high on this mountain."

"I see," I replied, lucky to get even one word out. My mind was racing. Could it be possible? No, of course not – but ...

We walked up to the cross and saw before us a beautiful panorama of the valley below. It was such a peaceful sight. We lingered until sunset, watching the sun splash pink, purple, and orange paints on its canvas in the sky. I was desperate to search around for the second report while we were there, but could think of no excuse to do so without appearing silly. I just had to find a way to come back.

* * *

During supper in Shenanigan's, a local sandwich shop in an old wooden building, several of Elizabeth's friends asked us to come to a Halloween party that night. They were regaling us with tales about the numerous ghosts, like the Headless Gownsman, which were rumoured to haunt Sewanee.

Later, I escorted Elizabeth to the party. We had no costumes, but were definitely the exception. The students appeared as pumpkin heads, scarecrows, witches, a headless gownsman, Frankenstein, Napoleon, and even Elvis. After being there for a while, I saw that Elizabeth was having fun with her friends, as well as filling them in about our mother's condition.

"Elizabeth, I'm pretty tired. I think I'll go back to Monteagle and call it a night."

"Don't you want to stay here with us and enjoy the party?"

I could tell, however, that she was not desperate to have her older brother around, and I knew it wouldn't be hard to slip away. I replied, "No, y'all have fun. I need to get back to Atlanta first thing in the morning, so I can pack for Oxford."

"Okay," she said, giving me a hug. She then whispered, "Thanks, Cade, for being there for me. Mom's accident ... and all ..."

I gave her hand a tight squeeze, saying, "I know. I love you, Sis. Now, you take care, and I'll see you soon."

As I got to the car, my heart was pounding. Could it be possible this isolated mountain in Tennessee was Soulbane's High Southern Cross? Surely not! But, then again, Malta had seemed pretty improbable, too. At any rate, there was no harm in looking. A thick cloud had descended on the campus, forcing me to drive very slowly. As I neared the end of the road, there was a strange white glow ahead. The cross was not visible in the fog, but spotlights created a surreal aura of light. I walked up to the cross and began searching everywhere, although it was difficult to see much in the dense, soupy fog. Nothing unusual stood out, however. After about a half hour, I knew it was useless to continue and that it had been too much to hope for anyway. It was getting quite chilly, and the dampness made it worse. I sat down on a bench to think and pray, realising how exhausted I was after the grind of these past several weeks.

Because there was nothing else I could do, I dejectedly got up to walk back to the car, then abruptly stumbled and fell over a stone near the base of the cross that was apparently protruding above the other stones. There was a wrenching pain in my shin, and I was on the verge of cursing when I saw something on the ground where I had dislodged the stone. I crawled over and pulled the stone away. Under it was a flattened packet of papers – wrapped in red ribbon! I grabbed them. My fingers began to tremble as I clumsily untied the ribbon and read what was now a familiar writing style. Unbelievably, I had found another Soulbane letter! It had never even crossed my mind that I would literally stumble upon it here on this mountain in Tennessee.

I had brought my laptop with me to Sewanee, in order to try and catch up on some of my tutorial work. Because of the fog, I decided it would be best if I just sat in the car and typed them, so I picked myself up and started toward the car. A pain shot up my leg, and I looked down to see blood staining my trousers. I took out my handkerchief and tied it around my shin midway between my ankle and knee, to stop the bleeding. I had no time to worry about an injury now.

I hobbled to the car and turned on my laptop. As the screen began to light, however, it suddenly went dark again and the familiar whirring stopped. I pulled the power switch again, and the whirring faintly started and then stopped. A dead battery ... I couldn't believe it! I looked at my watch and saw it was almost eleven-thirty. I didn't have a lot of time to type all this and return it by morning. I certainly didn't want to meet up with whoever or whatever had been in the cave in Malta. I tried to recall my tour with Elizabeth around campus. But everything would be closed now.

I began driving at a snail's pace, and pounded on the steering wheel in frustration. It was too far and too dangerous to drive back to my hotel room in Monteagle. Where could I go? I saw some lights on in a building to my right, stopped the car, and got out. As I came closer,

I realised it was All Saints' Chapel. Could it possibly still be open? I pulled on the large wooden doors at the front entrance, but they were locked. Then, I heard organ music. Where was it coming from? It had to be inside the Chapel. I walked around the side and found another door. It was open! I stepped inside quietly. The Chapel was dimly lit, and I could see a huge circular rose window at the rear of the church. The tall arched ceiling and beautiful stained-glass windows reminded me of some of the French cathedrals I had seen. To my left was the altar, with a large white sculpture of Christ. Several Halloween revellers were in the Chapel, and one of them, dressed as Count Dracula, was playing some eerie music on the organ. They were oblivious to me, so I slipped unnoticed into a dark corner. I was sweating profusely and my leg was throbbing with pain.

The people in the Chapel wore a variety of sinister-looking costumes and masks, and I had momentarily shuddered at the sight of them. One in particular had an almost evil look about him and I was beginning to fear I would never get the report typed. Finally, the organ became silent, and they departed laughing. As they neared the door I had entered, I remained hidden in a dark corner, so close that I could almost reach out and touch them. I held my breath as they passed by and left the church. Then, as the door was closing, I heard it: a high-pitched cackle. I froze and gasped involuntarily as the hairs on my neck stood up. It was identical to the hideous laugh I'd heard in the Malta cave. Could he – or it – have just been here? Was he on his way to look for the report? What if he found it missing? I began to breathe heavily and felt faint.

The Chapel was now as silent as a crypt. It was urgent that I got the typing done, but could I find a power source? I heard the bells in Breslin Tower chiming twelve. I frantically searched the walls, and finally, up in the choir stalls by the organ, I found an outlet. I plugged the computer in, turned on the switch, and it purred perfectly. As I sat down in the wooden organ seat, a creepy low moan filled the church. I nearly screamed, and my heart felt as if it was in my throat. Then I laughed with giddy relief, realising that my foot had stepped on a pedal, causing the organ to emit the long, low groan. I carefully moved my feet and hands away from the organ keys and pedals.

I glanced over at the nearby baptismal font. It occurred to me that I had never been baptised. Amidst the choir stalls of All Saints' Chapel, All Hallows' Eve turned into All Saints' morning, as I typed the second instalment of the Soulbane Report. It took most of the night, and when I emerged from the church, I could tell, even in the thick fog, that morning was approaching. I drove back to the cross to put the packet back where I found it under the stone. The visibility was only slightly better than the night before.

As I walked, limping, toward the stone, I thought I saw something move out of the corner of my eye. I wheeled around, but saw nothing. My heart began to race. What if I were to meet Foulheart here? It was a prospect I did not want to face. I replaced the packet and moved the stone back on top of it. Only then did I notice for the first time there was a dark red mark on top of the stone. Blood? No, it was a marking of sorts – strange in design, but nevertheless clearly a symbol. A signal perhaps? I had the eerie sense that I was being watched, but neither heard nor saw anything. I raced back to the car, hardly aware of the pain in my leg. I was shaking violently by the time I reached the car.

The fog had begun to lift. As I drove through the two stone columns at the entrance to the university, I put my finger to the roof of the car: taking a guardian angel with me couldn't hurt, I told myself.

*   *   *

When I reached Atlanta, I drove directly to the hospital. Mom was sitting up in her bed, reading a novel.

"Hello, Cade," she said with feeling. "It's good to see you."

"You, too, Mom." She was still pale and thin, but some colour had returned to her cheeks and a number of bandages had been removed. She looked infinitely better than when I had first seen her in the hospital.

"Did you enjoy seeing Sewanee?"

"Yes, it's beautiful. I see why Elizabeth loves it there."

"I want you to know how much I appreciate you coming from Oxford," she said after a long silence. "I've never before come so close to death, and this accident has made me think about lots of things. Mainly about you and Elizabeth. I'm afraid of dying, Cade."

"I know, Mom, it's been a wake-up call for all of us." I took her hand and squeezed it, and then bent over and kissed her on the forehead.

She began weeping quietly. I felt words were not necessary. We remained silent for a few minutes, and then talked for a while. It was the best conversation I could remember having with my mother in years. Finally, I could tell she was getting tired. I kissed her on the cheek and quietly left her room.

*   *   *

I was dead tired, having been awake for almost thirty hours. But, there was one thing I had to do before I went to sleep. I picked up the phone and dialled England.

"Hello," said the voice on the other end.

"James, it's me, Cade."

"Oh, Cade, my dear boy, how is your mother?"

"She's going to be okay. She had a pretty rough time of it, but she's doing much better. The doctor says she should be able to go home in about a week."

"Excellent news."

"I have more news, too," I said excitedly.

"What's that, Cade?"

"I found Part Two of the Report!" I almost shouted. There was a long silence, so I said, "James, are you still there?"

"Yes ... yes, of course. Cade, you're surely joking."

"No, I promise. I really did find it. I'll tell you all about it when I return."

Please contact Rachael for me and tell her when I'll be back. I'll call you when I get to Magdalen, and bring you the report."

"I'm a bit at a loss," he said haltingly. "I look forward to hearing all about your latest adventure. Tell me, the report ..."

"It's about the Church," I interrupted him. "I had to type it fast, so I couldn't take time to study it. You'll have to help me understand it. There are a lot of things I want to talk to you about ... you know, my mother's accident …"

"I understand. I want to help any way that I can. In the meantime, since you seem to like Lewis, as I do, you might take a look at his book, *The Problem of Pain.*"

"Okay, I'll give it a try." It was the other book I had packed.

"Oh, James, I have one other favour to ask."

"You know I'll do anything I can to help you."

"Will you baptise me?"

"Cade, it would be an honour and privilege to do that."

*   *   *

At the Atlanta airport several days later, I said farewell to my father. In some ways, he was a stranger to me. He had worked most of the time I grew up, and I had never spent a lot of time with him. In the four years I had been at Virginia, he had come up only a few times, and one of those was because he was on business in Charlottesville and another was for graduation. We had not seen a lot of each other these past five or six years, and I knew we had grown apart. In other ways, I admired and looked up to him.

"Cade," said Dad as we sat waiting for my plane, "I've been doing a lot of thinking lately, since your mother's accident. I realise now how short life really is. You and Elizabeth are grown, and it seems like only yesterday when you both were tiny. I'm not sure of myself anymore. I thought I had life all figured out, but almost losing your mother has hit me hard. I want to spend more time with you. I know you need to get back to school, but maybe when your mother gets stronger, we can come see you." Tears were welling up in his eyes. I wasn't sure that I'd ever seen him cry before.

"Dad, it would mean a lot to me for you to come. There's so much I want to show you."

The plane was boarding now, and for the first time, I didn't want to leave. I lingered until the last call. We embraced, and my father said, "I'll see you soon, Cade, I promise. You mean the world to me."

I hurried onto the plane, holding the green backpack containing my computer in one hand, while using the other hand to wipe my blurred eyes with my handkerchief, still stained with blood from my fall.

15

A Plot to Remember

I WAS SHAKEN by the events of the past weeks, and I had a dozen questions for James. My mother's accident and her pain did not make sense to me. But with a lot of time for reflection during my trip home, I had also felt strangely drawn to pray. I realised that life is truly a gift, and that there are no guarantees or security outside of God.

On the overnight flight to London, I pulled out my computer and began reading more closely what I had typed. I had the disturbing sensation several times that someone was looking over my shoulder, but each time I turned around, no one was there. I shrugged it off and tried to concentrate on the Soulbane Report. The next thing I knew, however, the flight attendants were awakening us as the captain was announcing our upcoming landing. I realised how exhausted I had been. I looked out the window just in time to see the pink dawn rising over London, with Big Ben and St. Paul's silhouetted in the distance. I could hardly wait to see Rachael, and I was eager to tell her and James how I had literally stumbled upon the second instalment. I turned off my computer, reminding myself that I needed to recharge the battery when I got back to Oxford and make a back-up disk of both reports, which were all on my computer's c-drive. I had shredded the paper copy of the first report and letters before I left for the States, so that no one would find them while I was gone.

* * *

When I arrived at Heathrow, it was crowded and noisy. I was still groggy from the long flight. The bustle of the crowd carried me along toward baggage claim. I looked up and at first thought I was imagining things: there was Rachael waving. I certainly didn't expect to see her at the airport, and my heart skipped a beat with excitement. I had never felt like this about anyone before, and the sensation was at once exciting and unsettling. Then, I realised her ever- present smile was gone.

"Rachael, why are you ..." I started.

"Cade, it's James," she said, interrupting me. "He's had a heart attack. He's in the John Radcliffe hospital in Headington."

"When did it happen? How is he?"

"It happened the day before yesterday. The church gardener found him unconscious at the vicarage."

"Have you seen him yet?"

"Yes, I saw him yesterday. He knew who I was, but he was too weak to speak much. He whispered to me that he wanted me to bring you to see him as soon as you returned."

"What does the doctor say?"

"He's only given very guarded comments, but it doesn't sound good. I have James's car. He has limited visiting hours, but we can see him around one. I'll take you to Magdalen and let you drop your bags and get a shower, and then we can go see him. That is, if you feel up to it."

"Of course."

I was bumped several times by people in the crowded airport and was glad I had my backpack hung on my shoulders. I tugged at it to make sure it was secure.

Just as we stepped on the down escalator, I jerked my head around to look up.

"What's the matter?" asked Rachael.

"Oh nothing," I said, not wanting to alarm her. I certainly did not tell her that I was sure I'd just heard that terrible shrill laugh. I gripped the handrail tightly to conceal my shaking hands. I glanced back several times as we walked through the airport, but saw nothing unusual.

On the way to Oxford, I gave Rachael a step-by-step account of my amazing discovery at Sewanee. Jet lag was catching up with me, however, and I began to nod off in the car. The next thing I knew, Rachael was shaking my arm.

"We're at Magdalen." I looked up to see that we were indeed near the entrance to the Magdalen lodge.

I shook my head vigorously, then said, "Okay, sorry for not being better company." I still felt very groggy.

"That's fine. I know you must be exhausted."

I jumped out of the car and retrieved my bags from the trunk. Rachael rolled down the window, saying, "While you take your bags up to your room and get a shower, I'll run fill up on petrol and get us some sandwiches. I'll meet you back here at half past twelve, and we can stop at Headington Hill park and eat before going to see James."

"Sounds good. I'll see you then."

The mid-morning bustle of students crowded the sidewalk in front of the college. As I walked into the stone entranceway next to the porter's lodge, Robert Thompson waved from inside the lodge and came out. I dropped my bags, and we greeted each other with a bear hug.

"Welcome back, Cade. I've thought of you often. How is your mother?"

"She's much better, thanks. Mom had a rough time of it, but she's going to be okay. She gets to go home soon from the hospital."

"Splendid," he replied, smiling his warm, broad smile. "I've missed you."

"I've missed you, too. How's Clive?"

"He's well, thank you. He asks about you every day. You look tired. Let me help you with your bags."

Ordinarily, I would have protested. But I was so tired that, this time, I was grateful for the offer. Mr. Thompson was his usual cheery self, and he filled me in on various events I had missed. I told him about my mother and James as well. Over the summer I had told James and Mr. Thompson about each other, and I was looking forward to introducing them soon. As we got to my room, I felt almost overwhelmed. Mr. Thompson must have sensed it, because he put his arm around my shoulder and said, "Now, you get some rest. We'll count on seeing you soon," he yelled as he left my room. I could hear him bounding down the stairs, whistling.

After the hot shower, I felt much better. As I pulled on my sweater, I glanced at my watch and saw it was almost twelve thirty. I was eager to see Rachael. I took my backpack with the computer and hid it under my bed, before heading to the lodge.

When we arrived at James's hospital room, I was very apprehensive as we entered quietly. The room was dark, and at first I had difficulty seeing him. There was an unpleasant, antiseptic smell that immediately brought back memories of the hospital I'd so recently visited. As my eyes adjusted, I could see James propped up in the bed. Tubes were attached to him, and there was a monitor beeping above him, with green dots and lines moving from left to right. James waved weakly for us to come in.

"Greetings, my dear friends," he said softly. "It's so good to see you. Please turn on the lights."

Rachael flipped on the lights, saying, "James, how are you feeling today?"

"Better." He pushed himself up higher in the bed, and there was a grimace on his face. He was very pale and his grey whiskers showed several days' growth.

"So, Cade, you indeed found something interesting on Halloween?"

"That's right. I had given up any hope, and then I literally stumbled over them. These discoveries are really incredible."

"Yes," he replied quietly, "we've seen some pretty unbelievable 'coincidences,' haven't we?"

James looked so sickly, I had to catch my breath.

Rachael smiled, and said, "James, are you too tired for us to visit?

We can come back later."

"No, no. I want to see you young folks. You mean the world to me."

We visited for a good while, and I told the Sewanee story again. Just as I finished, a doctor and nurse came in. The doctor told us that the vicar needed to rest now, as the nurse took out a hypodermic needle and began filling it with some fluid.

"We'll come back tomorrow," said Rachael.

"Good," James replied, smiling. "I'll look forward to it. And, Cade, I want you to bring me the report. I can't wait to see what you found. Bless you both."

As we neared the door, James called out feebly, "Rachael, I almost forgot, I need you to get some things for me from the vicarage."

Rachael walked back to his bed, and they spoke in low tones that I could not overhear. She then kissed him on the cheek, and joined me again at the door.

*   *   *

When we arrived back at Magdalen, Rachael parked the car on High Street and accompanied me to the College. The day was turning to twilight. As we entered the main entrance, I saw Mr. Thompson in the lodge, and he and I waved simultaneously.

"Rachael, come meet Mr. Thompson."

Before we could enter the porter's lodge, however, Mr. Thompson had come out to greet us. Just as I was about to introduce them, Mr. Thompson said, "This must be Rachael. Hello, my dear, I'm Robert Thompson. I feel as if I already know you from all that Cade has told me. You're even more lovely than I had imagined."

Rachael blushed, and said, "Thank you, Mr. Thompson. Cade has spoken so highly of you. It's a pleasure finally to meet you."

"How is your friend, the vicar?"

"He's a little better today, I think," replied Rachael, and added with a note of urgency, "Thanks for asking. Please keep him in your prayers."

"I'm just off work now," said Mr. Thompson, "and thought I might go into the Chapel for Evensong before heading home. Would you care to join me?"

"That would be lovely," said Rachael, and I mutely assented.

When we entered Magdalen Chapel, a few dons and students were seated up in the tiered, dark wooden pews on the left. On the right side sat the Magdalen boys' choir, arrayed in bright red robes with white surplices. An imposing white marble sculpture was illuminated above the altar and two sets of seven tall candles flickered as the College chaplain, dressed in a black robe with a white surplice and clerical collar, walked in and began the service. I had never before witnessed such an ancient and beautiful ritual. The spoken liturgy was punctuated with several beautiful anthems sung by the choirboys in their high-pitched, melodious voices, and I felt transported to another realm. As the remaining daylight streaming through the windows slowly disappeared, the small pew lights and candles cast a warm glow throughout the chapel. After kneeling in prayer, we sat for one of the anthems, and I took Rachael's hand. She smiled, her face alight again.

We quietly departed the chapel at the close of Evensong. It was now dark, and there was a cool, gentle breeze swirling around the Magdalen buildings.

"Rachael, I'm famished," I said. "Would you like to grab a bite to eat?"

"Sure, that sounds fine," she replied. "Mr. Thompson, will you join us?"

"Thank you, love, but I've a few things left to do in the lodge, and I suspect Rose will have something for me when I get home. You two run along and eat. I'm sure you have a lot to talk about." He smiled and winked at me.

"Why don't we just go to the Magdalen dining hall, since we're already here?" I asked.

"I'd like to, especially since I've never seen it before," said Rachael.

"All the best," said Mr. Thompson, who half-turned and waved, as he began walking toward the lodge.

As we arrived at the steps to the dining hall, I turned to Rachael, saying, "We're lucky. There's usually a line this time of night, but it looks like we'll get right in tonight."

After we picked up our food, we entered the dimly lit, cavernous dining hall. The large figures in various portraits hanging high up in the hall, looked down at us, while the usual buzz of dining chatter echoed around the dark, wooden panelled walls. We found a place at the end of one of the long wooden tables, just as the dons began entering from a side door at the far end of the hall, to be seated at the high table. As one of the dons finished saying the traditional Latin blessing, I looked across at Rachael. Her delicate pink and white complexion glowed in the light of the small table lamp, and I caught myself staring at her blue eyes.

"Cade, hello," said a voice, interrupting my thoughts. Peter Mizzi was standing behind me, apparently on his way out of the dining hall.

"Oh, hi, Peter," I replied, smiling, and shaking his extended hand. "Peter, I want you to meet my friend, Rachael Adams."

"I'm so glad to finally meet you Rachael. I've heard a lot about you."

I felt my face flush.

"The pleasure's mine," said Rachael, in a friendly, dignified tone. "Cade has told me all about Malta and your wonderful family. I hope I can visit your country some day."

Peter beamed and replied, "You're welcome anytime. Cade, it's good to see you back at Magdalen. How is your mother?"

"She's much better, Peter. Thanks for asking. She had a nasty accident, but the doctors say she is going to be okay."

"Really splendid news!" Peter exclaimed. "I've been thinking of you."

"I appreciate that very much, Peter," I replied.

"Say, Cade, now that you're back, ... well, the Wilde bunch has an important game tomorrow against St. John's. I hope you'll plan to be there, that is, if you're up to it, I mean. We really need you."

"You bet I'll be there," I said quickly. I could have kissed Peter for mentioning our rugby team.

Peter added, "Guess I'll see you tomorrow then. Rachael, it's nice to meet you, and I hope you'll come to our game, too."

"Thanks," she replied. "I might just do that." Her radiant smile made me wish this night would never end. It was a wish I would soon come to regret.

We quickly finished our meal, as I told Rachael more about how awesome it was to suddenly come upon the huge Sewanee cross on that beautiful fall afternoon. I could feel jet lag beginning to catch up with me, however, and had to make an effort not to yawn in front of her. We left the dining hall and walked through the ancient passageway in Cloister Quad, past the Chapel, and into the open air in St. John's quad. The overcast sky blanketed any stars. As Rachael and I walked to my rooms, we held hands and talked about our excitement over taking the new report to James the next afternoon. One of the haunting and beautiful melodies from Evensong continued to flow in my head, and despite my exhaustion I felt an almost tangible sense of peace.

Rachael had offered to help me unpack, and we had a lot of catching up to do after my trip to the States. As we reached my staircase, it was dark. I reached over and flipped the switch, but nothing happened.

"The bulb must be out," I said. "I'll have to get them to fix it. Anyway, come on up."

As we started up the stairs, I could hear someone bounding rapidly down the stairs. The person came quickly around the corner of the staircase, where it turned sharply halfway between the ground and first floors. It was too dark to see his face.

"Hello," I said as he started down the last flight.

There was no response. Instead, he quickened his pace and bumped Rachael roughly as he passed rapidly by us.

"Hey, buddy!" I shouted. "Wait a minute!"

He did not turn around, nor slow his pace. From the light outside St. Swithin's, I could see that he had on a dark coat and a hat that covered his head.

"Forget it, Cade," said Rachael softly, holding my arm as I started to pull away to go after him.

Despite my anger, I nodded in agreement, and we headed up the stairs to my room. The staircase was completely dark, and I was holding Rachael's hand to guide her. I reached in my pocket to get my key as we arrived at the landing on the third floor. I started to put the key in the keyhole, but when I put my hand on the doorknob, the door swung open.

"That's odd. I'm sure I locked it when I left."

I turned on the lights, and Rachael gasped, "Oh, dear Lord, Cade, what's happened!"

I turned to see my room in complete shambles. Everything I owned was tossed about the room. Drawers were open with clothes spilling out. The floor lamp was overturned. I was stunned, and for a moment stood there motionless. Finally, I rushed to my bedroom and flipped on the light. The mattress was halfway off the bed, and clothes and books were strewn everywhere. There was complete chaos in the room and in my thoughts. I sprung over to my bed and fell to my knees to peer under the bed. The backpack was gone!

"Foulheart!" I screamed.

"What are you talking about?" asked Rachael anxiously as she came into the bedroom.

As I dashed to my window, I yelled, "My computer's been stolen!" I looked out and saw the man from the staircase exiting the college at the porter's lodge gate and walking briskly up High Street. He appeared to be holding something on his left side under his coat. I tried to think. How could I catch him? All of the Soulbane Reports were on my computer, and I had no backup!

"Rachael," I said quickly, "I can't explain right now. I think that man we just saw has stolen my computer. You stay right here and don't move. And, whatever you do, lock the door and don't let anyone in but me."

"But ..."

"I don't have time to explain," I gasped as I reached the door. "Just do as I say. And, under no circumstances are you to call the police. Just wait 'til I get back."

I flew down the stairs. I had one chance. I might be able to go out the side door on Longwall Street, and possibly intercept him. I ran through St. Swithin's Quad into Longwall Quad, and reached the door that opened onto Longwall Street. As I went through the door, the man was just crossing Longwall Street, still on High Street. I was in luck. I began to run after him, and got to High Street just in time to see him turn on New College Lane. All of this had started with that winter's solstice walk on this small lane – was it going to end here as well? When I got to the Lane, he was turning the corner to the left. *This winding street is a perfect getaway place*, I thought. I continued to run and spotted the thief again. He turned around and apparently saw me, because he began to run. I could see him under a street lamp holding an object that looked to be about the size of my backpack.

Oxford was probably the worst place to try and catch someone, I thought desperately as I ran. It has so many nooks and crannies, so many side streets and little-known corridors. It was all too easy for someone familiar with the University to escape. And, I had heard tales of secret passageways and hidden rooms. My only hope was that I knew more than this strange man.

After the man ran under the Bridge of Sighs, he headed left toward the Bodleian. I had not expected that. Surely I could trap him if he went into the library. He would immediately be noticed, unless ... what if he was one of the librarians ... or, an Oxford don?

I hurried through the Bodleian quadrangle past the statute of the Earl of Pembroke. Once inside the Proscholium, I could not see him anywhere. I walked quickly toward the entrance into the library, noting that no porter was there to check reader's cards. I looked around frantically. Nothing. The reports could be lost forever! I heard a noise and looked towards the Bodleian shop, where in a nearby corner, a door was closing. I began to stride toward the door, when a porter started up from his desk and said, "I'm sorry, sir, but I need to see your card first."

Fumbling in my pocket, I could find nothing but at that moment two other readers crowded at the desk to have their bags checked, and as he was distracted I darted towards the doorway. Straight up the stairs was the lower reading room, but to my left I noticed a door which read 'restricted to library personnel'. It was ajar, and led directly to a stairwell. I rushed down – I didn't have any time to lose.

If this was the way the stranger went, he would soon be out of reach. When I arrived at the bottom of the steps, however, I stopped cold. There were two different passageways before me, and I had no idea which one to take. They were both dimly lit and afforded no helpful view. I started to go down the one to the right, when I heard a strange sound that startled me. As I turned around, I heard a creaking sound and saw a conveyor belt behind an iron grid moving in the other passageway. I realised then that I was standing before the underground tunnel that passed beneath Broad Street, connecting the old and new library buildings!

I ran down the passageway, trying hard not to lose my balance on the steep slope beside the conveyor carrying its cargo of requested volumes. Suddenly, I was out of the dark tunnel and in a cavernous room, with rows and rows of shelves stacked floor to ceiling with books. The lighting was still rather dim and I doubted my ability to find anyone in this maze. Nevertheless, I began to run from one row of shelves to another, hoping to catch a glimpse of the elusive burglar. I tried not to think about losing all the Soulbane reports now, after coming this far. How could I have been so stupid as not to make a disk and preserve them?

Row after row revealed nothing but books and empty space. Then, I heard a rustling noise. I stopped and listened, hoping to get some sense of where the noise came from. I heard something again, across the room. I silently walked toward the sound, and peered down a long row. There was someone with their back to me, kneeling on the floor. I tiptoed down, thankful that my running shoes made no sound on the concrete floor.

I grabbed the person from behind, saying, "Got you now!"

A female voice screamed and startled me so much I let go and stood back. A thin woman in her mid-fifties, with greying black hair and wire-rim glasses stared at me. I then saw that just past her was a cart with books, which she was obviously reshelving. Her face was ashen.

"What's the meaning of this?" she shouted.

"I ... I'm so sorry ... I," I stuttered. "I thought you were someone else ... I ..."

"What are you doing down here?" she continued the interrogation. "Only library staff are permitted here."

"Well, I got lost and must have ..." I was trying desperately to think of something. Just then, I heard another noise and recognised it as the sound of a lift. Without waiting to explain further, I turned and ran.

"Wait, stop ..." she yelled, but I did not heed her command. Instead, I ran to an exit door and up the stairs. When I arrived on the next floor, the lift door was standing open, but the lift was empty. I recalled from my orientation as a Bodleian reader that this New Library building I must now be in had eleven floors, three of them underground. I feared I would never find the stranger amongst the stacks of that many floors, but I had to try. I could hear no sound on this second basement level, and began again to search the stacks of books. Nothing. I went down one long aisle, hoping to find some way to get a better view of this floor, when I heard an odd wheezing, whistling sound. I stopped to listen. As I turned in the aisle toward the sound, a rumble startled me. It was a full bookcase falling in on me! I dived out of the way, narrowly avoiding being buried by an avalanche of old, thick tomes.

I lay on the floor, my feet covered with heavy volumes. Kicking off the books, I struggled to stand. I heard footsteps running, and realised they were going down the stairway. I rushed down in time to hear the echo of someone running back down the tunnel, and I quickly resumed the pursuit. As I began to run down the dimly lit tunnel, it suddenly became pitch black! Then, that same blood-curdling laugh reverberated in the tunnel. I shuddered, but kept running. A sudden rolling sound confronted me, but before I had any time to react, an impact knocked me to the ground. As I got up, I could feel one of the book carts I had passed by when I had run through the tunnel the first time. I took a deep breath and shook my head to clear it, then continued down the dark corridor, until I found the stairs.

When I arrived at the door at the top of the stairs, I grabbed the doorknob quickly and almost fell backwards when the door did not give. It was locked! Desperate now, I knocked, but no one came. He was getting away. Then, I did my best movie hero imitation and kicked the door. It came loose, and I thrust it open. Several people were staring at me in shocked amazement. I heard something and looked to the left to see the female librarian I had startled standing at the entrance into the Proscholium, calling indignantly, "You, sir, come back here!"

I ran down the hall and brushed past the outraged woman. I arrived in the quadrangle just in time to see the mysterious figure running through the arched passageway on my right that led to the Radcliffe Camera. I heard the librarian shouting at me, too, but I dashed toward the stranger without acknowledging her. It was very dark now, and the sky was completely overcast. The man dodged to the right, around the Camera. I was getting quite hot and tossed my coat off on the pavement near the Brasenose entrance. I spied him again as he ran into the Church of St. Mary the Virgin. When I arrived inside, it was dark, and the only light was what came from the outside street light that shone through the church windows. I looked around for him, then heard a sound of footsteps on my left. He was going up into the tower!

I dashed up the steps of the dark interior of the tower. I could hear the man above me, screaming wild curses. The footsteps stopped, and I slowed my pace. Where was he? I then heard a sound that made me shiver – a low, wailing moan, followed by a sinister, shrill laugh. The same sound I'd heard in the Malta cave! I resumed my ascent.

When I reached the stone balcony, I saw no one. I was gasping for breath. I glanced quickly both ways, with the bird's-eye view of Oxford all around me. Then, I saw him lurking in the shadows. I rushed to the right, just in time to glimpse the stranger moving the other way around the steeple. I cut back to the left. This cat and mouse game reminded me of seeing a Mardi Gras Order of Myths parade once in Mobile, Alabama. The lead float had two costumed figures, Death and Folly, and Folly continually chased Death around the top. Who was folly and who was death up here? I didn't want to think about that.

As I turned a corner of the balcony, I saw my quarry standing motionless in the shadows, waiting silently. He was trapped. I heard heavy breathing, that made the same wheezing, whistling sound I'd heard in the library. I began advancing toward him, anxious to get a glimpse. Did I know him? Suddenly, there was a deafening roar, and I instinctively put my hands over my ears. It was the church bells signalling the quarter hour. Before I could duck, the man stepped forward and swung the backpack against my head, knocking me to the ground. I was stunned by the hard blow and grabbed my head, feeling a lump already forming. He gave that hideous laugh again, and before I knew it, he had gone around to the door and was running down the stairs. I had missed him again.

I stood up woozily, taking deep breaths. I was having trouble focusing my eyes, reminding me of the symptoms of a concussion I'd had after a sporting accident years ago. As my head cleared, I looked down into the courtyard and saw my attacker making his way down Catte Street. He appeared to be limping slightly. I figured I had lost him, but I wasn't going to give up now. I went down as fast as I could, trying not to stumble in the darkness. When I emerged into the courtyard facing Radcliffe Camera, I resumed running. My head felt as if it was splitting, but I kept going.

Just past the Bridge of Sighs, I stood in the middle of the large intersection, looking in all directions: down Holywell Lane, then down Broad Street past Blackwell's, and then down Parks Road past Wadham College. No sign of him. Breathing heavily, I slapped my thigh. I had missed him. My best guess was that he would have gone back down New College Lane, and I started to head that way when I heard the now-familiar, ear-piercing cackle. It was as if the stranger couldn't help but taunt me. It came from somewhere down Parks Road, so I began to run again in the direction of the sinister laugh.

I could not see or hear anyone. Then, down about one hundred yards in front of me, there he was standing under a tree near a wall. He turned around and looked at me, and once more stabbed the night with his laugh, as he tossed the backpack over the wall. I heard a soft thud when it landed. My spine tingled and panic swept over me. Should I pursue? Did I want to catch him? Pope's phrase came to mind, "... Fools rush in where angels fear to tread." Consistent with that aphorism, I resumed the chase. I had to have that computer back.

The man was now scaling the wall, which I recognised to be around Trinity College. This was my chance to get him, and I was gaining on him. He had pulled himself up almost to the top. I grabbed one of his legs and began to pull. I had him!

Suddenly, as I was about to pull him down off the wall, the mysterious stranger turned and looked at me. The shock of what I saw stunned me so completely that I let go of him and fell to the ground. I sat there paralysed, confused, and sick. Surely, this was all a nightmare. Then, my shock gave way to anger, and I leapt to my feet.

In a rage now, I jumped up and grabbed the top of the wall. I somehow pulled myself up high enough to see the dark figure racing far across the grass at Trinity and disappearing into the shadows. Simultaneously, I felt a piercing pain in my left hand and remembered too late ... the top of this wall had thousands of pieces of sharp broken glass cemented in it! The pain in my hand was excruciating. I dropped to the ground, angry and defeated. I heard that sinister laugh once again echoing in the distance and pounded the ground in frustration with my right hand. My left hand was bleeding profusely from a cut across my palm, so I attempted to wrap it tightly with my handkerchief. I could feel warm blood soaking into the handkerchief and the sting of a deep welt on the side of my head. I sat on the ground, leaning against the wall, so out of breath, I felt faint.

With intense effort, I tried to focus my mind on what to do next. I had one last chance. If I continued down Parks Road, I might still find him if he circled around that way from Trinity. It was a long shot, but I decided to try it. I had nothing to lose. The street was dark, and the traffic had quieted. I walked at a brisk pace, still trying to catch my breath. My hand throbbed. I had to find him because, I realised with a sinking feeling, it was now or never to retrieve the Soulbane Reports.

As I strode down the pavement, however, I suddenly heard rapid-fire gunshots. I instinctively dove to the ground, landing in a mud puddle. Could someone actually be shooting at me? I didn't dare raise my head. I hadn't really stopped to consider how dangerous this chase could be. I dragged myself along on the ground, out of the puddle, now covered with mud from head to toe. I lay still, praying I would not get shot.

I wasn't sure how long I stayed down before I began to think I heard the shrill sound of singing. What could that be? Then more shots. I was totally confused and kept close to the ground, trying to figure out where the shots were coming from. Then, I heard several people screaming in unison, "Please to remember, the fifth of November. Gunpowder, treason, and plot ..."

Guy Fawkes' Day! This was Guy Fawkes' Day! And those weren't gunshots, they were fireworks! I got up and looked around. Sure enough, off in a nearby field there was a bonfire going, and I could see a crowd of people around it. By now I was shivering from the frigid air, and decided to go warm myself by the fire. I was feeling faint and confused from the combination of my injuries, the chase, and jet lag. I could see several people staring and pointing as I stumbled toward the orange glow, but scarcely cared what I looked like. I huddled as close to the bonfire as I could, trying to get warm and dry. There must have been a hundred people around the fire, laughing, singing, and drinking. I glanced around at the faces illuminated by the firelight, but did not recognise anyone.

I decided to move to the other side of the fire where fewer people were, so that I could move closer to the fire to get one last burst of warmth before walking back. Glancing over at the coals, I saw just out of reach of the fire what looked like books. I instinctively stooped over to look and picked them up. They were *my* C.S. Lewis books! The ones Rachael had given me, that I had put in my backpack for my trip to Atlanta! I grabbed them and began milling in the crowd, desperately looking for the strange man. No one there had on a hat like that of the stranger, and I could see nothing unusual about any of them, nor did I spy my backpack. Was he here, and I just didn't see him? Had I already missed him? I was furious at the thought of being this close, and yet having nothing to show for it.

The fire began burning down to deep orange coals, and the people began to disperse. I lingered for a while longer, hoping against hope that my computer was not melting in the ashes. In a futile effort I poked at the smouldering rubble with a stray piece of wood. Finally, I reluctantly began the walk back to Magdalen. The throbbing in my hand and head was all I could think about. As I walked back, I thought over the tumultuous events of this evening. I had been so close to having the Soulbane Reports, and now they were gone, perhaps forever. Without the reports, no one would ever believe my story – neither the events in Malta nor Sewanee – and I could never reconstruct the reports without my computer. That terrible laugh echoed unceasingly in my head. But it was the haunting vision of Robert Thompson's face looking down at me from the top of the Trinity wall, that flashed continually in my mind like lightning.

16

SIGN OF THE CROSS

A S I LET MYSELF in the door from Longwall Street, the Magdalen bells signalled it was eleven. I'd been out for several hours and was completely wiped out. Rachael! I'd forgotten all about her. What if something had happened to her? She could be in real danger! I forced myself agonisingly to run. When I reached my staircase, the light bulb was on. I hurried painfully up the steps. My whole body ached, my hand throbbed, and I felt dizzy and confused.

When I opened the door, I noticed immediately that my room was almost tidy, in stark contrast to its condition when I left earlier this evening. I heard a noise in my bedroom.

"Rachael, is that you?"

My bedroom door pushed open, and out walked Robert Thompson. I stood there momentarily stunned, then angrily rushed forward, hands clenched.

"Where's Rachael?" I screamed. Gasping, I continued, "I can't believe you of all people ..." But the room began spinning, and the world went black.

I became vaguely aware of being jostled, but my mind was in a fog. Where was I? My head felt as if it were splitting open. As I opened my eyes, I was astonished to see two men clad in dark uniforms strapping me to a stretcher.

189

"What are you doing?" I cried in alarm, aware that my voice seemed strained and hoarse.

"Looks like you've had a nasty time of it," said one of them, as he tightened a strap across my chest.

I tried to sit up and found, to my great consternation, that I was completely restrained. I looked around quickly to see I was still in my room, and Mr. Thompson was standing near the doorway. They lifted the stretcher, and I protested, "Wait! Where are we going? I . . . don't listen to that man." I gestured toward Mr. Thompson.

"He's a bit delirious, I'm afraid," said the man standing next to Mr. Thompson, who nodded gravely.

Before I knew what was happening, I was carried down the stairs onto the green. A small crowd of students stood there gawking, but no one said anything. I was carried through the college, out the main gate at the porter's lodge, and thrust into the back of an ambulance.

"Where are you taking me?" I demanded again.

"To hospital," said one of the men, as he jumped into the back with me. "Now, you just relax."

Relax! I was petrified. What was happening? I was still disoriented, but the events of this evening began to come back in fits and starts. I recalled the run through the underground tunnel ... the Death and Folly chase on top of St. Mary's steeple ... and Mr. Thompson staring down at me and laughing derisively from the top of the wall at Trinity. Damn! Was Mr. Thompson really Foulheart? A sudden sharp turn by the ambulance brought me back to reality, and I cringed at its loud, obnoxious siren.

In a short while, we stopped abruptly under some bright lights. The back door opened, and I was quickly carried inside. There was a lot of commotion, and I saw one of the ambulance attendants talking to a woman dressed in green surgery clothes, with a surgeon's mask hanging down from her neck. I couldn't hear what was said.

"Wait!" I said. "What's going on? Let me up!"

The doctor came and bent over me. "Calm down, sir. You've got a fairly deep cut on your hand, and we need to stitch it up." She touched the bump on my head, and I winced.

"But, the man who was in my room ... he's ... he's," but I just couldn't bring myself to say it. They would really think I was crazy.

"Everything will be all right," said a nurse, as I was taken into a curtained cubicle. They lifted the stretcher and put me on a table. Bright lights over the table almost blinded me, adding to my paranoia.

I began to struggle again, saying, "Don't ... don't touch me! This is all a mistake."

"We'll have to sedate him," said the woman doctor. I glanced over and saw the nurse filling a syringe. I tried again to sit up, but was unable to move my chest. Someone else was standing at my side, holding my arms down.

As the nurse approached me, I screamed again, just before she plunged the needle in my arm. I struggled furiously, wondering if I was about to be part of some diabolical experiment. Slowly, however, I felt myself going limp. I looked over to see the doctor pull the mask over her face, and pick up a shiny metal object. As extreme drowsiness began to creep over me, I saw the doctor moving toward me, the instrument in her hand. Was this the end? I wondered. The hissing oxygen machine in the room seemed to become louder. Finally my panic dissipated as I seemed to hear the gentle swell of the ocean ... peaceful ... soothing ...

*   *   *

"Cade ... Cade ... it's Rachael," I heard a voice somewhere in the distance. I blinked open my eyes, and saw Rachael standing over me, concern written all over her face.

"Where ... what ..." I began to say. I shot up with a start, only to feel a sharp pain in my head. I quickly laid back down.

"You've had quite a night," replied Rachael. "You're in hospital at the John Radcliffe."

I looked around then and found myself in a hospital room, similar to the one James was in. Before I could get my wits about me, the door opened and in walked Robert Thompson.

My heart began to race and a fight-or-flight instinct sent adrenaline pumping through my system. "You … it was you …" I began to say accusingly. Rachael and Mr. Thompson both had startled looks on their faces.

"Cade, it was Mr. Thompson who called the ambulance that took you to the hospital. In fact, he's been here all night with you."

Rachael's stern rebuke took me by surprise. I felt embarrassment, coupled with confusion. Mr. Thompson smiled and looked down.

"I … I'm sorry," I said. "It's just that, well, I had the strangest night." I wondered if it could all be a bad dream.

The door opened again, and a nurse asked if I wanted anything to eat. I realised that I was ravenous after my ordeal.

"What time is it?" I finally inquired.

"Oh, it's almost noon," said Mr. Thompson. "The nurse told me that she's been checking on you through the night and doesn't believe your concussion is serious. The doctor came in about twenty minutes ago and said you could be released assuming you feel up to it."

"I can't get out of here soon enough," I replied, as I sat up in bed. I felt a sharp pain in my left hand, and looked down to find it heavily bandaged.

"You had a nasty cut," said Mr. Thompson. "The doctor last night said you'd lost some blood and were in shock. And, you were delirious, screaming something about a foul heart and Guy Fawkes. So, they decided to keep you overnight for observation."

Rachael came over and stroked my head, smiling. "Cade, I've been dreadfully worried. After you ran out last night, I finally went and found Mr. Thompson at the lodge. Fortunately for us, when he returned to the lodge after evensong, he had to assist the night porter with a problem, so he was still in the college. I was pretty shaken, so after we tidied your room up a bit, he took me to his home in James's car. Mr. Thompson went back to Magdalen to see about you, and then called later to say you were in the hospital. His wife insisted I spend the night with her last night. What in the world happened after you left me in your room?"

"It's a long, long story," I said. "Let me get my wits about me, and then maybe I can tell you about it."

* * *

After lunch, I felt infinitely better. Mr. Thompson went to see about checking me out of the hospital, and Rachael decided to look in on James, while I showered and changed into some clean clothes Mr. Thompson had brought me. Just as I finished getting dressed, someone knocked on the door, and Rachael entered.

"How is James?" I inquired immediately.

"He's doing better this morning. James is anxious to see you, Cade, but I haven't told him about your injuries. You don't have to go if you're not up to it."

"No, I'm going with you," I said emphatically. "But Rachael, you know my computer was stolen last night. It had all the Soulbane letters and reports on the c-drive, and I didn't have a back-up. I can't believe after all this I've lost them. I ... I don't know how to tell James."

Rachael was silent for a while, then said, "Well, there's nothing we can do about it. We need to see James, and ..."

Just then Mr. Thompson returned to the room, smiling and saying, "Everything's all set. We can leave whenever you're ready. The nurse at the main desk on this floor said for you to come back in a week to be checked, and in the meantime, to let them know if you have any problems."

"I'm more than ready," I said, managing a weak grin. Rachael and I gave each other a knowing glance, and then I said, "Mr. Thompson, we're going to see Rachael's vicar, James Brooke. Why don't you come along with us? I want you to meet James." He hesitated a moment, then nodded in agreement.

As we walked through the hospital corridors, my sense of relief at being free turned to a sickening feeling of despair that the reports were gone, with no hope of being recovered.

"Cade," said Rachael softly as we turned into the cardiac ward, "I know you're down, but please try to be upbeat for James. The last thing he needs is bad news."

"I know," I said, with a grimace.

James was sitting up when we entered, and he smiled immediately as we introduced Robert Thompson.

"Welcome," he said. "I've been looking forward to your visit. Robert, it's a privilege to meet you. Cade has told me all about your lovely family."

We all expressed concern about James' health, but he brushed off our inquiries. "I had a good night's sleep; I mustn't complain. In any case, I can't wait to see the new report you found. Oh, Cade, my dear lad, what in the world happened to you?"

"It's a long story," I said.

Rachael and I looked at each other, and then she said, "I'm afraid we have some bad news. Someone stole Cade's computer."

James's face fell. Finally, he said, "Well, that's not the end of the world now, is it? Cheer up. At least we have part of the report, the first instalment."

I looked at Rachael in desperation, and wanted to crawl away. Finally, I said, "I hate to tell you, but we don't have that either. I shredded it before I went to the States."

"I see," said James. He had a distant look in his eyes. "Tell me about your hand."

"James, I ... I don't even know where to begin. It's a bizarre story, and Mr. Thompson has no clue about any of this." I nodded in his direction.

"Oh, I'm happy to leave," said Mr. Thompson hastily, starting towards the door.

"Not at all," I said. "You deserve to hear this, too ... especially after last night!" I proceeded to tell the story beginning that winter's solstice night in the Magdalen library. This time I did not leave out any significant events, including the strange incident in the Malta cave. Rachael audibly gasped when I described my experience there. Up until this moment, I had never breathed a word to anyone about my second visit to the cave, afraid that I would sound completely crazy. After the previous night's adventure, however, I began to believe that my brush with Foulheart had not been a dream. I told them everything, including the ghastly image of Mr. Thompson's face at the wall.

I concluded by saying, "And that's the whole truth and nothing but the truth, so help me God. Unfortunately, I'll never be able to prove it without the reports. I can't believe I lost them after all this."

Mr. Thompson smiled, saying, "Don't be so hard on yourself, Cade. What you've done is nothing short of heroic. We believe you. And let me assure you, I could never have climbed so nimbly over Trinity Wall, much less outrun you in the chase you described!" We all began to laugh at what now seemed an absurd idea.

Then, Mr. Thompson continued, "I remember once, after I got to know Mr. Lewis well, I asked him about *The Screwtape Letters*. He wouldn't really talk about them. I even asked him if he had ever met Screwtape, but he only replied that he could in a sense see him everywhere he went but he he wouldn't go as far as saying that he would know Screwtape if he walked in the through the door. He just wouldn't talk about Screwtape, and I always thought that was odd."

James shook his head and said soberly, "Powers and principalities at work in this world. It's spiritual warfare you've been up against."

"And the worst of it is," I interjected, "I still don't know who he is or what he looks like."

"That really doesn't matter, Cade," he answered. "The devil is a master of disguise. St. Paul said in his letter to the Corinthians that the devil can disguise himself as an angel of light. Even if you had seen him, he would be different today, and something else yet again tomorrow. Just look at the face he showed you at the wall. Now, don't fret about that."

"But what about his voice? I thought I somehow recognised it."

"Yes, that does raise interesting possibilities. But, without a better idea of who it might be, we have nothing to go on unless you hear the voice again."

"What can we do now?" asked Rachael.

"I don't know," said James. "When I'm lost or befuddled, I turn to prayer . . . that great mystery of our interaction with our Creator. Just remember, even the devil is but a fallen angel ... he's not the equal of God."

"I'm so sorry – about everything," I said.

"Not to worry, Cade," he replied. "Look at how you've grown

through all this adversity. And besides, there is something much more important to me right now than these reports."

When I looked at him quizzically, James turned to Rachael and added, "Did you bring me the items I talked to you about yesterday?"

"They're right here," said Rachael, as she reached for the tan canvas bag she had brought in with her. "Mr. Thompson came home this morning after the nurse told him Cade was not in any danger. I took your car and went over to the vicarage to pick these up for you."

Rachael handed James a small black book with a gold cross on the front, a bowl and a towel. Then, she pulled out a small container with clear liquid in it.

"Cade," said James, "It's time you joined our family. Are you ready to be baptised?"

"Well, yes, I guess so," I said. I had forgotten all about my request.

"Good," he said quietly. "Robert, if you, Rachael, and Cade share the other prayer book, I will read from mine. I'm afraid I don't have a third prayer book."

"Not to worry," replied Mr. Thompson, with a wink to Rachael and me. "I've been to a few baptisms in my time."

James then resumed, "Cade, this service has been used by the Church of England since 1662." He then began to read from the *Book of Common Prayer.* After a number of prayers, exhortations, and Scripture readings, James looked at me and said, "Dost thou renounce the devil and all his works, the vain pomp and glory of the world, with all covetous desires of the same, and the carnal desires of the flesh, so that thou wilt not follow, nor be led by them?"

"I renounce them all," I responded with conviction, as I glanced down at my bandaged hand.

"Dost thou believe in God the Father Almighty, Maker of heaven and earth? And in Jesus Christ his only-begotten Son our Lord? And that he was conceived by the Holy Ghost; born of the Virgin Mary; that he suffered under Pontius Pilate, was crucified, dead, and buried; and that he went down into hell, and also did rise again the third day; that he ascended into heaven, and sitteth at the right hand of God the Father Almighty; and from thence shall come again at the end of the world, to judge the quick and the dead? And dost thou believe in the Holy Ghost; the holy catholic Church; the communion of saints; the remission of sins; the resurrection of the flesh; and everlasting life after death?"

"All this I steadfastly believe," I said with a gulp at the awesome ideas I was professing a belief in.

"Wilt thou be baptised in this faith?"

"That is my desire."

At last, James said, "Cade, this water comes from the River Jordan, where Jesus was baptised. I have been saving it for a very special occasion, and this is it."

I bent my head over the hospital bed. James then trickled the water over my head, saying, "Cade, I baptise thee in the name of the Father, and of the Son, and of the Holy Ghost. Amen."

"Amen," said Rachael and I together. Mr. Thompson quickly echoed us.

James then marked the sign of the cross on my forehead, saying, "We receive Cade into the congregation of Christ's flock; and do sign him with the sign of the Cross, in token that hereafter he shall not be ashamed to confess the faith of Christ crucified, and manfully to fight under his banner, against sin, the world, and the devil; and to continue Christ's faithful soldier and servant unto his life's end. Amen."

When we came to the end of the liturgy, James added, "You are now part of an ancient sacramental tradition going back to Christ. You have been marked with the sign of the cross and are his child forever. This sacrament of baptism is an outward and visible sign of an inward and spiritual grace. Blessings upon you, my son."

Rachael brushed away a tear and squeezed my hand. I then bent over the bed, put my arms around James's neck, and hugged him. Mr. Thompson chuckled happily, and I was glad he had been a witness. He then shook my hand vigorously, while congratulating me heartily.

We had stayed far beyond our allotted time. James was obviously exhausted, and the events of last night were beginning to catch up with me, too. Rachael suddenly spoke up, however. "Before we leave, can we say a quick prayer for you, James?" We then prayed for James, and Rachael added on a request that my computer would be recovered. I privately concluded that this was only a placebo to make us all feel better. We then all bade James farewell, promising to come see him again the next afternoon.

*   *   *

The only reason I slept at all that night was that I was overcome with fatigue from the long trip and my harrowing Guy Fawkes' night. As I lay in bed, my bandaged hand throbbing, I kept replaying in my mind the events of the previous night. It was infuriating. I had been so close ... I tossed and turned for several hours, but finally fell into a fitful sleep.

When I awakened, it was nine-thirty the next morning. Rachael had agreed to pick me up at one, so that we could visit James again. I felt drugged and heartsick. I berated myself again and again for my stupidity, first in not being more careful with the backpack, and second in not making a back-up. I had lost the chance of a lifetime.

I forced myself to get out of bed and get going. The lump on my head had receded, but my hand was still sore. After getting showered and dressed, I went up to a coffee shop on High Street for breakfast. I sat there in the corner, mute and stunned, continuously stirring my coffee. I tried to read the morning paper, but couldn't concentrate on anything. All I thought about was my lost computer.

As I returned to Magdalen, Mr. Thompson waved me into the lodge.

"Cade, I've been looking for you. I went up to your rooms, but you weren't there."

"I stepped out for some breakfast," I replied mechanically. "Why were you looking for me?"

"Some unsavoury character came to the lodge asking for you. I tried to get rid of him, but he kept insisting on seeing you. He wouldn't say why."

"What did he look like?"

"A homeless beggar. Old, dirty clothes, beard, and ... he was blind."

"Blind? Was his name Newt?"

"Yes, now that you mention it. The man did say his name was Newt. Do you know him?"

"Yes. It's another long story. Where is he?"

"He had a friend with him. I sent them over to the gardens while I went to look for you."

I walked across the street to the Botanical Gardens and looked around. Newt was nowhere to be seen. I was curious why he was looking for me, and suspected he was looking for money. I realised it had probably been a mistake to tell him who I was and where to find me. I got more and more frustrated as I walked through the gardens. With the current state of affairs I hardly needed vagrants wandering into the College and embarrassing me. I finally spied Newt and his friend sitting on a bench back in the gardens near the river.

"Newt," I said tersely as I got close to them. I was ready to tell him off.

"Cade, is that you?" he asked, turning his head in the direction of my voice. His companion was equally dirty and unkempt, and I recognised him as one of the men I had seen at the shelter in October.

"Yes, I heard you were looking for me," I said irritably. "Listen, I don't want you to ever ..."

"I ... I have something that might be yours," he said, before I could finish telling him not to come looking for me again.

"What's that?" I replied, beginning to backtrack from my intended tirade.

From under the bench, Newt pulled out a green backpack. It was dirty and the worse for wear, but it was *my* green backpack.

"Where did you ...?" was all I could stammer out. I felt my face flush with shame at what I had almost said to Newt.

"A couple of nights ago, a strange man came to the shelter boasting about stealing a backpack," said Newt. "He was a real braggart. Me friends said they had never seen him before. I just remember his voice. A high, squeaky voice that grated on me ears. And, a weird laugh. He kept gloating over stealing the backpack, saying something about, 'I really showed that American imbecile. That'll teach him to fool with

me.' He was an arrogant fellow. I didn't pay no attention until I heard
him say your name and congratulate himself on taking your
computer, saying something about some reports. When I heard your
name, me ears perked up. I called me mates over and told them you
were me friend. I asked them to get your backpack for me and make
sure everything was left in it. Jimmy here can tell you the rest."

Newt's companion nodded, and then said, "I went over to the man
and asked for the bag. He screamed at us and got up to leave. Several
of us surrounded him, and, well, let's just say a little force got his
cooperation. He cussed up a storm, but gave it to us and left ranting
nonsense about soul something or other."

"What did he look like?" I was dying to know.

"Don't reckon I remember much. He was a strange man, with dark
features. Kept his hat on the whole time and stayed in a dark corner.
Never really got a good look at him. Can't say as I ever seen him
before." Jimmy's broad smile revealed his missing front tooth.

"I ... I can't begin to thank you," I said to them both.

"I might be poor," said Newt. "But, I got me dignity. I don't like
no stealing. I wanted to be sure I brought this back to you." His
hands fidgeted nervously.

My heart was pounding, and I felt as if I would float away as Newt
extended the backpack out to me. I grabbed it and quickly opened the
flap. Inside was my laptop computer, apparently miraculously still
intact.

"Newt, I can't thank you enough. You don't know how much this
means to me. You, too, Jimmy." I shook Jimmy's hand and then
embraced Newt.

"Cade, you've already thanked me. You're the first person outside
the shelter who's treated me as a human being. I have feelings like
everyone else. That night you carried me back was the nicest thing
anyone has done for me since I became blind. I'll never forget what
you did."

"I can assure you that I've been paid back a thousand-fold."

We sat together in the gardens for a good while, then I insisted on
bringing them some lunch. I ran down the street and bought them

sandwiches and fruit. As they ate, I promised Newt I would look in on him soon. When we said good-bye, I pressed a twenty-pound note in Jimmy's hand and asked him to share it with Newt.

I was giddy as I walked back to Magdalen, clutching the backpack tightly.

*   *   *

"Cade, you're joking!" screamed Rachael when I told her after she pulled up in front of Magdalen. She jumped out of the car, hugged me, and we both laughed. As we drove to the hospital, I told her the whole story of each of my encounters with Newt, beginning with the first time I had cussed at him. I could scarcely believe myself that the computer was safe on my lap.

When we arrived on James's floor, the duty nurse told us that James had left instructions to be awakened when we got there. He was asleep when we entered, and as Rachael gently shook his arm, he opened his eyes and smiled weakly.

"How are you today?" she asked him.

"Fine, fine," he said unconvincingly. "Help me up." We got on either side of him and cranked his bed up, holding him steady. The monitor above him provided a steady beep. We propped some pillows under his back and poured him some water.

"James, we have some good news," Rachael finally said, when he appeared comfortable. "You won't believe this, but Cade's computer was returned to him!"

"It's a miracle," said James in a tone of astonishment. "How did it happen?" I again told the story.

James grinned and some colour came into his face. "Did you bring the rest of the report with you?"

"Of course," I said. "Do you want to read it now? I only hope it is still there ... and that my computer still works."

"Well, let's give it a try," said James, as he shuffled in the bed, trying to make himself more comfortable.

17

SPIRITUAL GUILLOTINE

I PLUGGED MY LAPTOP in and placed it on a table near the bed. With a tremendous sense of relief, I retrieved Part Two of the report.

"Rachael, I'm a bit frazzled. Do you mind reading this for James?"

"Not at all." Rachael sat in front of the screen and began to read:

To Soulbane,

I have read Part One of your Report, and it shows real promise. Nevertheless, I am deeply grieved at the trouble I had to go through to find it.

Can you imagine the intense agony I encountered in having to scour that bloody awful cave looking for your Report? I couldn't find it ANYWHERE on Carnival day. You stupid wretch! Were you drunk again? Being down there with those candles and crosses and prayer requests, not to mention the statue of the Enemy's own Mother, was more than I could bear. It was excruciating! I even had to come back on the day of ashes to look for them. You idiot! What if I had been blessed? Gadzooks! Or what if someone else had discovered them – or me? After what happened with Lewis, it would be a daymare of the worst kind. I finally found it in the cave, but in the wrong spot.

Be more careful! Even the red ribbon was torn, you imbecile. And, be on time with your next instalment. My anger was appeased only by observing the maturity shown in your Report.

Skoal,

Foulheart

To the most dishonourable Foulheart,

I cannot imagine why you had the difficulty you describe. Just as we planned, I left the Report on Carnival Day at the appointed spot in the cave. Perhaps you participated too much in Carnival yourself? Attached is Part II of our Report. I feared it might not be on time. Slobglob and Scrunchmouth got into a vicious fight over who would have to visit the Enemy's churches and report on the sermons being preached. Of course, that was a terrible task. Why did they think I assigned it to them instead of going myself?

I happened along just before they devoured each other, and I had to threaten a visit from you to get them to come to their senses. I then thought about splitting their duties, but that seemed to me to be too close to the Enemy's concept of fairness. So, instead, I assigned the entire project to Baldface. He was gratifyingly furious!

To summarise this Report: one need only visit the empty, lifeless churches all over the western world to know the state of the modern Church. Europe has huge cathedrals and numerous churches spread out all over its cities and countryside, but many are now nothing more than graveyards and tourist attractions. There is little real spiritual life in them, and their physical decay mirrors their spiritual decay. In America, materialism, wealth, and self-centeredness are the order of the day. The churches there are largely full, but, I am pleased to note, spiritually bankrupt. The modern Western Church no longer knows who it is, what it represents, or in many cases, why it even exists, and this is reflected in the fact that there is little more than superficial commitment and faith among churchgoers. We can all rejoice in the fact that much of the Church no longer has any meaningful voice in modern-day culture.

One of the most despicable parts of our job in compiling this

Report was that we had to attend hundreds of services in the Enemy's churches, in order to ascertain from inside Enemy lines how our strategies were working and to see if the Church posed any threat. Fortunately, after hearing their sermons (or, in many cases, sermonettes), it is clear our Homeland is in no danger.

The Enemy established his Son as the Head of the Church. We discovered, however, that the ingenious strategies of our Royal Hindness have resulted in a spiritual guillotine of the Church, whereby the Head has been virtually severed from the body. Therefore, we are confident that the body is dying. What a glorious funeral it will be!

I will await further instructions from you.

Ever yours,

Soulbane

Report to Base Command

II. THE CHURCH

A. The Great Denial

The Church has done a great deal of harm to its own cause, much to our delight. Of course, the Enemy's religion is not really a religion (or set of beliefs) at all, but a relationship. That relationship centres on the Enemy's Son, yet the Church itself is casting doubt on who this Being was – some of its scholars and priests even question whether he ever existed. The more we can help this along, by painting him as a mythical figure, or a figment of the imagination of the apostles and early evangelists, the sooner our Royal Hindness will know complete victory.

The Church has many who are questioning whether the Bible is even accurate, let alone authoritative, and there are many attacks by theologians themselves as to the sayings and teachings of the Enemy's Son. The further humans get away from the belief in the miracle of the Incarnation, the easier it is to whisper in their feeble minds the notion that this is all a myth anyway.

Of course, we've had much success in discounting the many miraculous events described in the Enemy's book. Therefore, we have been promoting the belief that a "virgin" birth is impossible and absurd, and that the miracles of the Enemy's Son are mere superstition, or pure fiction. Even more importantly, the Resurrection itself is under such fierce debate that its validity will soon be destroyed by our Forces. First, of course, we steer minds toward the idea that there was no bodily resurrection at all – which many in the Church have already accepted – and that the eyewitnesses somehow merely felt that the Son was still somehow there in Spirit. The more vague and "spiritual" the Resurrection, the better for us. It doesn't take much then to promote the "fact" that the Resurrection was nothing more than wishful thinking by some of his dejected followers. Once the Resurrection is at best a ghost story, these humans can be easily persuaded that it is all hogwash anyway. The Resurrection is at the heart and core of Christianity, so with it out of the way, there is really nothing left of the Enemy's religion.

Even if we have some who think the Son did actually exist, then our strategy is to convince them that, at best, he was only a good teacher. This is not ideal because his teachings certainly point people in the direction of the Enemy. On the other hand, if the Son's words are viewed as mere teachings, it is not hard – especially in the pluralistic society that has developed in the western world – for us to get these people side-tracked onto other roads and onto other "great" teachers who espouse "truth," instead of Truth.

The result of all this is that in modern western culture, the Enemy's Son is merely an interesting but irrelevant character of ancient history, if not simply a figure of myth and superstition. Part of the Church has helped enormously in this regard. The attention paid to him now is usually in the form of exposing the myth of his existence, or the fabrication of his supposed moral teaching, or denying his supernatural Being. As a teacher, he is but one of many, with no more standing than any other human teacher. He is now outdated and irrelevant to modern society and thought. To be sure, we had some setbacks due to Lewis, whose articulate books addressed these issues so well, but we've redoubled our efforts to have his books viewed as the ranting of an old, misguided, ivory-tower fool.

B. The Bible as Fiction

For centuries, the mainline Church recognised that the Bible contained the Enemy's central message to his creatures, and was both inspired and authoritative. Now, however, not only are there so many differing interpretations as to render the Scriptures ineffective, but there are numerous attacks within the Church itself as to the authority of the Enemy's word. The western Church is now engaged in a huge debate over the authority and interpretation of the Scriptures. Our job has been to ensure that the Enemy's dangerous words are watered down or ignored. Our research indicates that we have been stupendously successful.

As the Base Command is well aware, I am not allowed to quote any specific examples, because even the mere recitation of the Enemy's word is intolerable to us. In general terms, however, some vague references will suffice. Some of the western Church, for instance, is arguing over whether the world was created in seven days, or whether the world and man evolved over the course of millions of years. This debate has caused much division and dissension among the Enemy's children, and it has diverted them from getting to know the Creator, because they are so bogged down in fighting about this issue. This example points up one of our major successes: we have convinced these humans that they must either believe in religion or in science – but not in both – since the two subjects are "obviously" incompatible. This has been one of our great victories, because it separates the spiritual from the material world – something of utmost usefulness to our cause. The Enemy, of course, created both, and he desired, for some unfathomable reason, that these realms should together form part of a whole; we, however, have striven to have the humans think of them as completely separate and mutually exclusive. Pure science, of course, seeks to know truth (that ugly word again!), and mere Christianity seeks the same object, just from a different angle. Now, we have succeeded in causing a huge rift in these two camps of religion and science. It's like setting two divisions of the same army face-to-face: they attack each other and ignore the real enemy. Hell forbid if these two disciplines ever recognised their complementary natures and instead collaborated to understand better the Creator and his creation.

Furthermore, as the vermin have come to think of themselves as so much more advanced and better educated (*i.e.*, more "civilised"), it is no longer fashionable to believe in miracles. Now, they have a "rational" explanation for every event, and there is no room for a supernatural explanation of unusual events. In fact, rationality has totally supplanted revelation in the modern world. This thinking has led to the watering down of the Scriptures, which are filled with stories of incredible (and, unfortunately, true) miracles performed by the Enemy. It has proved rather a cakewalk to nudge the Church itself, not to mention those outside the Church, to discount any notion of miracles. Whether the so-called miracles are viewed as myths, or whether they are given some rational or purely "scientific" explanation, really makes no difference to us. As long as the parting of the Red Sea, the manna from heaven, the story of the loaves and fishes, and turning water into wine, are viewed as anything but supernatural miracles, then our purposes are met. All of Christianity rises and falls on two historical concepts: the Incarnation and the Resurrection. Obviously, if we can convince these creatures that the various miracle stories are mere poppycock, then it is easy for us to get them to conclude that these two major tenets of the Enemy's religion are "impossible." Once this is accomplished, we have won, because without the Incarnation and the Resurrection, nothing is left of Christianity and the Scriptures but a fairy tale.

It has been said by some of these humans that if someone doesn't read, they are no better off than someone who can't read. This little maxim is certainly appropriate when it comes to the Church and the reading of the Bible. As we observed over and over, very few of the Enemy's creatures ever bother to read his message to them. There have been times in past generations where his word was read and put into practice, but that is no longer true of this western culture. Our research showed that actual reading of the Bible, even by people who profess to be Christians, is down drastically. Moreover, even on the rare occasions when they open the Book, they virtually never take the time to truly study and inwardly digest it, much less to apply its teachings in their lives. Therefore, our once terrible obstacle of doing battle with humans armed with the Enemy's words, is a thing of the past. His Scriptures, never being read, much less studied and applied, pose no threat to us now. Illiterate or ill read, it's all the same to us.

Finally, even the Enemy's own "theologians" are stripping away any usefulness of the Scriptures by attacking the authority and reliability of the Scriptures. Thus, with our prodding, the Bible has become either just a human account of events and myths, or a work of fiction with no real significance. With this accomplished, it will not be long before the Bible is rendered completely irrelevant, and read only by a small group of scholars who study the myths and legends of ancient civilisations. Thus, his living word will be synonymous with the Dead Sea.

C. The Tower of Babel Revisited
On the question of basic doctrine, much of the Enemy's Church is in shambles. Not only is there a chasm between liberal and conservative theologies, but there is everything in between. In addition, there are numerous cults and sects with all types of varied doctrines, each nevertheless holding themselves out as the sole possessors of the truth. No wonder the little vermin are so confused – even the ignoramuses who acknowledge the Enemy have so many doctrines and theologies thrown at them, they don't know what to believe. It is just as effective to our plans to send the Enemy's followers off on tangents and wild goose chases – so that they remain forever confused or are constantly searching without ever really getting to know the one who was crucified – as it is to have them never acknowledge the Enemy in the first place.

Of course, the Enemy's doctrine used correctly would be devastating to our cause. He wants his Church to recognise "One

Lord, one Faith, one Baptism." Hah! Bloody little chance of that with these morons. Fortunately, time has become our great ally. For two thousand years, the overwhelming majority of his Church recognised a basic core doctrine, which was articulated in the creeds, that served to draw them ever so close to the Enemy and act as a unifying force. It gave our Hindom Forces real trouble. Even with minor differences, where his Church in the past rallied around the central tenants of the Enemy's faith – such as the Trinity, the Incarnation and Resurrection, original sin and the fall of man, atonement and forgiveness, the inspiration of Scripture, and grace – we had a real battle to fight in the world. According to Foulheart, at that time, the Church was a formidable force to be reckoned with, and our Royal Hindness led our forces into many titanic spiritual battles. Now, however, some parts of the Church have abandoned their own two-thousand year teaching and wisdom, because they no longer attach any importance to the creeds. "Archaic," "old fashioned," "misguided," "myth," "superstition," "irrelevant," and even "barbaric," are words we have whispered in their ears, to great effect.

Not only have we weakened the Church in any attempt to unify itself around a central, core doctrine, but these imbeciles get so caught up in defending their own minor doctrines, that they lose the ability to learn what the Enemy has revealed to them. Thus, we can, in fact, easily steer them away from the Enemy and replace any semblance of faith and charity with our wonderful spiritual virtue-replacements, such as pride, greed, selfishness, and anger. They become so intent on defending "their doctrine" – meaning, of course, any trivial difference we can highlight – that they focus completely on that and not on the loathsome resurrected One. The *last* thing they think to do when defending *their* own particular doctrine is to love their neighbours. Doctrines and theologies and intellectual debates have replaced any ongoing, living relationship with the Enemy based upon a faith anchored in the creeds. Thus, Christianity now is really no different from other religions and philosophies which have various doctrines – but no personal Being – as their foundation. As long as doctrine is their god, we have nothing to fear.

We visited (ugh!) hundreds of churches during our research. One thing that was readily apparent after numerous visits is that the Church, merely a mirror of society anyway, is as segregated as society itself. There are rich and poor churches, white and black churches, blue-collar and white-collar churches, city and rural churches, and few of them contain any true cross section of people. In addition, of course, the Church is divided into hundreds of denominations based upon various doctrinal, liturgical, or external differences. Schism is the Church's real battle cry. Thus, there are numerous different kinds of churches: high and low, Bible and liturgical, post millennial, a-millennial, and pre-millennial, liberal and conservative, fundamentalist and charismatic, and untold other distinctions and denominations which we do not have the time to detail here. Any time there is some doctrinal difference among church members (much less good old standbys like greed, anger and envy), instead of either trying to resolve these differences or to recognise the central tenets of their faith with which he wants to hold them together, they split off and have nothing to do with one another.

It's like a modern-day Tower of Babel: the resulting chaos and division is a marvel to behold. The Enemy's weak army is disorganised and divided, it marches in opposite directions, and it spends its time shooting at each other, thus making our job easier by the day. It doesn't take an Archdevil to understand that such an army can never win a war of the magnitude of the one in which we are engaged. The Church gives lip service to unity and brotherly love, but worships at the feet of schism. His ingenious battle plan, outlined in the creeds, is now in shambles. The result, of course, is that our once noble spiritual warfare is really only an afternoon skirmish. Our Royal Hindness hardly even bothers to come and observe these one-sided battles anymore. Our Forces trained strenuously for thousands of years in preparation for a grand battle called Armageddon. Now, however, our military operation is a mere shadow of its former greatness. Our Royal Hindness believes we'll mark our final victory, not with a titanic cosmic battle with the Enemy, but merely by walking effortlessly and unopposed into an indifferent, weak world.

D. Bah Humbug

Some of the most fun for our Hindness's forces has been in
undermining the Enemy's own celebrations. Just think, the two
central events in the history of the world – the Incarnation and the
Resurrection – have been so watered down and trivialised, that they
are now nothing more than an excuse to have parties and to take
holidays from work. From early on, their children grow up believing
that Christmas is all about Santa Claus and receiving gifts. Even
adults – who are really not very far removed from these childish
notions – focus on their parties, clothes, and gifts. Commercialism is
the true ruler of Christmas. The Infant Child is either completely lost
in all this, or else relegated to a nice little tale of babies, mangers, and
wise men, while the earth-shattering concept of the Incarnation is
completely ignored.

Every Christmas we see many in the Church get further and further
away from the reason for the celebration of his nativity in the first
place. It used to be such a devastating time of the year for our Forces
and their efforts to obtain morsels were continually thwarted, but no
more. In fact, that time of the year now is as rich a harvest of souls as
any other time. There are still a few worrying skirmishes with the
Enemy, however. For example, the attention paid to that ghastly book
by Dickens, where humans are made to look upon the eternal and the
chance for redemption, no matter how late in life, has undone much
of our good work. We are also disturbed by the effects of films such
as "It's a Wonderful Life," where people are shown the parable of
sowing and reaping in vivid form. But, for the most part, these and
other forays by the Enemy are minor irritations.

Even the celebration of that terrible day that Foulheart has told me
about, when the one with wounded hands and feet visited our
Hindom and brought the infamous blinding light into our sacred
darkness – even that event today usually amounts to nothing more
than egg hunts, bunnies, and bank holidays. Just think – the greatest
event in all human history, and they hardly pay attention. The
Resurrection (that terrible, terrible day) forever changed our battle
strategy: of course, our Master has repeatedly assured us that it was

really part of his plan to let the Enemy think he had won the battle, all the while he was losing the war. Our research reveals this is in fact the case: most humans no longer pay any attention to the ramifications of the Resurrection whatsoever, and even those who do, either give it vague intellectual consideration with no corresponding action, or else they dismiss it as just a wild, imaginative tale – told by idiots and signifying nothing.

No wonder we will be victorious in our battle, if the Enemy's creatures can so easily forget his gift to them of his own Son, and if they can so easily trivialise his rescue mission designed to show them how to overcome our accomplice Death. Most wonderful of all to us is that the tremendous torture and suffering he underwent on the Day of the Cross, that most dreaded of days in our Calendar of Hell, was all for naught. The modern world couldn't care less, and that indifference marks perhaps our greatest victory ever.

E. The Password to Hell

Much of the modern-day Church ignores its Founder's stern warnings about our Hindom, preferring to focus only on the more palatable doctrines. The Church's teachings on our lower regions take a myriad of forms, almost all beneficial to us. Best of all are the ideas that a loving Creator would not allow hell and thus it doesn't exist at all, and that there is only a heaven where all of his human creatures will go, regardless of their thoughts, actions, and beliefs. Of course, thanks to our Royal Hindness, their free will is distorted and clouded by sin, but somehow – we have yet to understand this fully – the Enemy compensates for this when he issues his righteous judgement on these creatures. Apparently, he despicably gives them every chance to join him. Despite his weak underbelly, however, we have been receiving large shipments of souls, not because the Enemy no longer loves them, nor because he does not do everything to bring them home to himself, but because their own individual choices all during life have eventually led them to choose us over him. (Of course, we can hardly blame them, after our careful inducements!)

The little darlings live entire lives thinking only of themselves, establishing money, power, fame, sex, and material things as their gods. They nevertheless think they still deserve his kingdom – which he emphatically told them was not of this world – despite the fact that by their own actions and choices, they have moved further and further away from that Being who cherishes such useless things as sacrifice, unselfishness, charity, and generosity. These humans begin thinking they are somehow in control of their lives and masters of their fates. (Whenever one of them claims to be self-made, we know they're on the right path to our Hindom.) At first they merely ignore or run from the Enemy's voice. Later, as their hearts harden and their pride swells, they never even hear or recognise his call. The irony is that in his alleged wisdom and love in creating free individuals, the Enemy also necessarily created judgement. (According to our Royal Hindness, the Enemy's very nature means he is just.) Due to the Enemy's warped sense of justice, he decided it expedient to sacrifice his Son to pay for human misdeeds. He apparently only requires that people acknowledge his love and accept what he calls "grace," which we have never fully understood, although our Master shudders at the very mention of it. This is similar to the nonsense our Royal Hindness endured and has often spoken of when he, too, lived in the kingdom of light, before he so prudently revolted.

In this regard, the Base Command has worked hard to promote several distorted views of Christianity. One view is to persuade these slow-witted creatures to ignore the work of the Cross, and to make them believe they must earn their way to the Enemy's home. These humans lead wretched lives of misery performing endless "good" deeds, never experiencing the Enemy's unconditional love for them. Another wonderful distortion is one in which the Church constantly threatens eternal damnation. These scare tactics work occasionally, but generally have the opposite effect: like those mired down in earning their way to the Enemy, those frightened by hell live miserable and bitter lives. Not only are their minds obsessed with constant railings about our Homeland, but their hearts soon become hardened to the Enemy's compassion, love, and forgiveness, and they embrace only his anger and judgement. How many of these folks have we ultimately persuaded to join us? It's so easy, since they're already halfway to our Hindom anyway, walled off from other humans and from his grace. Fortunately, many of their fellow creatures hear this message as one of hate, and they then have nothing to do with the Enemy or his church.

Yet another view we have promoted to great effect is one in which people intellectually assent to the work of the Son on the cross, but it has no corresponding impact on their lives. They live seemingly happy lives because they assume all is well with the world, little realising that their failure to sacrifice and grow in the Enemy's likeness means they, too, become more self-centred and unloving. Any of these avenues suits our purposes just fine. Miserable followers of the Enemy, or self-centred intellectual assenters, are prime targets for our strategies. And, they fall so easily, it's almost not worth the effort any more.

Many in the western Church try hard to avoid unpleasant issues. So, they talk often about grace, seldom about sin. Forgiveness is an over-worn phrase, but repentance is hardly mentioned. Fortunately, the wretched concept of holiness is never discussed. The Church is eager to talk about a gurgling infant born in a stable under a bright star, but not about the pervasive, destructive evil that put that baby on a cross of torture. Thus, much of the Church only wants to talk about heaven or salvation or eternal life, but never about personal sin or the existence and consequences of evil. The Master's strategies are working to great effect everywhere, and the Enemy's Church has proved itself to be a less than formidable foe. Life is so much easier for our forces in the twentieth century, and it will be a walk on the beach by the twenty-first century.

It's really not so bad down here! The main thing is that he is nowhere to be seen, and none of his so-called virtues are tolerated. Apathy is the foundation of our Homeland. Besides, we almost always get what we want here, with little influence of the Enemy to ruin everything. What could be better than that? Our Royal Hindness has made sure that there is no hint of light or warmth, no horrid kindness or gaiety, and no community. It's marvellous to be left alone to our own devices, knowing that the password to hell is indifference.[HN]

F. The Prosperity Gospel

There is a marvellous development in some parts of the west, particularly the United States. This is what we call the "prosperity gospel," and it has served our purposes wonderfully well. While our mission is to bring all souls to our Hindom, we have not yet attained a one-hundred-percent success rate. That will come in time. Nevertheless, even where the Enemy has won some minor battles, we have still turned the war in our favour. A good method – one that has proven remarkably successful over the centuries – is the use of half-truths. Half-truths, masquerading as the entire truth, are subtly distorted by us so that the stupid creatures cannot figure out until it is too late that they have actually been walking down one of our pathways.

One such half-truth that has been especially useful is this health and wealth gospel. Many of the Enemy's churches have grown, it is true, but this causes us no disquiet when we examine the reasons for the growth. Just listening to their sermons, as distasteful as it was, provided us much merriment. Of course, some of the "telly evangelists" also gave us great delight in this regard. The major tenet of this prosperity gospel is that if you will only become a Christian, then the Enemy will forever bless you with material riches, a wonderful family, and perfect health. (The main ones getting rich are these preachers.) Thus, thousands, perhaps millions, have joined churches and professed allegiance to the Enemy for all the wrong reasons (wrong, at least, according to him). They become Christians thinking that will be the magic answer to all their problems, and that

[HN]Oddly enough, Foulheart informs me that he has never yet met a visitor to our Homeland who felt that the Enemy had treated him or her unfairly. They never rail at his judgement. Instead, they apparently always say they asked to be left alone by him, wanting nothing to do with him. It is they who turn their backs on him. They all bear the same trademarks: no passion, no spark ... just apathy, self-centredness, pride, and inertia. That's why they fit in so well here.

they will live in a perpetual comfort zone. They do everything in reverse: they seek to be happy, not to fulfil the Enemy's purposes. They never realise that the Enemy designed them to work in exactly the opposite way. It is unfortunately true that the Enemy (for some unknown reason) regards these vermin as his children, and that he desires to bless them beyond their wildest imaginations, but his idea of blessings has ultimately to do with matters of the heart and soul. He is primarily interested in developing them for the eternal journey, rather than for the grain of sand in the hourglass they spend on earth. We, on the other hand, have a different journey in mind for them.

Of course, he has blessed some of his followers with material riches, but that is, for him, a secondary matter. We have sometimes purposefully not stood in the way of such blessings, both because materialism allows us to easily guide their hearts away from him, and because it leads others to believe the prosperity gospel must be true. It also makes others so green with envy that it leads them to many other sorts of vices.

Once the prosperity gospel is in place, we can then have our fun. It is often difficult to know which way to go, and the Base Command has spent much time studying this issue. The easiest – and generally best – approach is to just leave them alone with their wealth, because usually they soon forget all about the Enemy and focus only on temporal things. Greed and pride have played into our hands for centuries, and the present time is no different. The one who became like them told them about where to store up treasures, but they pay no attention.

An alternative stratagem, terribly destructive to these two-legged animals, is to let them undergo some difficulty or tragedy. If they have bought into the prosperity gospel, then the least little adversity sends them into a tailspin. We have to be careful, because this can, in some instances, make them turn to the Enemy as a last resort. The way to avoid this is to make them think that the adversity must mean he does not really exist after all, or that he does not really love them, or, finally, that they must not be good enough, or must not have enough faith, or must have sinned terribly, or must not have prayed enough. The particular reasoning doesn't matter so much as the end result: that they give up and drop any semblance of faith in the Enemy. Any of these reactions suits our purposes perfectly well. If they have been indoctrinated thoroughly in this prosperity gospel, the least difficulty – much less a major problem – destroys what little true faith they may have had in the Enemy and make them easy targets for our trained tempter fiends.

One of the most desirable results (at least from the standpoint of our amusement) is the notion – frequently confirmed by their "concerned" friends – that if something bad has happened, it must only mean that the human has sinned, or is not praying hard enough, or doesn't have enough faith. This teaching is tremendously destructive to the creatures who took the bait of the prosperity gospel, and our Forces have had much fun in watching their agony as they try to understand what they have done wrong to bring this adversity upon themselves. Because they never bother to read the Enemy's book, they fail to understand that he never promised an easy ride in the fallen world caused by our Master, but simply his company and inner peace on the journey. We have seen how the Enemy shamelessly comes to his children when they need him, but fortunately, they are rarely aware of his presence and concern, and instead they just blame him for their adversity.

Many thousands have been duped by this spurious gospel, and the greedy imbeciles never seem to catch on. Obviously, they have paid no attention to what he has tried to warn them about in the Scriptures. We've watched with glee as people send in their hard-earned money to some of these preachers who make all sorts of promises on behalf of the Enemy that he never made himself. (Of course, since so few people bother anymore to actually read the Enemy's instructions, they can be led to believe anything.) Foulheart has described to me the sumptuous meals he has had of several of these prosperity preachers, and says that because they pretended to speak for the Enemy and perverted his message for their own gain, they have been particularly appetising morsels.

G. The Twin Towers of Hell: Ignored on Earth

It became readily apparent to us as we listened to all that was being spouted from pulpits that much of the modern Church has eliminated two words from its theological vocabulary: "sin" and "evil." These twin gates that mark the entrance to our Hindom have become non-existent in modern culture, and the Church is simply afraid to mention them. First, because the world no longer wants to acknowledge any moral absolutes, this necessitates that they ignore concepts like sin and evil. Taken to its logical conclusion, such thinking means that there is no meaningful difference between our beloved Adolph Hitler and that thorn Mother Teresa. Second, the Church is so intent on being all things to all people, that it dares not hurt anyone's feelings by talking about such unpleasant subjects. We actually found several churches that avoided even mentioning the Enemy's Son, for fear of offending someone.

The result is that, week after week, year after year, many of the sermons in the western world either ignore these concepts or trivialise them. Gradually, over time, the concepts of sin and evil have become almost extinct, and now, thanks to our help, they are virtually "unmentionables" in the Church. Occasionally, of course, some wonderful disaster occurs, like a bombing or a massacre or an outbreak of war, which for a day or two adds a flicker of talk about these outdated words, but these are quickly quelled with the help of our Royal Army for Global Emergencies, whose mission is to go immediately to such events in order to destroy any positive influence the Enemy attempts to exert. As soon as we have any hint that the Enemy's Angelic forces are at work anywhere in the world, the Base Command immediately dispatches RAGE to counter such activity. We witnessed several such missions first hand and were impressed with the effectiveness of RAGE. In addition, we should also mention that we found the Master's commando units, Special Church Obliteration Fiend Forces, were remarkably effective in their behind-the-lines sabotage operations within the Enemy's Church itself.

A tremendous additional consequence is that a human's private life and actions are never seriously questioned when it comes to his or her public life. Of course, our research shows that personal character is what the Enemy really cares about. With the help of our strategies, even when one of these vermin, like their politicians, commits a flagrant offence against decency, it doesn't take long for people to say that private behaviour has no bearing on public actions. How wonderful! As soon as we can divorce the two, we have won another battle. (Of course, as the Base Command has long recognised, we rarely even have to assign any assistants to these earthly politicians: many of them make it here without help.)

Because some of the modern Church offers no meaningful insights into sin and evil, it no longer offers any true solace when bad things happen, nor does it adequately explain so-called human nature in its fallen state. Moreover, the logical result of the elimination of sin and evil is that there is no need for a Saviour. The cross thus becomes meaningless and foolish in their eyes. Thus, parts of the Church have become a mutual feel good society, where people are not challenged with the difficult parts of life, and instead are made to feel that all's well, and they should be proud they are such good, religious people. And, besides, since the Church no longer deals with our Hindom, there is nothing for the creatures to worry about anyway. Such doctrines have allowed our Master to enjoy many a hearty meal.

The other thing that happened as sin and evil have disappeared is no one recognises that their actions have consequences. These humans have completely forgotten the Enemy's Book's instructions on the inevitability of sowing and reaping, which for some odd reason, the Enemy built into creation. These humans give no thought to the future or to the consequences of their actions, and they are ignorant of the dark ripples of black deeds that permeate history. They try to ignore or excuse their bad actions by talking about the Enemy's forgiveness. They fail to realise, however, that often even where the Enemy forgives them for the *fact* of their sin, he does not necessarily eliminate the *consequences* of that sin. In fact, I am told by Foulheart, who is privy to such information, that the Base Command is tracking a noticeable increase in these dark ripples in recent years, which must, of necessity (because of the natural laws

The Soulbane Stratagem

designed into his creation) have deliciously evil consequences in the future. The cataclysmic change occasioned two thousand years ago in the waves being tracked by the Base Command caused no little worry in our Underworld. Now, however, Foulheart tells me that the black ripples are increasing dramatically, such that we expect soon a tidal wave which will once and for all destroy these despicable creatures.

I should mention the other end of the spectrum, before we conclude this chapter. As mentioned in the chapter on our Hindom, the opposite response to ignoring sin and evil is to focus entirely on them. Thus, some parts of the Church emphasise sin virtually to the exclusion of all else. This results in the miserable and bitter people we discussed previously. They live in continued dread of judgement and punishment, and in a constant state of unworthiness. Such Christians are our entertainment, and certainly have no appeal to the world-at-large. Even those who slip through our grasp and join the Enemy are no real loss. Such rigid and miserable creatures, so focussed on their own sins, and so self-righteous and judgemental regarding others, would hardly make good appetisers anyway. The Enemy is welcome to them.

We'll accept either scenario: let the Church ignore sin entirely, or focus on it exclusively. The purposes of our Royal Hindness are served either way.

H. Holiness: A Modern-Day Dodo Bird
One of the reasons our Royal Hindness revolted from the Enemy was that our Master simply could not stand a Being who was by nature . . . holy. Hell is the antithesis of such a disgusting concept and, thank badness, Our Father Below has no such characteristics. For some unknown reason, the Enemy wishes his followers to exhibit his characteristics. His Son talked over and over again about holiness. While we cannot begin to comprehend why anyone would want to be holy, it is clear this is very important to the Enemy's plans.

Fortunately, in the modern-day western world, and in the Church itself, holiness is a concept rarely spoken of and never practised. With our help, the modern world abhors holiness and laughs at anyone who attempts to lead a holy life. How often did we overhear derisive gossip when one of his disciples tries to follow him, about how he or she is "holier than thou." No one in their society wants to be scorned, and certainly not for something as stupid as being holy.

Much of the Church has offered no resistance on this front. Virtually none of the sermons we listened to addressed this subject, and even when it was mentioned, it was always in passing or, at most, in some "intellectual" way. As long as we can keep Christianity at a purely intellectual level, with no corresponding action, we have accomplished our purpose. Holiness is now one such hypothesis: it is merely a theoretical concept that is much too hard or difficult for anyone to attempt. Because sin and evil are no longer treated seriously by the Church, they don't have to deal with holiness anyway. And, besides, relativism means holiness is not important, so why bother?

The little vermin never get to experience the apparently powerful support the Enemy gives to his children who seek holiness, because they never even give it a try. As long as we can keep them thinking that holiness is much too difficult, or not important enough, to attempt, then his creatures will not progress very far along their spiritual journey. Nor will they ever experience the supernatural strength he willingly supplies to them. Although he apparently realises his children will not be perfect, he nevertheless apparently expects them to strive daily with his help to be more like him. Because the Church has abandoned any pursuit of a holy life, however, we don't have much to worry about in this regard.

I. The Church's Theory of Relativity

Because much of the Church is now shaped by the World, it has fallen prey to one of our favourite strategies: relativism. By his very being and nature, the Enemy is a moral absolute. The little clever-clogs, however, have decided that they know better. Relativism is so much easier for them: they can do whatever they like and not feel guilty. With no eternal standards to judge thoughts and conduct, there is really nothing else for us to do but set the banquet table.

Much of the Church has almost unknowingly fallen prey to the siren's call of relativism. Without evil, there is no need for a Saviour, and without sin, there is no need for a cross. Then, of course, there is no need for religion at all, and no need to mouth such archaic and uncomfortable terms as guilt, sin, repentance and holiness. Consistent with this illusion are the subtle artifices we use to promote the notion that the Church is really nothing more than just another social club, on a par with the garden club or bridge group. It's simply another place for people to gather and visit. By adapting to its relativistic surroundings in the world, the Church has signed its own death sentence.

Rather than being counter-cultural, much of the Church has failed to stand up for the Enemy's values in any meaningful way, or even to take a strong stand against the Master's virtues for fear of hurting someone's feelings. Therefore, one of our key strategies has been very successful: the world is now shaping the Church, instead of vice versa. Western society is spiralling out of control, and the little darlings are hardly aware of it. We can state unequivocally that more and more each day, life on earth mirrors life in our Homeland: total victory will be achieved when they are one and the same. Their narcissistic and materialist focus has blinded them to any spiritual element of the Enemy's creation. The Enemy's Church often no longer stands firm against our Master's stratagems and attacks, and instead tries either to be "relevant," or to put up rigid walls of dogma, while ignoring the Enemy's teachings. Both stances mean that it is going right down the mudslide with all its bleating sheep.

J. Titanic Compartmentalisation

These humans have a wonderful propensity to compartmentalise everything. Instead of trying to find constants in their lives, they run hither and yon with no real idea of where they're going. We have used this propensity to great advantage, even in the Enemy's own back garden, the Church. The Master has been realistic enough to recognise that some of the stupid creatures will not see the darkness and, incredibly, will decide to follow the Enemy. Our Royal Hindness has devised plans to minimise this.

There are two types of compartmentalisation that have proved particularly useful to us: first, separating mind, body, emotions, and spirit, so that people view them as distinct parts of their being and therefore ignore the fact that the Enemy designed them to function as whole human beings, integrating each of these components into their lives. For instance, they ignore their bodies in their workaholic greed to get ahead, or they neglect to feed their starving souls by focusing only on material and temporal things. Second, we have strained hard at getting these humans to separate out events in their lives, so that there is no continuity or purpose interconnecting their lives. Thus, their lives are divided into separate sections: family, food, church, work, leisure, or other activities. Such compartmentalisation allows us to keep them from ever realising, much less experiencing, the wholeness envisioned by the Enemy for his creatures.

One such strategy we have employed to great effect has been to make the Church and the Enemy just one more compartment, and thus limit his impact. This has, in fact, been easier than we imagined. In those instances where we have been unsuccessful in totally preventing church activity, then the basic plan is to not let the Enemy play a role in their lives outside of an hour or so each week. Once we can limit his involvement to Sunday morning, we are well on our way to capturing another soul. We tempt them with reasons not to go, of course: that they are tired, or have chores to do, or that the Sunday paper, or television, or lunch is calling. Because he never forces himself upon his children, the choice is still theirs.

The plan, then, is simple: let them go to Church on Sunday, then make sure they leave any thoughts of the Enemy behind them when they leave. He, of course, desires to be the centre of *everything* they do: their work, their families, their recreation, their friends, and their thoughts. We, on the other hand, want these imbeciles to think he is only present inside an ecclesiastical building. It is amazing to see how easily even the churchgoers so quickly discard him once they leave the building. The dangerous thoughts and feelings they may have while at church – horrid thoughts of brotherly love, prayer, self-sacrifice, and compassion – must be quickly extinguished or else he can begin to work, and now that they have done their religious duties, they "deserve" to have the afternoon off to pursue their own interests. Thus, any dangerous notions they may have picked up that morning are quickly forgotten or at least put off until a more convenient time later in the week. Of course, it is never convenient. We can easily lead them to believe that he has no place in their work lives or their dull day-to-day lives. By Monday they are totally focused on work, or children, or problems, or activities, and it never occurs to them to involve him. Before long, missing a Sunday here or there no longer seems to matter, and church going is done only on "special" occasions, which are rare indeed. If we do our job really well, the only such occasion is their own funeral, which for many of them is like tossing the life ring into the water after the drowning has occurred.

Because this is the sound bite society, anyway, the Enemy at best gets a few seconds of their attention, even from those who pretend to follow him. The superficial faith engendered by this made us drool with anticipation. With their attention spans so short, their reading limited to a few seconds of headlines or summaries, their prayer lives mainly a quick blurb as they rush out the door, and their lives so busy and compartmentalised, our attacks on them are like shooting at slow-moving ducks in a game booth. It's almost too easy to even call it sport.

These mortals seem to be trying to replicate the design of the Titanic, foolishly believing that if they compartmentalise all aspects of their lives into airtight compartments, they are somehow unsinkable. Little do they realise that this is a recipe for disaster for them and a gold mine for us. Ironically, by striving so hard to make each compartment of their lives airtight (and spirit tight), these humans have sealed their fate. The result is no different than the Titanic: souls sunk into a deep spiritual abyss.

K. One Dimensional Christianity

There is another aspect of modern-day western Christianity that, while not ideal, has proved useful in some respects. This is the phenomenon that, even where there are followers who are, for some stupid reason, devoted to the Enemy, it is only a "one-dimensional" relationship: either vertical only, or horizontal only. Take vertical Christianity, for instance: these vermin spend their entire so-called spiritual lives devoting themselves to occasional, self-centred prayer, and reading only for the sake of more head knowledge, without ever taking action in the world around them. Many of them pride themselves on being "intellectual" Christians, whereby they spend all their time reading and debating about theological issues, and no time putting their beliefs or faith to work in the world. Thus, while they may be lost to us in an eternal sense, they never have any impact for good in the world or with their fellow humans. They are so proud of being "spiritual" and "pious" and "knowledgeable," they never bother to feed the poor, visit the sick or those in prison, or to help their neighbours. Such spiritual pride is so useful to us. Because they never test their faith, it actually remains weak and ineffective, just like muscles which are never used. Our job is to make sure they spend their lives in intellectual pursuits, and that they never get their hands dirty with the work of the Enemy.

The Son demonstrated that the Enemy wants his followers to be "in" the world, while at the same time not be "of" it. Fortunately, that teaching was a wasted effort. If we can't lead people astray completely, then the next best thing is to render them ineffective. Again, the Enemy's law of sowing and reaping is helpful here, because if his children do not sow at all, there is nothing to reap later. Plus, the Enemy has a strange concept: he uses these silly people to act for him in the world, and to be his hands and feet, so to speak. Our strategies have successfully paralysed the Enemy by preventing him from acting through these creatures. The modern churchgoer's emphasis on a vertical Christianity, to the exclusion of works, means that the world is ours for the taking.

The opposite, but equally useful, phenomenon, is "horizontal" Christianity. These followers spend their entire lives busy – they think – in his service. They volunteer for everything, and their main objective is to be busy. Often, this is a result of their perceived unworthiness, which we rush to promote whenever possible. They have missed the significance of his subversive action on the cross, so they spend their lives trying to work their way to him. Or, this is a result of another type of pride: they want to be seen and praised by others for their good deeds. These purely horizontal followers are easy prey for us, because they are too busy to pray or to read his words or to be still and seek him. Of course, this is right in line with one of our Royal Hindness's Thirteen Commandments: "Thou shalt always prevent prayer to the Enemy." Foulheart has gleefully told me of patients he has seen who spent years working for their church and yet literally only a few minutes of that was spent in prayer. Thus, they never stop to find out if they are doing what he wants them to do, and most importantly of all, they never get to know him.

Apparently, that is what he is all about: he wants these stupid creatures to know him, trust him, and become like him! We must try to prevent this outcome at all costs. Horizontal Christians miss the main point entirely, thank badness. Of course, when they never seek to know him, or to be guided or strengthened by him, our field forces have had remarkable success in whispering bitter nothings in their ears to the effect that they are "unappreciated," "ignored," "unrewarded," and "unnoticed" in all their busy activities, until they are finally "undone," and end up bitter, angry, and burned out. The best of it is – they blame him, when the entire time he was tapping and waving at the window asking to be let in, but they were too busy to notice.

L. Form over Substance

One enormously entertaining phenomenon in the western church is legalism. The Son attacked the rule-givers of Judaism, whose lives were governed by the oppressive religious laws no one could keep, and tried to show these creatures how to experience what he considers true freedom.

We have fought mightily in waging the war to counter this message. Of course, what the Son taught about how to live, was in fact to point the way to how they were actually created to function best. These imbeciles, however, never take time to think through the notion that maybe the Creator knows a little something about his creation, and that he might know better than they what they need. He promises that those of his creatures who are obedient to him, even if it seems difficult, will in fact experience his notion of joy (something we have not been yet able to replicate in our Hindom Laboratory). Such despicable creatures, who learn his kind of joy through their obedience to him, though few and far between these days, are one of the last real challenges left to us. Of course, we cannot begin to imagine anything so revolting as obedience to that Being, nor could our Master, which is why he mutinied in the first place. Now, however, some large segments of the western Church impose their own set of legalistic rules, to the end that the followers of the Enemy are heavily burdened by the Church's external trappings, rather than freed by his words and his wretched concept of grace. We always encourage superfluous rules about what does and does not make an acceptable Christian – the more pedantic and trivial, the better.

Another quite useful device for us is the employment of mindless ritual, long-forgotten symbols, and rote repetition of words in church services. I need not remind the Base Command that another of our Master's Thirteen Commandments is: "Thou shalt always exalt form over substance." It's such sport to observe these creatures struggle under the weight of rules, rules, rules (with their attendant guilt and condemnation), or ritual, ritual, ritual (which engages the mouth and eye, but not the heart and mind), when they are not connected in any meaningful way to the awful Risen One. We found a few outposts where the Enemy's spirit is bringing the symbols and rituals alive in prayer and worship, which is disastrous for our purposes. But these pose little danger, because we have surrounded them with the hardness and scepticism of the secular world, so that his holy flame – the most despicable and dangerous cancer in the universe – does not spread. With our forces victorious on every battlefront, we'll soon overrun these few remaining pockets of resistance.

Any time we can divorce the rituals or practices imposed on them by the Church, from what the Enemy thinks is true spiritual life and grace, we have advanced the cause of our Homeland. "Don't" and "can't" are the watchwords of legalism, and we couldn't have structured it better ourselves. As long as his grace and joy are completely hidden, and his wretched spiritual fire of love is smothered, while the Church's rules and rituals are venerated, we have little risk of losing the war. Ritual or legalism, without his spirit, are like a lighthouse with no light: it looks majestic and safe, but it leads to shipwreck.

M. Tromp l'Oeil

Finally, we are delighted to report that a centuries-old strategy is still continuing to work in the world and church today: hypocrisy. This, of course, results when we get people to focus on the actions of other Christians as the deciding factor in whether Christianity itself is true and valid. Historically, the Church has been enormously helpful to us in this regard: the wars, Crusades, Inquisitions, oppression, abuse and misuse of wealth and power – the list goes on and on – coupled with the failure to feed the poor, tend to the sick, and care for their neighbours, have wreaked havoc on the Church's attempt to attract new followers.

From the very earliest beginnings of the rude outbreak of the Enemy's kingdom, right after the Son appeared to his disciples and then ascended to that horrendous world of eternal bliss, our Royal Hindness has focussed the attention of would-be followers, not on the Son and his book, but on the failings of the Church. That timeless stratagem has worked wonders for our cause, and continues its success up to the present time. We lost count during our study of the thousands of vermin who turned away in disgust from the Enemy for just this reason. Of course, as our Master so wisely realised, they invariably witness actions that are anything but what the Son taught. Thus, these potential followers quickly conclude either that there is nothing of substance to the Enemy's religion, or that it makes no tangible difference in the lives of people who claim to worship the Enemy.

We found that, as long as our fiendish forces can maintain exclusive focus on the actions of other humans in the Church, most of the battles are ours. Because they are human, and thus subject to weakness, even those who seek the Enemy invariably fail to live up to the highest standards of moral behaviour. We particularly like to direct the attention of seekers on the superficial followers, including some who claim the authority to speak for the Church, who are as much a part of this world as any atheist. In this way we can whisper deceits into the ears of these searchers concerning the hypocrisy of the Enemy's followers, and the "obvious" falsehood of his religion. Meanwhile, we try to make sure that they notice nothing of positive Christian activity around the world. Rumour and hearsay are such invaluable tools for our Hindom!

Our greatest danger, though thankfully seldom faced by our forces in the modern world, is when one of the vermin who is seeking to learn about the Enemy, by-passes observing fellow humans, and instead focuses his or her inquiry on the words, deeds, and life of the Son. We found disastrous consequences whenever the Founder himself is studied, because of his damned appeal to their hearts, minds, and souls. Thus, our Forces must take whatever steps are necessary to prevent humans from studying the Scriptures and learning about the Enemy first-hand, because we cannot dare let anyone discover the Person revealed in the Scriptures. Instead, we must continue to put before them the delightful *trompe l'oeil* that the only "truth" to know about the Enemy is to be gained by observing the Church and individual Christians, and then to insure that what they observe are the most hypocritical examples. Of course, care must be taken that under no circumstances should we point them toward those extremely rare individuals who seek the Enemy daily and follow him unreservedly, yet with full humility, joy, and love. Such horrid creatures are as dangerous to us as fire is to ice.

CONCLUSION

Our Forces are on the verge of victory! The Enemy is fast losing the war, both in the Church and in the World. Our strategies are having a tremendous effect, and in fact, based upon our research, we are confident that the projections by the Base Command of the timetable for world domination should be shortened considerably, given the speed with which the Enemy is losing ground daily.

The best part is that, thanks to the genius of our Royal Hindness, all of this has been accomplished incrementally – so gradually that they don't even see the final tidal wave coming their way. We have paved the road to our Hindom stone-by-stone, and they have unwittingly walked down the pathway right behind us.

On behalf of Baldface, Scrunchmouth, Bleakblab, and Slobglob, I wish to express our gratitude to the Base Command for allowing us to undertake this research. We enjoyed immensely the opportunity to study the western world and make this Report, because we learned that with each passing day, the world is becoming more and more like our beloved Homeland.

VICTORY IS OURS!

Respectfully Submitted,
Soulbane
Captain, Junior Devil Corps

18

THE END OF THE BEGINNING

WHEN RACHAEL finished reading, she looked up. James sat motionless in his hospital bed. He had a faint smile on his face, and a tear was rolling down his cheek.

"Cade," he said softly, "I want to thank you."

"Why?" I asked puzzled.

"Because you have given me new life with your discovery of these Soulbane Reports. These dark reports have brought me back to my senses and have reminded me of God's goodness in the midst of evil. I have not truly lived these past six years since my Anne died. I got angry with God, and finally just ignored him, going joylessly through the motions at work and in my life. Despite all that, God has blessed me by letting me be a part of your remarkable discovery. Like the ghosts who visited Scrooge, God sent you and Rachael to me to bring me back to him. I feel like Simeon: now, I can die in peace."

"Don't talk about dying," said Rachael anxiously. "Not now after all you've done to help us."

"My dear Rachael, I know my hourglass is almost empty. But I'm not concerned about dying because I'm at peace with God and with myself. I know he will be there to greet me, and that is a priceless assurance. Besides, I want to see Anne again, and even that rascal Lewis. It will be a joyful reunion. Oh, I almost forgot. Rachael, did you bring Cade's baptismal gift?"

Rachael smiled and produced a book from her canvas bag, handing it to James.

"I want you to have this now," said James. He handed me his copy of *The Screwtape Letters* signed by C.S. Lewis.

Tears welled in my eyes and a lump grew in my throat.

"I don't know what to say," I finally whispered. "This means more than I can tell you."

"Come closer, both of you," whispered James. We went on either side of his bed, and James held out a hand to each of us. We took his hands, and he closed his eyes, saying, "Dear Heavenly Father, thank you for the gift of these young people, Cade and Rachael, and for letting me see these reports. Bless these two on their journey through life and be with them always. In Christ's Name. Amen."

"Amen," we both repeated.

"Now, Cade, I want you to promise me something," said James.

"What's that?"

"I want you to promise to publish these letters and reports so that the world can see this. It is a big responsibility and it rests on your shoulders now. Will you grant this final wish for me?"

"Of course," I whispered.

"Rachael, please see to it that Cade makes good this promise."

Rachael nodded, tears flowing down her cheeks.

James continued in a soft, yet firm voice, "What Soulbane reports is frightening. Of course, we can't take all he says at face value, and I certainly don't agree with everything he says. While I admit that the Church has many failings, at the same time the Church has done an incalculable amount of good in this fallen world. Besides, the Scriptures recognise that the devil is a liar. Soulbane has his own political agenda, and he is shrewd enough to know what to report and not report, as well as how to characterise it. Remember, too, we've heard only half the argument – we haven't heard the Archangel Michael's side. Never, never underestimate the power and resilience of God's love in the world. However, although Soulbane often presents a false slant, we can't afford simply to ignore his comments on the western world and the state of the Church. He also often hits the mark painfully accurately. This report should be a wake-up call for all of God's faithful."

"I'll do my best," I said softly.

"I'm afraid I'm quite tired now," he said finally. "Please take care of old Zeke for me. He's my best friend, and he'll be wondering where I've got to. Also, I have little in the way of possessions. See to it that my church gets them. I have no family apart from you and my parishioners. I love both of you very dearly. Blessings to you." He smiled slightly and began to doze off.

Rachael and I stood there for awhile, until James had drifted into a deep sleep. We crept softly out of the room, and as we reached the hallway, I took Rachael's hand and held it tightly. Spoken words would have been impossible at that moment. Instead, I found myself saying a silent prayer.

*   *   *

As we rode back to Oxford, my mind was filled with many different thoughts and emotions. As if reading my mind, Rachael said, "What are you thinking about?"

"Oh, James is such a dear man, and I've really grown to love and admire him. I hate to see him in the hospital like that."

"Yes, he's a remarkable person. I vividly remember him from when I was a child. He was always so joyful in those days, and, to be honest, I hardly recognised him that first time you and I went to see him. Obviously, your discovery really meant something to him. Cade, are you going to publish these Soulbane papers?"

"I don't see that I have any choice. I've come to believe in God, thanks to you and James ... and C.S. Lewis ... and I have to believe he allowed us to find these reports for a reason. The coincidences are all just too incredible. James talked about my responsibility, and I guess he's right. You know, Rachael, if it were up to me, I would rather just keep quiet about all this."

"Why?"

"Because, no one will believe us. This story is so incredible. They'll think we've lost our marbles."

"Cade, I'm proud of you. I hope you'll publish these reports."

I could feel my ears burning. "Rachael, I've fallen in love with you." I couldn't believe the words had just come out, but instinctively I knew they were true.

Rachael frowned slightly, saying, "Cade, please don't say those words unless you mean them. Those are serious words to tell someone."

We got quiet then, and I watched as first Magdalen Tower, and then other ancient Oxford buildings, came into view as we travelled down from Headington Hill toward the city. I wondered if I should not have blurted out my feelings.

Rachael broke the silence, saying, "I'm so worried about James. He seemed as if he feels he is going to die. I care so much for him and don't want to see him go, not now."

"I feel the same way. We'll go out and see him again tomorrow."

"That would be nice. I know you must be shattered. I'll meet you in front of Magdalen at, say, half past twelve tomorrow afternoon."

"That's great. I guess I'll see you tomorrow," I said as I stepped onto the pavement, hesitating and hoping for something more.

"Yes, I'll see you then," was all she replied, however. Rachael began to put the car into gear, so I reluctantly shut the door. I waved as she drove off, wondering why she had not responded to my confession of love. I could hardly bear to think of her rejecting me now.

Mr. Thompson was not in the lodge, but there was a note in my cubby hole. I smiled when I opened it to find a message from Clive welcoming me back and inviting me and Rachael to come out for dinner the following Saturday.

As I walked out of the lodge, the tower bells began chiming, as they have done for hundreds of years. It was four in the afternoon, and I took a deep breath of the refreshingly brisk November air. The day was beginning to pass into twilight, and the bells brought to mind James's favourite poem, Gray's *Elegy*, which I had read several times after our talk in the graveyard. The opening stanza flooded my thoughts:

The Curfew tolls the Knell of parting Day,
The lowing Herd wind slowly o'er the Lea,
The Plow-man homeward plods his weary Way,
And leaves the World to Darkness and to me.

I wondered at the extraordinary events of the past year and pondered the future. Would a knell soon be tolling for James? Based on the Soulbane Reports, would one also be tolling for the world and for Christianity? Was the future one of darkness or of light? What should I do with these mysterious and ominous reports I had discovered?

I walked down to the deer park and leaned against the iron fence. The deer were grazing silently as a full harvest moon rose in the east, illuminating the dusk. I was lost in thought for who knows how long. I finally began to walk toward New Buildings, having decided to wander around Addison's Walk. I was indeed a pilgrim on a journey, and that journey had taken me on roads I would never have guessed. This was, in some ways, like Churchill's famous speech, just "the end of the beginning" for me.

I stopped under the Great Plane Tree and looked up into its enormous leafless branches. Hearing something behind me, I turned and in astonishment saw Zeke was loping down the path toward me, barking hoarsely, with Rachael walking behind him.

I knelt down on one knee and called to him. "Hello, Zeke, old boy," I said as he came up, nuzzling his head in my arms and licking my face. "Where did Zeke come from?"

"Don't tell anyone, but I've had him in my room the past several days so I could take care of him. My scout, bless her soul, promised to keep my secret." I stood up to see a shy smile on Rachael's beautiful face. "Cade, I came back to tell you I love you, too."

I grinned with relief and joy and gave her a kiss, my heart racing with excitement. I wanted this moment to last forever. She took my hand, and the three of us strolled toward Addison's Walk in the twilight. As we passed C.S. Lewis's old rooms in New Buildings, I nodded and smiled, as if greeting an old friend. The Magdalen bells began to mark the passing of another hour. Silhouetted against the fading purple sky, Magdalen Tower stood majestically, as it had for over five hundred years.

EPILOGUE

T HE WEATHER was overcast and blustery as I stepped off the bus, pulled my coat tighter to ward off the chill, and walked briskly to the village church. I pushed open the creaking iron gate with one hand, papers clutched in the other, and hurried into the churchyard. Brown leaves rustled as they swept across the ground.

"James, I wanted to read you this letter that I discovered in the Magdalen library! I found it, just like the first ones, on the winter's solstice ..."

I then read aloud the new letter, my voice slightly hoarse:

My dear, my very dear Soulbane,

Your Report has been submitted to the Base Command and it was quite well received. In fact, given that it reached the correct conclusion that our Master's forces are victorious on every front, in both the battle for the Church and the battle for the World, the Base Command decided to pass your Report on to our Royal Hindness. As you know, this in itself is an extraordinary compliment, because the Base Command takes great pains to let only the most optimistic reports reach the eyes of Our Father Below. The Base Command has given me a special commendation, which I readily accepted, as I've taken full credit for your labours.

Of course I am gratified to see that you have learned a great deal from my personal tutorials. You have progressed magnificently, and your Report gives hints of possible greatness to come if you continue in your current fiendish ways. A job well done, my fine fellow.

Because of the depths which your Report has plumbed, it appears that our Master has taken special notice of our efforts. Thank badness for that. To reward you, the Base Command has decided to send you back into the field for a mission of downmost importance. I shall be in touch with you soon to deliver your next assignment.[HN]

Very, very affectionately yours,
Foulheart

H.S.   Soulbane,

This "hindscript" is for your eyes only. Your carelessness may have almost caused another debacle of untold proportions. If so, we narrowly averted a disaster that would have finished us both.

Due to my superior insight, I began to suspect we had been found out. You will recall I had a similar premonition with Lewis, when I had an intuition that Wormwood had screwed up, but ignored that to my deep regret. Can you imagine the damage it would have caused our Hindom if your Reports on our plans for world domination and for the final overthrow of the Enemy had been discovered? Egads, it's unthinkable!

At any rate, I had reason to suspect that a ninnyhammer Oxford student, who had recently converted to the Enemy's camp, had uncovered these Reports. (Thank badness, neither of us was assigned to him. I understand Slayspark was severely reprimanded for letting his patient be won over – and on top of Magdalen Tower of all places! Apparently, Slayspark had been ignoring his patient: after observing the student's behaviour, friends, and reading material during his first year in Oxford, Slayspark thought it was quite safe to leave him

---

[HN]*You may now inform your urchins, Baldface, Scrunchmouth, Bleakblab, and Slobglob, that their excellent work has also not gone unnoticed, and that their reward will be sent shortly; namely, several of our choicest and juiciest morsels.*

alone. Damn Slayspark! Will you junior fiends ever learn? Haven't I said over and over, never to underestimate the Enemy's ability to work in the lives of these humans, especially when it appears they have no interest in him? The damned Enemy can fan even the faintest spark into a flame. Gadzooks! Will I forever be surrounded by incompetence?)

While I always located your Reports in the prearranged place (notwithstanding some quite unpleasant episodes in the Malta cave!), my instinct told me something was amiss. Therefore, I stole the clod's computer just in case. It was great fun to be back in the field again for a little larceny, and we had a marvellous chase! It reminded me of the good old days before I got kicked downstairs. I took it to one of my favourite visitation spots, a homeless shelter, because I so relish the misery and despair in such places, intending to see if there was anything on the oaf's computer. Before I had a chance to confirm whether this Oxford dunce indeed had the Reports, however, some foul vermin in the shelter pirated the computer from me! Despite my fury, I had to grudgingly admire their despicable behaviour. Besides, what better place to ensure the computer never resurfaced than leaving it with a bunch of drunkards and reprobates? No doubt those thieves sold the computer on the black market and it will never be heard of again. Our secret is safe!

As I finished, I added, "I knew you would want to hear the latest letter." The silence was disturbed only by the brisk wind whispering in the large yew tree standing nearby. I remained facing the new granite gravemarker, which was conspicuous amidst the crumbling, illegible stones around it. The dates of Rev. James W. Brooke's birth and death were separated by a dash – a mere punctuation mark which told nothing of this remarkable man's life. Underneath the dates was the inscription: *John 11: 25-26*, shorthand for Jesus' promise of the resurrection for believers. Standing side by side was an almost identical marker, though somewhat more weathered, with the name Anne S. Brooke.

Before I turned away, I pulled a smaller, folded sheet from my inside coat pocket, glancing at the pink scar across my left palm. As I read Gray's *Elegy*, I had to pause a few times. When I finished, I placed the poem beneath an urn containing a few faded roses, then turned and walked slowly out of the churchyard.

I reflected on this newest letter and knew I would have to make good my promise to James, who had died a few days after we had read the second Soulbane Report. While urging me to publish them, he had nevertheless reminded Rachael and me that we cannot take them simply at face value. As Jesus said about the devil, "When he lies, he speaks according to his own nature, for he is a liar and the father of lies." It is evident that Soulbane has his own agenda and selfish well-being in mind, yet I decided to make no attempt to correct or edit any of his words, but to present them simply as I found them.

Ever since my adventure on Guy Fawkes' night, I've listened everywhere I've gone for that odd shrill voice that so chilled my bones before. Once or twice, late at night when Oxford has calmed its hectic pace, I've thought I heard that eerie cackle in the distance, echoing off the ancient stone walls. Was it my imagination playing tricks on me? I wonder if I will meet him again. Not that I desire ever to do so ...

THE END

Acknowledgements

As Tennyson said so eloquently in *Ulysses*:

> I am a part of all that I have met;
> Yet all experience is an arch wherethro'
> Gleams that untravell'd world whose margin fades
> For ever and for ever when I move.

Which is to say, this book owes a tremendous amount to countless people, who in one way or another have contributed to it, and acknowledging all of them would be impossible. This book would not have been possible, however, without the assistance and friendship of several special people. My wife, Kelli, constantly encouraged me during the writing process and contributed numerous suggestions for improvement. I owe a particular and deep debt of gratitude to several people. Without the advice, encouragement, and prayers of The Very Rev. Dr. Paul F. M. Zahl and The Rev. Canon C. Frederick Barbee, this book would never have come about. In addition, the following people gave generously of their time to read draft manuscripts and counsel me about this book, offering invaluable insights and encouragement: The Rt. Rev. Henry N. Parsley, Jr, Frances A. Cade, Colin Nutt, The Rev. R. Leigh Spruill, The Rev. Dr. Russell J. Levenson, Jr., and Frances A. Alexander. Special appreciation goes to

Susan Cuthbert, an excellent and patient editor. In addition, Carol B. Crawford and Nida M. Hammond patiently typed many revisions during their off-time after work. Robert E. Fraley, D.J. Snell, Richard E. Neal, and John Hunt gave a first-time author a chance to be published. Thanks also to the Muscats in Malta, Dolly, Louis, Andrew, and James; to Michael and Margaret Comely of Abingdon, England; and to Mary Clapinson, Keeper of Western Manuscripts for the Bodleian Library, all of whom provided me with factual, pictorial, and geographical assistance, to the Friday morning Cholesterol Club for our many discussions about and struggles with faith; and to Rotary International for giving me the opportunity to live a dream and study in Oxford. My parents, Ruth and Norman, have always been there for me. My precious triplet sons, Jonathan, Taylor, and Nelson, gave me a reason not only to attempt this book, but to persevere during those times when Soulbane whispered in my ear that such an undertaking was pure folly. I can only offer my heartfelt thanks to each of them. Any deficiencies in the text, however, are solely mine and Soulbane's.

Finally, like Cade Bryson, I give a smiling nod to C.S. Lewis. His writings have not only influenced and shaped me enormously, they have provided many hours of entertainment and enlightenment.

– Norman Jetmundsen, Jr.
Birmingham, Alabama